STRARYS

CORA BRENT

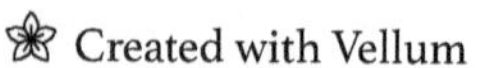 Created with Vellum

STAY IN TOUCH!

Make sure you sign up for my newsletter to receive updates on new releases, sales and giveaways.
CORA BRENT'S NEWSLETTER SIGNUP
You can also find me here:

Check out what's happening on Facebook:
www.facebook.com/CoraBrentAuthor

Join my exclusive reader Facebook group: https://www.
facebook.com/CoraBrentsBookCorner

Add future releases to your TBR list:
https://www.goodreads.com/CoraBrent

Follow me on Instagram: CoraBrentAuthor

ALSO BY CORA BRENT:

GENTRY BOYS (Books 1-4)

Gentry Boys Series

DRAW (Saylor and Cord)

RISK (Creed and Truly)

GAME (Chase and Stephanie)

FALL (Deck and Jenny)

HOLD

CROSS (A Novella)

WALK (Stone and Evie)

EDGE (Conway and Roslyn)

SNOW (A Christmas Story)

Gentry Generations

(A Gentry family spinoff series)

STRIKE (Cami and Dalton)

TURN (Cassie and Curtis)

KEEP (A Novella)

TEST (Derek and Paige)

CLASH (Kellan and Taylor)

WRECK (Thomas and Gracie)

The Ruins of Emblem

TRISTAN (Cadence and Tristan)

JEDSON (Ryan and Leah)

LANDON (Coming Soon)

Worked Up

<u>FIRED</u>

<u>NAILED</u>

Stand Alones

<u>UNRULY</u>

<u>IN THIS LIFE</u>

<u>HICKEY</u>

<u>SYLER MCKNIGHT</u>

<u>LONG LOST</u>

<u>THE PRETENDER</u>

PROLOGUE

RAFE

5 years ago

I've been free for less than twenty-four hours.

Getting used to life on the other side of the bars takes time, whether I've been inside for a week or for five months. The noise and smells of the jailhouse rot stick to my senses like glue and nothing except the passing of days shakes them off. Right now I'm still in the stage where I keep my back to the wall, ball a fist at any loud sound and sink only halfway into my dreams in case someone goes nuts.

I don't know how it is for other men. I would never ask.

Usually when I get out I'm in a hurry to use my dick and fuck up my head for a few hours. I'll get to all that.

First, I've got a situation to deal with.

The truck I'm driving looks like it was assembled from rusted scrap pieces and duck taped together. I can't sit here for long with the engine running while black exhaust clouds puff out of the tailpipe. This is the kind of neighborhood where people notice things like shitty trucks hanging out beside the curb for no particular reason. The truck's not even mine. It belongs to a sad sack named Dempsey who still owes me two grand and is terrified that I'll do something meaningful to extract it now that I'm out.

"Sure, you can use my truck, Rafe. It's got a full tank and hey, take your time."

Ha! I'll do that. And maybe I'll even bring it back in one piece before I start stepping on his nuts in order to squeeze some cash out of him.

Before I walked into the cage to serve time for this latest piece of bullshit I had a truck of my own and it was a few sturdy notches above this junkyard carcass. But the garage where I'd arranged to park it for my five-month vacation went belly up and the owner is long gone. As for the truck, there's no trace. Dempsey heard a rumor that the guy went way up north to one of the Dakotas and I'm thinking if he wants to keep his fingers attached then he'll stay there. Of all the things I don't have the patience for, being ripped off is at the top of the list.

I need to just go knock on the motherfucking door and get this over with. The house is exactly what I expected, with infinite tall windows fronting its many rooms and boxy front yard hedges that someone spends a lot of time shaping. There's even a damn balcony, a cup-shaped space jutting out above the entry, complete with fancy wrought iron scrollwork in front of double glass doors.

As if those glass doors have felt me staring, they crack open. A second later a woman floats through them. She's wearing a floor length purple robe and one hand holds a purple drink tumbler while the other scrolls through her phone. She steps over to the railing and it's easy to see that this is really her natural habitat, but then again I knew that. I never even bothered to look for her at Spit, a rat trap of a country bar that serves an uneasy mix of hardcore criminal types, dumbass college pricks, and the occasional upper crust wife in search of a decent dick.

Guess which category she falls into.

She kept me busy for a few months and it was all kinds of hot but we weren't built for anything special. I've had better than her before and I could be having better right now.

No, I'm here because of what she told me on my last night of freedom.

When I get out of the truck I shut the door loudly enough to catch her attention. She looks down from her balcony perch. She freezes. Her lips form a soundless word that might be my name or it might be *"Fuck."*

She disappears and I wait right where I am. This is a risk. She could be calling 911 and saying anything she wants. With my record I'm not the one who will be believed.

The front door is a mammoth iron monstrosity and it creaks open. Dana Walsh steps outside with the diamond Rock of Gibraltar on her left hand while her right hand cradles her swollen belly.

"Rafe," she says.

Dana closes the door behind her but stays where she is. This is not a conversation to have from thirty feet away so I trample her lush front lawn to get closer. Along the way, my foot accidentally kicks a double-bowled dish filled with pet food and water. Everything spills. Not my problem.

Her eyes are wide and she nervously tucks an escaped strand of artificially red hair back into place.

The hand returns to guard her big belly. "I didn't know you had been released."

"Just yesterday." I gesture to the reason I'm here. "You look like you're about ready to pop."

A smile flashes. "Eight more weeks." The smile fades. "I didn't think I'd see you again."

My fingers itch to hold a cigarette. Or a bottle. Something, anything, to shove away whatever emotion is bound to develop from this moment.

"You tell me you're having my kid but you didn't think you'd see me again?"

"Hush." She waves her arms and looks behind her as if the closed door might get its feelings hurt. "Kevin's inside."

I'm not keeping my voice down. "I couldn't give less of a fuck."

Her brow furrows. "How on earth did you find me?"

Either she thinks I'm as dumb as a dog or else she forgot that the Internet exists. Took all of sixty seconds of online searching to discover her address. Dana liked to run her mouth after getting her brains fucked out. When she wasn't going on and on about her boring charity work that has something to do with stray animals she was blabbing about her husband's law firm in the city's pricy new business park and the custom, marble-floored McMansion she'd designed here in the land of Real Housewives Of Clueless Rich Bastards.

Dana doesn't await an answer to her question. "If you need money-"

I cut her right off. "I don't."

She nods. Another pat to the belly. She stares down at it fondly. "Look, Kevin knows about you. He's been very understanding. We're going to raise the baby together."

I feel like being mean. "It's nice to hear I was able to give you something that your dickless wonder of a meal ticket couldn't."

Her head snaps up. "Rafe, you understand nothing." She's about to say something else but then she sighs and deflates a little. "It's not your fault. You're a kid, haven't even reached your twenty-first birthday. My god." She sniffs. "I turned forty last week. Old enough to be your mother."

My laugh is as sharp as a bark. "You didn't think I was a kid when you were choking my cock down your throat."

She can't stop herself from flinching. "That's not necessary."

"Truth hurts. Why'd you tell me you couldn't get pregnant?"

"That's what I thought. I didn't lie to you. We tried IVF. It didn't work. Kevin refused to consider adoption and-"

"I really don't fucking care."

"Then why are you here? What do you want?"

My eyes shift to her belly. There's a quick ripple beneath the satin. I was careless about many things but I always wrapped up my dick before sticking it in new places. Then one time I didn't and now here

I am, staring at the consequences. If Dana had it to do over again I'm sure she would never have told me. She would have just waved farewell on the morning I needed to report to lockup in order to serve time for a fight that I didn't even start. Life is less fair than it is on the grade school playground and judges don't care who hit who first. I would have forgotten about her on the inside while the days passed with unbearable slowness and I would have just assumed she'd moved on too.

But she did tell me.

She'd pressed my hand to her stomach and her eyes misted as she said, *"I'm pregnant, Rafe. It's yours."*

And for a hundred and fifty three days I had lots of time to think about that.

"I don't want anything," I tell her, my eyes still on the ripple in her satin robe as the piece of me inside her belly shifts again. "I just needed to see if you were all right."

She relaxes slightly but she doesn't quite believe me. She's spent enough time in my company to understand I'm not made of tender feelings.

Her nerves are betrayed by the shake in her voice. "Kevin will take care of me. He'll take care of both of us."

Kevin Walsh's photo is on his law firm's About Us page. He's even older than Dana, with a face like a pale weasel with bad hair plugs. One of his suits is likely worth more than I've ever owned at one time. Yeah, he would be the kind of man to take care of businesses and wives and even a kid that's not his.

I'm only good at looking after myself and even on that count the results are kind of sketchy. I was a rotten kid, a hellacious teenager and by most standards I'm on my way to becoming a shitty man. Quick tempered, in and out of prison, making money through less than legal means and then blowing it all on nonsense before I've finished counting it. I have nothing to offer that kid in her belly. I was even the worst of big brothers, always lashing out with misplaced fury at a scrawny boy who didn't even know how to fight back. There aren't many memories that really bother me but the ones that do always involve Jonathan. Wherever he is I hope he doesn't think of me too often. Since I could never even treat my little brother right then I have no business trying to be a father.

"Is it a boy or a girl?" I ask and it makes no difference. I just want to know.

Dana hesitates, afraid the answer will mean something to me. "It's a boy."

A boy.

A boy who might have my eyes and enjoy playing football just like I used to.

A boy who won't grow up with the stink of the Hempstead name following him around.

A boy who will be raised here, amid sparkling affluence, instead of the grimy landscape of the small town trailer park where I grew up.

A boy who will likely never even know that I exist.

"Take good care of him," I say and then I turn my back. There's no point in emptying out the few crumbs in my wallet or making promises that I'll give things I don't have. She knows that, just like she knows our son will be much better off without me.

And I know it too.

This is why I won't think twice about climbing into Dempsey's truck and driving away without looking back.

1

———

IZZY

My dad operates under a clear set of life rules.

One of the cardinal bullet points is: Look a man in the eye and tell him you won't accept his bullshit.

That's undoubtedly good advice.

But when the bullshitter in question is staring somewhere south of your eyes then it's difficult to apply.

"I find this completely unacceptable." I snap my fingers in the hope that his eyes get startled away from my tits. "We had a verbal agreement, Lou."

Lou, the pink-faced, thin-haired landlord who might require a power tool to pry him from his undersized desk chair, scratches an itch on the right side of the broad belly that threatens to split through his red polo shirt. His nasal wheeze of a voice follows. "You didn't give me a deposit."

Another of my dad's rules: Keep your temper in check. Unless you have no choice.

I'm rapidly reaching the summit of no choice. I've been driving for two days, I smell like cheap roadside motel soap and all of my treasured belongings are currently stored in the trunk of my car. Granted, the car is a gleaming new Escalade, a gift from the devoted father whose advice follows me everywhere. But still. I'd much rather have a roof over my head tonight in a place that doesn't offer to charge by the hour. Right now Landlord Lou is interfering with my plans.

Alas, I am not my father. Deck Gentry could lean in and utter a few meaningful words that would give Landlord Lou an anxiety attack. I suspect the effect would not be the same coming from a five foot two redheaded female.

So instead of blowing a fuse and knocking Lou's pencil jar over, I sit up straighter and offer him a smile.

"Lou, you told me to give you the deposit when I arrived. Well, here I am. And in my purse is the cashier's check for the one bedroom apartment I had reserved online and then confirmed with a direct call to you. Do you recall our conversation? It was eight days ago. You chewed on potato chips the entire time. Or perhaps it was crackers. I can't be sure. You did belch twice and failed to excuse yourself but I didn't complain. Then you promised that my apartment was located close to the pool. You said the keys were in your hand. I'd like to know what happened to them since then."

Lou's eyes are the color of limp spinach and they blink. "Hey, it's nothing personal. I got an offer to pay more rent."

"I could have paid more rent."

He shrugs and his fat fingers play with a ballpoint pen. "Eh, it's just the way it works. There's never enough apartments in Hutton to deal with all the damn college kids coming back."

"Fascinating summary of the local real estate market. Technically I'm one of those college kids. Except I'm not a kid. And I'm enrolled in grad school for speech pathology. But that doesn't matter. I need a place to live. I drove all the way here from Arizona with the expectation that one awaited me. I could sue you, you know."

My understanding of the legal system is dim. But Lou's limp spinach eyes bug out.

"There's no need for that kind of talk, Isabel."

"It's Isabella. My friends call me Izzy. But you can't. You haven't even apologized yet."

He loses his alarmed expression, perhaps realizing that I am not about to mount a legal challenge. "I am sorry."

"I don't forgive you."

The man sighs. He shifts in his chair and a fart-like noise follows. "You ought to check out the HSU online forums. Sometimes people post there in search of roommates. Good looking girl like you should have no trouble finding a place."

"Thank you for the encouragement. But despite my visual appeal I am somehow particular about where I sleep at night."

"Oh." He's confused. "Okay."

I stand up. "This has been a complete waste of my time." A candy dish made of blue crackle glass sits on his desk and I point to it. "Are those root beer barrels?"

His head bobs atop his fat neck. "Yeah, my wife always buys these huge containers of them from Costco."

"Then you won't miss these." I dump the contents of the candy dish into my purse because I like root beer barrels and because I've decided I'm owed something for my troubles. If I cannot have a place to live then I will at least have some decent candy to comfort me in my hour of misfortune.

He stares at the empty candy dish after I place it back on his desk. Then I change my mind and stick the candy dish in my purse too before swiveling to make an exit. The moment might have felt semi-triumphant, except I manage to crack my right knee with the office door when I fling it open. I bite back a curse of pain and make an effort not to limp my way outside and to my car.

I've barely got the engine started when my phone pings. I'm not surprised to see a text from my dad. I would not even be shocked to learn that he was already aware that I've been dicked out of my apartment and stolen a candy dish. This may sound paranoid but anyone who is acquainted with Deck Gentry understands that the man possesses an uncanny level of perception. When the rest of the family calls him 'King Gentry' they are only halfway kidding.

Hey, kid. You must be there by now. How's the apartment?

The easy fix would be to hit the call button and whine out my brand new plight. My father can find a solution to any problem. By the end of the business day Lou would be jobless and I'd have the keys to the fanciest apartment within the borders of Hutton, Texas. I would go to sleep tonight secure and content and unworried.

And cowardly.

Because I'm well outside the boundaries of childhood and I can no longer expect my daddy to iron out all the wrinkles in my life.

Apartment's great. Moving in now. Talk more later.

I stare at the words I have just sent. I picture my dad in his Arizona backyard, perhaps sitting on the patio beneath the overhead misters and frowning over the lie that has just reached him from hundreds of miles away. I do not believe that my lovable father has supernatural abilities and I'm quite aware that he's been wrapped around my finger since the day I was born. Yet I chew the tip of my nail and suffer a few seconds of anxiety as I stare at the little text screen dots and await his reply.

Let me know if you need anything. Always here for you.

For a fleeting moment I wish I was there, back home, at the house where my untouched bedroom awaits and blooming rhododendrons climb an arched trellis outside my window. I could have gone to grad school at Arizona State and lived in one of the many sprawling apartment complexes surrounding the university, only a short drive away from my father's overprotective care and my mother's gourmet cooking.

Instead I'm here, in this dusty armpit of western Texas with no friends within five hundred miles and no place to live and no positive developments except for the acquisition of a purse full of root beer barrels. I pop one into my mouth and a hideous noise rumbles out of my stomach, warning me to do better. Breakfast, eaten many hours ago, was an inadequate portion of soggy French toast sticks served through a drive in window. I'm sure I'll be in a happier mood after I've filled my stomach. Maybe I'll even have some good ideas about what the hell I'm supposed to do next when my life skills are ill suited to fending for myself.

While in search of a place to eat, I take note of the fact that

Hutton appears to be a completely ordinary and not altogether attractive college town. If I'm being honest then I can admit that I didn't exactly have my pick of graduate university programs. My first two years of college were an orgy of sorority social engagements and various short term boyfriends who all kind of run together in my head when I think back. I had fun. My grades had less fun. By my third year I started to shape up and get a better idea about which direction I wanted to take but repairing the damage to my GPA was a challenge. After the souring of yet another ill-fated relationship I decided that I needed to go somewhere new, somewhere unfamiliar, and HSU has a high quality speech pathology program. Eventually I'd like to work with children. There are few skills more critical than the ability to communicate and I believe I have something to contribute in the world. Isn't that what we all want? To be useful.

My eye catches on a small, mustard colored building embellished with an ugly red lettered sign that says 'Greasy June's'. Since someone took the trouble to paint the words 'Best Burgers In Hutton' on a large front window I decide that my stomach and I can probably do no better than this. I pull into the parking lot.

The interior of Greasy June's proves to be far more cheerful than the exterior. The décor has a country yesteryear atmosphere with flowered china plates hanging on the walls beside rusted implements that might be kitchen antiques or might be torture devices. I can't tell the difference. The hostess looks cute in a retro style flared apron and her nametag says (of course!) June, although I have my doubts that she's THE June since she looks to be about my age. As the hour is late for lunch and early for dinner, there aren't many other customers and I'm seated at a prime window booth before June urges me to try the apricot lemonade.

I don't glance at the laminated menu in front of me. "What's your biggest, most exceedingly messy burger?"

She grins. "That would be the Gutbuster. A double decker with bacon, avocado and Monterey Jack cheese. Trust me, it's enough for two meals."

"Sounds heavenly. I'll also take one of those large lemonades."

June scribbles on a tiny notepad that fits into the palm of her hand. "Coming right up."

After she scuttles away I'm left with a choice between staring out the window or staring at my phone. These last two days on the road have been the loneliest in my memory. While it's true that I like my personal space, I'm not a girl who is used to going out to a restaurant and eating alone.

The last text message from my father haunts me so I turn my phone face down on the table. I haven't lied to him since I was six and denied climbing onto the kitchen counter to eat all the frosted Christmas cookies. He would have known I was lying even if red and green sugar crystals weren't clinging to my chin. There are other messages on my phone that I haven't responded to yet. Hopeful encouragement from my mother, safe travel wishes from my Aunt Promise, a good luck text from my cousin Thomas. Before nightfall I'll answer with artificial cheer but right now I just want to stuff my face with something fried and wallow in my problems.

At the very least I'll be stuck getting a hotel room for the night. Instead of settling in and shopping for furniture this weekend I'll be searching for a place to sleep this semester. After Lou's short lecture on the scarcity of housing in Hutton I feel a little uneasy about my prospects. There are only five days until classes begin and I'm carrying my life around in my Escalade.

Plus my knee hurts.

I'd forgotten about how I crashed into the door while trying to exit Lou's office but now I see there will be an ugly bruise there. My stomach rumbles once more and I'm about to push another root beer barrel into my mouth when June swings by to rescue me with a plate of food.

"Wow, you weren't kidding." I eye the glistening tower of meat and cheese and onions and bacon and other parts I'm not sure how to identify but will surely taste splendid.

"Enjoy." June also drops off a frosted glass filled with orange tinted lemonade. "Would you like some utensils? This sucker is messy."

"No thanks. But I'll take a few more napkins."

I've barely sunk my teeth into the dripping monstrosity when I realize that Greasy June's will be my restaurant of choice as long as I'm in Hutton. It's true that food tastes better when you're hungry but this gorgeous blend of meat and grease and melted things deserves a prize. Sure, burger juice dribbles down my chin and cheese sticks to my fingers, but who cares? No one is watching.

Except the absurdly hot guy two tables over.

He is watching.

He must have arrived during my brooding spell. Usually I'm observant enough to notice a tall, muscle-stacked hunk of manhood but today I have other issues. Artistically complex tattoos curl up his thick arms before disappearing beneath the sleeves of the black t-shirt that has seen one too many washes. Generally my jaw doesn't drop over the sight of ink. I'm too used to seeing it on the men in my own family and it strikes me as nothing special. But as I dab the burger grease from my mouth I find myself placing internal bets over how much of this guy's impressive chest is covered with ink. I bet it's a lot. And I wouldn't complain about confirming this theory. His blue eyes conduct a sweep; obviously he doesn't care if he's caught checking me out.

Then I notice that he's not alone at the table. A little boy with the same shock of black hair sits across from him. I would guess the child's age to be around five. He's a little older than the preschoolers I worked with at my internship during my last college semester.

The man's attention turns back to the kid. He frowns. He says something and picks up a crayon that was lying on the table. He seems to be trying to interest the boy in drawing on a piece of paper. It's kind of a cute scene. They are obviously father and son. But the little boy stubbornly crosses his arms and looks away, refusing to answer. The man drops the crayon and leans back in his chair with a sigh of frustration.

The man's eyes shift and he notices that I'm still staring but there's no flicker of emotion. He yawns and rakes a hand through his hair. I get the impression he'd rather be anywhere else but here. June stops by and deposits a pair of lemonade-filled glasses on the table. Within seconds the boy reaches out and intentionally knocks his glass over, causing lemonade to spill all over the table, the floor and June's white sneakers.

"Oliver," says the man but there's no anger in his tone. He sounds tired, exasperated.

For a second I consider approaching them. Children always like me. But the guy doesn't strike me as the type who would welcome interference from a stranger. He grumbles as he mops up the mess, despite June's appeals to allow her to clean it up. Then he balls the wet napkins up, grunts out his order and looks at the kid as if he's never seen a child before and worries it might bite.

In the end I decide the politest course of action would be to finish my sloppy meal in silence and leave the two of them alone with their awkward family troubles. Shockingly, I'm still hungry when I finish and I'm no closer to any solutions regarding the small matter of where I should live.

The good news is that I recall seeing a bakery just down the road.

Perhaps a cupcake or two will lead to an epiphany.

I'm willing to give it a shot.

It's not like I have any other ideas.

2

RAFE

Getting this kid to eat is tougher than holding a handful of sand. Last night I let him have ice cream for dinner because I didn't know what the hell else to try. After a three day crash course in babysitting I still don't know much about children but I'm pretty sure they're supposed to eat regularly.

This morning I packed him into my truck two hours before the sun came up and we drove five hundred miles to get here to Hutton. Along the way I bought him plenty of snacks but he rejected them all except a bag of M&M's.

After spending the entire day squinting through a dirty windshield and watching a good portion of Texas roll past I need a break. Because I'm still not sure about this next step. Because I'm sick of shoving gas station beef jerky in my mouth. And because somehow I have to get the kid to consume something that's not pure sugar.

"We'll stop here and eat," I say as I turn into some dive called Greasy June's.

He doesn't answer, which is no surprise. So far he rarely strings more than three words together. Perhaps he's more talkative around people other than me but there's been no chance to test this out. On the first day I was afraid he couldn't hear very well. Since then I've caught on that he can hear just fine. Plus he's answered enough direct questions that I believe he both understands everything that's happening and has the ability to speak when he chooses to.

I set the truck in park and tilt the rearview mirror so I can see into the backseat. He's staring out the window even though there's nothing to look at except an ugly parking lot. The Marvel sticker book I bought him at a rest stop two hundred miles ago sits in his lap. Something deep in my chest hurts when I look at him. He's had a lot of terrible news to get used to in a very short period of time. There's no way to know if anything I'm doing right now is correct and I've got no one to ask. Packing up my life in Houston and heading here was a move of desperation. The kind of people who tend to populate my life aren't the sort that qualify as role models. I'm no role model myself but I need to pretend like I'm better than I am. In this whole world I've got one person who might be able to help me figure out what to do and he's here in Hutton. He's also not expecting to see me now. Or probably ever again. We haven't laid eyes on each other since we were kids. And the one time we spoke, about a year ago, he wouldn't even be straight with me about what city he was living in. It's possible he'll flip his shit and clobber me in the jaw when I show up on his doorstep. That's a risk I have to take right now. After three days of sleepless misery and searching for a moral center I don't recall ever having, I can't think of a single other plan. This kid's stuck with me and I've got no clue how to do right by him.

I'm still staring at him in the mirror and finally he turns his head. Our eyes meet in the mirror I see myself in his flat glare.

"Do you like hamburgers?" I ask him. "I can get you something else if you don't. Just say the word and I'll get you anything you want."

What a goddamn liar I am.

I can't give him what he certainly wants above all else.

I can't give him his mother back.

"I want ice cream," he says.

Four words. A possible new record. I'm just happy to hear his voice.

"Yeah, you can have ice cream after you eat some real food."

He scowls and snaps his head to the side once more to glower out the window. The sticker book in his lap gets flung to the floor, landing with an angry thud. A message, I guess. His way of saying that he doesn't want anything from me. I don't blame him. He got a complete shit deal. If someone had told me three short days ago that I'd be on the other side of the state after becoming the sole guardian of a kid I was never supposed to meet then I would have laughed the bastard right out of the room.

Even as I pressed an elevator button to the top floor of a fancy office building I had no clue that my world was only minutes away from going completely nuclear...

After being harassed for days I finally got curious about what the hell this guy could want. I'm led straight to his office where he waits for me at the door.

"Rafe." He heaves a sigh. He's got a lot of nerve acting as if this is a huge inconvenience for him but I'm not here to pick a fight. He steps back and gestures to a long conference table in an office that's bigger than my current apartment. "I didn't think you'd show up."

"Yeah, neither did I." I sit down hard in one of his pricey leather chairs and hear a crack. Then I go about slowly lighting up a cigarette. I don't even smoke that much anymore. I just always keep a pack around and right now I want to piss him off.

Kevin Walsh hates me. That much is clear in his puffy fifty-something face as he drops into a chair across the table. It's true that I thought about blowing off this meeting. Then I got to thinking that this must be important and it must have something to do with the kid, like maybe he needs a kidney or something. If that's the case, then I'd say that I'm not doing anything important with either of mine and he could have his pick. But if this dick drumming his fingers on the table insults me by trying to offer up some cash then he might get some cigarette ashes shoved down his throat. I'll check into the hospital today and volunteer to let them cut out whatever part the boy needs but I can't be fucking bought.

Kevin holds my eye and delivers the blow. "Dana's dead."

"Shit." I don't like hearing this. My mind searches for her face and can't find it, which seems weird. It's been too long and over the years I've tried too

hard to blot her out of my head. Instead of her face I see a bland oval void surrounded by red hair.

"It was quick." Kevin exhales and laces his fingers together. "An aneurysm last Tuesday."

"I'm sorry to hear that." And I am. Not just because Dana wasn't a terrible person but because somewhere out there is a little boy who's lost his mother.

Kevin nods and straightens his back. "And the reason I called you here is because you have the opportunity to finally take responsibility for your son."

"My son?"

"Yes. I know Dana told you about him."

"I was told you were raising him as your son."

"No. Dana and I split up four years ago and I'm about to get remarried. Dana has no other family. Her will stipulated that I'm to receive custody of the boy but that's impossible. I hardly know him and I'm certainly not going to take over raising him now."

"You son of a bitch. You think he's some fucking dog you can pass off?"

Kevin is annoyed. "I can't stop you from turning your back on the boy. In fact, from what I know about you he'd probably be better off if you did. But then I'll have no choice but to place him in the foster care system."

My ears ring with rage. He's lying for sure. With all his connections and his money he could figure out another way. He wants the kid gone, out of his life completely. Seriously, fuck this guy. Fuck him and his puffy face and his puckered lips and his broken down dick. Maybe a swift kick in his miniature balls would get the message across.

But his last sentence makes me stop and think for a minute.

I've heard too many stories about what happens to kids who get caught up in the system. A roll of the dice if ever there was one. The kid could very well end up in some picket fence happily ever after. Or he might wind up getting trafficked by perverts.

The kid. MY kid.

The closest I've ever come to him is that morning five years in the past when I stared at the shape moving in his mother's pregnant belly.

I don't even know his name.

No, I can't storm out of here. I can't push Kevin Walsh out of his expensive chair and tie his testicles in a knot. All I can do is crush my cigarette on the surface of his polished conference table and hope that I've ruined it. He doesn't notice. He's too busy pushing a yellow folder in my direction.

"I've taken the liberty of having his birth certificate changed to reflect his proper paternity. Most of Dana's assets, once liquidated, will be placed in a trust for the boy when he comes of age but you are free to petition the trust for access to the necessary funds to help raise him. In fact, I think you should do that." He opens the folder and thumbs through the papers before raising an eyebrow at me. "You'll find all the proper documentation inside."

I get it. He wants to wash his hands of the situation and yet be able to sleep at night. He figures that if I turn out to be a scumbag who will drain the trust and abandon the kid anyway then it's not his fault because at least he tried. Every word out of his mouth is dusted with arrogance, like he's expecting gratitude.

I swallow. "Where is he?"

Kevin Walsh is pleased that the matter is going to be settled. It's still early in the day. He can go celebrate with a lunch of martinis and caviar, or whatever the fuck these kind of people eat. He reaches for a black box on the table and presses a button. "You can bring him in now."

Seconds later the door opens and I stare into a face that takes me back in time. If we were in my hometown of Arcana then people would know him at a glance. They would nod their heads and whisper that he's inherited the angry face of a Hempstead male. It's true. He looks like me. I've thought about him a lot more than I wanted to since the day I jumped into a borrowed truck and left him behind.

"Say hello to your father, Oliver," Kevin urges in a snotty voice that reminds me why he's a lousy motherfucker.

I hold out my hand. How do you introduce yourself to your kid? "Hello." I try out his name. "Oliver."

He looks up at me. There's anger and confusion in his eyes. His hands are balled into little fists.

Instead of answering with words or a handshake he kicks me. Hard.

The three days that have elapsed since then have not gone much better. At least Oliver hasn't kicked me yet today. But I'm not kidding myself that he's a member of my fan club either.

I hop out of the truck and walk around to the rear passenger side. I'm glad I don't need to worry about the truck breaking down. It's fairly new, bought with funds from a legit job I had making custom furniture, something I'm unexpectedly good at. Maybe the skill lives in the family blood. With a few tools and some sweat my dad was able to turn a simple hunk of wood into a freaking work of art. He used to let me and my brother pound away with hammer and nails in the garage until our mother had fits. The guy could probably build anything. He just wasn't good at holding down a job. Other shit got in the way. Alcohol. Women. Gambling. My grandfather was good at woodworking too. In my parents' closet there used to be a hand carved wooden box made by my grandfather in a high school shop class. It might have been the only physical thing my dad had left of his own father and it disappeared around the time he died. After that my mom lost the house, moved us to a trailer park and became a raging asshole.

I haven't thought about that stupid box in years. It's only on my mind now because I've been thinking about family. And about the things we inherit, both good and terrible.

The Hempstead men.

We can make coffee tables and we can kill.

What a legacy.

I wonder how long I can keep my son from finding out what kind of people he comes from.

Oliver squirms when I hold his hand on the way into the diner but after he tried to bolt at a gas station this morning I'm not taking chances.

The diner is practically empty. The waitress is charmed by the sight of us, assuming we're some everyday father/son duo out for an ordinary meal. She supplies crayons and a paper menu that's supposed to be scribbled on and I thank her even though Oliver makes a face.

"Okay." I peer at the menu and make my voice sound cheerful.

"Lots of good stuff on here. You can have a burger or you can have chicken nuggets. There's mac and cheese and-"

He snatches the menu. "I can READ."

"That's great." I didn't know he could read. I can't remember if I could read at that age. My brother Jonathan probably could. He was always the smarter one. "You're pretty smart if you know how to read already."

He doesn't answer. He wipes his nose with the heel of his right palm and lets the menu flutter back to the table.

"Did you decide what you want, Oliver?"

"Chicken."

"Good, that's good. I like chicken too. Today I'm in the mood for a burger though. I'm gonna get the biggest burger they've got." I'm still talking in a voice that's all high and ridiculous. I sound like a woman for fuck's sake.

The kid's face remains blank. It hasn't occurred to him yet that I'm all he's got. I hope it doesn't occur to him for a while. The thought even depresses me. And I'm used to living with me.

The waitress takes our order and disappears. The diner looks like it was decorated by someone's color blind grandmother. Lots of frilly shit all over the walls. In its own way it's kind of homey though. It's probably been here for fifty years and has a small town vibe even though Hutton is not really a small town. Not like Arcana where the 'everybody knows your name' garbage becomes suffocating. At least it does if your last name is the same one shared by the town's most infamous murderer.

Oliver won't pick up the crayons while I'm watching so I try to look at something else. There are only two other tables in use and one of them is occupied by a redhead. She's alone and she's practically got College Girl stamped on the pink shirt stretched across her perky tits. The sight of her reminds me that it's been months since I had any fun. In another setting I might help myself to an empty seat at her table and find out if she has a thing for filthy talking ex cons with short attention spans.

That, of course, is out of the question right now. Or probably anytime in the foreseeable future. It's a good thing I have a healthy imagination when it comes to beating off. That talent will be useful.

She's shoving a greasy, dripping burger into her mouth like she hasn't eaten in a month. I think I can even hear her say, 'Mmmmm' as she chews a bite.

Her eyes shift my way and she covers her mouth with a napkin. Some burger juice has dripped onto her shirt. The polite thing to do would be to look away but I've never been a polite kind of guy. She shifts in her seat. Her eyes flicker to Oliver and then back to me. She draws a conclusion and relaxes, probably thinking that there's no reason for her to worry about looking cute in front of a dad out to lunch with his kid. The waitress arrives with a couple of tall lemonades and then I have to forget about College Girl because Oliver pushes his glass over. Now there's lemonade all over the table, lemonade in my lap, and lemonade on the floor.

I want to belt out a curse but I manage to bite my tongue. He's looking at me, chin up, awaiting a reaction. The waitress is fussing over him as if he got hurt. I sigh out his name and seize every napkin in sight to try and clean up. Everything is still sticky when I finish.

By now we've received a pair of new drinks and this time Oliver's comes in a plastic cup with a lid. College Girl is still here but it looks like she's getting ready to leave. She passes her credit card to the waitress and smiles. She must be having a better day than I am. Good for her. And I'm probably a creep for wondering if she is flexible enough to throw her ankles over my shoulders but so what. She can't read my mind.

I forget about the cute redhead and face the wrath of a five-year-old. He sips his drink through a straw and eyes me warily.

I heave a sigh. "Oliver, I know you're pissed off."

No, that's not the correct way to talk to a little kid.

I start again.

"What I meant to say is that I know you're angry. And upset. And we don't really know each other yet. Just please try to behave, okay?"

He probably wouldn't have agreed to the request anyway but the food arrives so he doesn't have time to say anything.

"Just look at this yummy plate. I wish I could eat every bite of this myself." The waitress is proud as she sets down Oliver's food. Someone, probably her, has arranged the nuggets in a smiley face.

I figure there's a fifty percent chance the boy will hurl the food on the floor or maybe throw it in my face but out of nowhere he smiles up at her and says, "Thank you."

Well. Smack my ass and call me Sally. I don't know where these good manners came from. And now I'm actually a little jealous of the beaming, round-faced waitress. I have yet to coax a smile out of the kid.

He ignores me while I watch him nibble the edge of a chicken nugget. I'm relieved he's finally hungry enough to eat something that's not a bagged snack food. I don't want to jinx it by reminding him of my existence so I remain silent and dig into my own meal. It's pretty good, the food. I'll come here again if we stay in Hutton. And my hope is that we will stay in Hutton because I have no other plan.

"Why are we here?"

At first I'm startled that he's asking me a question. I need to swallow the lump of food in my mouth before I can answer. He waits while I chew, his expression somber, maybe a little bit worried.

I wipe my mouth with a napkin and edit the words in my head so I don't accidentally spit out profanity. "We're eating a late lunch. Don't you like your chicken? I can get you something else."

He sighs with annoyance, a sound that belongs to someone far older. "No. I mean, why did we drive here?"

I thought I explained to him why we came to Hutton. Maybe I didn't. I'm not used to answering to anyone else. Besides, since the first time he kicked me in Kevin Walsh's office I've been spending most of my energy trying to avoid setting him off.

I ball the napkin in my hand and try to talk to him in a way that he'll hopefully understand. "We're here because this is where my brother lives. I don't have any other family and I know you don't either. I thought this might be a good place for us to live. If not, we'll go somewhere else. Jonathan, my brother, is your uncle. Because I am your father."

The words still sound strange, awkward. *I am your father.* Now I'm thinking of Star Wars. Crap. I wonder if I seem sort of like Darth Vader to him.

"Oliver." I try to look into his eyes. "I know you really miss your mother. And I'm sorry."

His expression shutters. He inhales sharply and picks up a fork, which he uses to stab at the chicken nuggets on his plate.

I suck at this.

But I'm hungry so I finish my burger while the kid destroys his food. At least he's not throwing shit on the floor.

A teenage boy appears and cleans off the table where College Girl was sitting. She's nowhere in sight. Even if I had time for women she probably wouldn't be my type. Still, I don't mind looking at what I can't have.

Oliver has sufficiently wrecked his chicken nuggets and now he pouts, staring at a bunch of empty tables just so he doesn't have to look at me. He reminds me of Jonathan right now with that lost little boy expression on his face.

In my mind my brother is still thirteen, small and skinny for his age. The last time I saw him he stole some money from our mother's purse and gave it to me. She'd just kicked me out but I thought it was just one of her tantrums. I didn't really believe I'd spent my last night at home, or that I wouldn't be seeing my brother again.

The minutes tick by and I know I'm stalling. There's nothing to be gained by wasting anymore time in here. I pay the bill and get a firm grip on Oliver's hand.

"Let's go meet your uncle," I say, not adding that Jonathan has no idea that I'm within five hundred miles. He's changed his name. He's started a new life. I could have called him first instead of just crashing into his world like a bad dream. I found his phone number on his business web site. But there's a better than average chance he would have told me to fuck right off if he knew I was on my way.

I don't know what kind of man he is. I'm hoping there's still something left of that quiet, sensitive kid who used to read comic books and rescue small animals. That kid would offer help to anyone who asked. Right now I need his help.

So does Oliver.

Jonathan was always better than I am. With all my might I'm wishing that he still is.

Because I've never known how to help anyone except myself.

3
____

IZZY

Ruby's Bakery is a fitting follow up to Greasy June's. It's cheerful to think that the small city of Hutton is home to a small army of female entrepreneurs with old fashioned names.

The bakery is small and very pink and smells like the interior of a jelly donut. There are no customers and I don't see anyone behind the counter but the sign on the door was flipped to 'Open'. With regret I can see that I've arrived late in the day. There aren't too many options left in the glass showcases beneath a long counter.

I'm examining the contents when a girl appears in a doorway that must lead to the kitchen. She's wearing a sky blue polo shirt with the bakery name stitched into the upper right corner. And she's gorgeous. Her shiny black hair is tied back and when she smiles at me I'm reminded of all the beautiful women who were around every corner when I vacationed with my parents in Oahu.

She steps up to the counter. "I'm so sorry I didn't hear you come in."

"Oh, not at all. I just got here. Everything looks delicious. If ever there was a day I was in need of dessert it's today."

She backs up, looks down at the contents in the display cases and wrinkles her nose. "Afraid there's not much to choose from at this point. A woman stopped by about half an hour ago and bought up most of what we had left to bring to the nurses who run the NICU ward at the hospital."

"I'm sure they deserve it more than I do. Do you have any cupcakes lying around?"

"Sadly, no." She pauses and then gets excited. "You know, I totally forgot. My boyfriend made a batch of lemon scones before he left. I think they're still cooling on the rack. They are to die for."

"Perfect. I'll take three."

She dashes through the doorway again and returns within twenty seconds. She sets down a basket filled with perfect pastry triangles. "Try one right now. I insist. These beauties instantly turn any bad day around."

The Gutbuster still sits in my stomach, deciding if it wishes to digest peacefully, but I'm not one to turn down scones or kindness so I pluck one out of the basket and bite down. "You're right. This is amazing. So amazing that I'm forgetting my manners and talking with my mouth full."

She laughs and passes me a napkin. "Have another. I'm Lana."

"Izzy."

"As in Isabel?"

"Isabella. If I'm feeling pretentious I drag out every syllable when I introduce myself."

She laughs again. "I haven't seen you around. You go to HSU?"

"I will. I'm starting the Masters program in speech pathology. Can I have another scone? I'll pay for them all."

"No need. We close soon and they would have gone to waste."

Lana likes to talk and she's easy to talk to. In a very short period of time I learn that the bakery is owned by her boyfriend and they live together in a house not far from here. She's also a student at HSU but she's switched her major so many times that she still has no graduation date. She's cool. I like her.

And in turn I tell her all about my first day in Hutton. She becomes furious on my behalf at Landlord Lou. I leave out the part about the candy dish I stole. It would sound weird. Because it is weird.

Then Lana's face lights up because she has an idea. "Shane owns the house. It's actually divided into two apartments. My BFF and I used to live in the second one but a few months ago Caris moved out with her boyfriend. Well, he's her fiancé now. And he's actually Shane's best friend. Isn't that amazing the way it worked out? Anyway, we planned to rent the second apartment to a couple of college girls this semester but they've decided to go live in the sorority house instead."

I hope I know what's coming. I hold my breath.

Lana is practically bouncing. "So the apartment is available if you're interested. It's a two bedroom but fully furnished and I'm sure we'll have no trouble finding a girl to take the other room."

It sounds unbelievably perfect. Except I don't do well with the roommate thing. I've tried. Horror ensued. "I am definitely interested. I can give as many references as you want and I can cover the extra rent for the two bedroom."

She's amazed. "But I haven't told you how much the rent is."

"I'm sure I can handle it."

She laughs. "Independently wealthy?"

"A beloved only child with excessively indulgent parents."

"Just as good." Lana holds her hand out. "Shake on it?"

I pump her hand. "You've just saved my life. I thought I would be sleeping in my car or in the gutter like a stray dog or worse, in another cheap motel. But don't you have to ask your boyfriend?"

"Nah. Shane is great and he's kind of left the tenant hunt up to me. He'll be happy to know that I've found someone respectable."

"I promise I am respectable. I'll sign a vow not to party or play loud music."

"Not necessary." She winks. "We're not that stuffy. We even have fun now and then. Oh, and there's a pool. Use it anytime you like."

"Lana, I am immediately inducting you into best friend status."

"You may have to fight my girl Caris for the honor. Izzy, this is going to be great!"

She's a dream come true. She really is. I'm sure I've been touched by the benevolent hand of fate. In the space of a few minutes I've gone from being homeless and despairing to being handed a fully furnished two bedroom apartment, complete with an awesome new friend and a pool. Yay me!

Lana decides that her boyfriend won't be upset if she closes up the bakery a few minutes early. She doesn't work here very often. She was just filling in because Shane's regularly scheduled employee called in sick and he needed to go help out his best friend, Jay. Boyfriend of Caris. Lana has already spoken of them so much that I feel as if I know all of these people already.

She gives me the address and says Shane will be around later to help unload my car. She wraps up all the scones and insists that I need to take them with me.

"Fair warning. You'll be getting all the baked goods you can eat and then some. It's a perk of having a bakery in the family."

I accept the bag of scones. "Lana, are you sure you don't operate as a fairy godmother in your spare time?"

"Maybe. I do like sparkly dresses."

She needs to lock up so we agree that I'll meet her at the house in twenty minutes.

My state of mind has improved so dramatically I nearly skip to my car. Once I'm closed inside with the air conditioner on blast I decide to let my dad know of these fantastic new developments.

Guess what? I found a better apartment. Tell Mom I'll send her the details later.

He answers immediately, as if he was just sitting around waiting for my text, a funny thought because Deck Gentry is too busy fixing the universe to sit around and wait for anyone.

That's great news, kid.

And then...

Lou will be relieved.

WHAT???

After I called and said some words to him he decided to locate an apartment for you.

My dad knows I lied. He knows I was screwed out of my apartment. He freaking already talked to Landlord Lou. And he has one more thing to say.

Maybe now that you found another place you can mail Lou's candy dish back to him.

Holy shit. There's nothing the man doesn't know.

Maybe I ought to be annoyed. After all, I moved all the way to Texas to 'assert my adulthood,' as I explained it my mother. Independence is tough to come by when you're the daughter of Deck Gentry.

However, I'm not annoyed. I'm loved. I'm lucky. Everything has worked out just marvelously for me.

But Lou isn't getting his candy dish back.

Fuck no.

4
___

RAFE

This is his mailing address. I was able to find it by looking up his business on the county website. It's only by sheer chance that I found out what city he's in and what his name is now.

The house isn't large, but it's a house. It's nice. There's a colony of clay pots by the front door, all of them overflowing with flowers, mostly pink and white ones. I would bet that a woman lives here with him.

There's no car in the driveway and this is something I failed to consider, whether I'd have to wait a long time for him to show up. I wouldn't mind waiting but I can't expect Oliver to sit in the backseat for hours on end. He's already been cooped up in here all day.

Jonathan is a couple of years younger than me and I guess we got along all right when we were really young. He didn't change. I'm the one who changed. By the time I reached middle school I was constantly furious. I was furious that we lived in a shit trailer in a shit town. I was furious that my father was dead and my mother couldn't stand the sight of me. I was furious that the sun rose and set and that other families lived in real houses and were happy. I took my rage to the football field and earned the nickname 'Killer'.

Everyone knew why. Decades earlier, long before I was alive, my grandfather, Billy Hempstead, murdered two people. A young couple. She was a former prom queen and also his ex girlfriend.

As the story goes, they dated all through high school. Then high school ended and she married someone else and so did he. I don't know what happened to flip Billy's switch to raging evil and make him commit two violent murders. My own dad was a little kid when it happened. The murder scene on the edge of Arcana became a place where teens would go to fuck and to party. I did too. Every time I got shitfaced or had my dick sucked out there I would think of Billy Hempstead and there was always just a little piece of me that was afraid. Afraid that I would someday become like the grandfather who died in prison long before I was born. Afraid that my mother's meanest accusations were correct and something wicked lived in my blood, waiting to come of age.

That hasn't happened. I'm no killer. I'm also no hero but I've never hurt anyone who didn't deserve it.

Except Jonathan.

Mostly I ignored my quiet, sensitive younger brother but sometimes I didn't. I would push him around until he pushed back and then I used that as an excuse to punch him until he hit the dirt.

For a long time I've been ashamed of that. I should be.

And honestly, I've missed him. After all, he's my only brother. At least the only one I know about. My father wasn't shy about where he stuck his dick so there might be a few DNA companions running around in the world but I'll never know for sure and Jonathan will always be my only brother. Our mother didn't feel much love for me but she did like Jonathan so I figured he'd be doing all right wherever he was.

I was just shy of my sixteenth birthday when I was arrested for attacking an old woman in her home. Not just any woman. A member of the Chapel family. As in Richard and Nancy Chapel, long ago murder victims of Billy Hempstead. Jesus. What a fucking soap opera. There was no one willing to post bail and it was my first real contact with the grubby reality of incarceration. I was scared. Varina

Chapel didn't die but she didn't remember anything about the attack either. No one visited me while I was locked up. Not even my own mother. I sat in a prison cell for weeks before the cops found out that I wasn't the one who'd clubbed Varina Chapel half to death.

Then came the day when the worn out, cheaply suited public defense attorney announced that I was free to go. The woman's sleazy ass boyfriend had confessed to the attack. As for me, I didn't even get an apology. All I got was a brown bag filled with the random shit I'd been carrying in a backpack when I was arrested, along with the news that my mother had fled the area and taken Jonathan with her. She didn't wait around to hear my fate. I'm sure she assumed I was guilty. My brother probably did too.

What happened to them after that I never knew. I had my own problems. I ran the hell out of town before I could get scooped up by the child welfare vultures. Life was no picnic for a while and I try not to remember the details. Survival isn't easy when you're a teenager on the streets. I did things and I had things done to me. But I managed to live. Not everyone can say the same. And aside from a few brief vacations behind bars, I was mostly free.

Now and then over the years I'd try to look for Jonathan online. I couldn't give a fuck about the bitch who had the nerve to call herself a mother but I would have liked to know what happened to my little brother. He just disappeared. There was no Jonathan Hempstead anywhere.

He stayed in the back of my mind but I'd given up finding out what became of him. If he didn't want to be found then that was that.

Then, out of the blue a little over a year ago, I received a phone call.

I don't know how in the hell he came by my cell number. He said he was doing all right. He just wanted to know if I was all right too. The call was over before I knew it and afterwards I stared at the phone in my hand. I understood why he refused to tell me where he was. I wasn't fooled by his vague reference to living somewhere in Arizona. He didn't want to see me. Even his phone number had been blocked out so I couldn't call him.

But at least I knew he was alive. And he said he was okay. That would have to be enough.

About three months ago I was on break at a job site. My phone battery was very low and I didn't want to use the last of it. A pile of magazines had been left beside a nearby recycling bin and I grabbed the first one on top of the stack, a glossy copy of something called Texas Trades. I nearly choked on my burrito lunch when I turned a page and saw my brother's face staring back at me. The man in the photo had little in common with the skinny kid who kept to himself but I had no doubt he was Jonathan. Little Johnny. The boy I used to call Limp Dick. He was being highlighted in an article about new up and coming small businesses.

"Jay Phoenix, owner of Western Farmhouse Designs in Hutton, calls his brand new custom woodworking venture a 'dream come true'."

So he was in Texas after all and he'd changed his name to Jay Phoenix. No wonder why I found no trace of a man named Jonathan Hempstead. He no longer existed. Good for him, I figured. Against all odds he'd become a regular upstanding citizen. I had no plans to interfere in his life. If not for Oliver I wouldn't be interfering in his life now. Instead, here I am, lurking outside his house like some random stray hoping to be let in.

Oliver kicks the back of my seat while I keep watch.

"I don't think anyone's home," I say out loud. "We'll just wait here for a little while and if no one shows up we'll go get ice cream and come back later."

No answer.

Kick. Kick. Kick.

I grit my teeth. I haven't yelled at him once and I won't start now.

Doubt creeps in.

This Jay Phoenix person is a mystery and I don't have another card ready to play if he shuts the door in my face. I dragged this kid to the other side of the state because I'm not a good guy and there should be someone in Oliver's life who *is* a good guy.

I close my eyes with a heavy sigh.

Kick. Kick. Kick.

"Oliver. Could you please stop that?"

Kick. Kick. Kick.

I open my eyes and see a blue car slowing down before turning into the driveway. There's a girl behind the wheel. My brother is nowhere in sight but it's stupid to sit here all day with Oliver kicking my seat. If she knows Jonathan, then her heart might be soft enough to feel some pity when she sees the kid.

I open his door and reach for his hand. "Come on."

He resists, crossing his arms and glaring. Shit. I hope he's not about to have a tantrum.

I unbuckle his seat belt. Chicken nugget crumbs are still stuck to his shirt. "Oliver, please."

He jumps out and thankfully doesn't pitch a fit when I take his hand.

The girl in the blue car steps out, oblivious to the world as she examines her phone with a smile on her face. She looks like the type of girl who's always coaxing everyone to look on the bright side. She takes no notice of us and I don't want to startle her but now she's reached the door and is fumbling with her keys, ignorant to the fact that I'm standing a few feet behind her.

"Hello there," I say, in as nice a voice as I can say anything.

She spins around and her phone falls out of her hand. Her jaw drops. She's wide-eyed with disbelief. And something else. Something I've seen plenty of times before, just not usually in the eyes of women.

Fear.

I glance down at Oliver and hold up my other hand, a surrender gesture to prove that I'm not about to do anything fucked up.

"I'm just looking for somebody," I tell her. "I'm looking for my brother."

She continues to gape. There's something about her, something about her wide eyes and silly glasses that pricks at me. She's familiar somehow.

"Rafe," she croaks and cups her hand over her mouth.

I'm surprised to hear my name. She's got to be Jonathan's girl-friend. Sorry, *Jay's* girlfriend. I'm sure she's the one who planted all these flowers and he must have told her about me. Yet that doesn't explain why a distant part of my mind somehow recognizes her. And the way she's looking at me, like she thinks I'm about to cut her throat, is throwing me all the way off course. Women aren't afraid of me. Women fucking love me. The only time I make a woman cry is when I take my dick away because I'm tired of letting her play with it and want to move on.

Oliver yawns at my side and the girl's eyes flicker to him. Her expression changes in an instant. This gives me an opening.

"I'm looking for Jay Phoenix." I pause. "If you already know my name then you must know I'm his brother."

She nods, still looking at Oliver. "Yes, I know that."

"And this is my son." Have I said that out loud before? I'm not sure that I have. Oliver tries to pull his hand away but I keep a grip on him. The last thing I need is for him to go running down the street. I notice that her phone is still on the ground where she dropped it so I bend over to pick it up. She hesitates for a moment when I hold it out. The screen is cracked.

Finally she reaches for her phone. She looks up at me, clear eyed and sincere, and I understand what my brother would see in her. She's gentle and she's pretty. "I'm your brother's fiancé. My name is Caris."

The name is not a common one and it means something to me. I just can't remember what.

"We've met before," she adds. "A long time ago."

"Limp Dick's got himself a girlfriend."

I have no talent for remembering faces. There's no reason for me to remember hers. She was of no interest to me years ago, that last summer in Arcana. She was just some little girl that my brother was hanging out with.

By sheer coincidence, or perhaps not because the cosmic powers operate under a fucked up set of rules, she's also the granddaughter of Richard and Nancy Chapel. Maybe that's why the image of her face had survived somewhere in my head, long dormant and awaiting the inevitable day when we would meet again.

"Holy shit," I say because I can't believe it but with a nod she confirms the truth.

Oliver is fidgeting. I don't know if he's even listening to the conversation. The Velcro fastenings on his little black sneaker hang open and he steps on my foot.

Caris bends to his level and she smiles. "Hello. What's your name?"

He quits fidgeting and stares at her. A few seconds later a soft word emerges. "Oliver."

"It's nice to meet you, Oliver." She looks up at me. "He's not here."

"We can come back later."

"No, no." She stands and opens the front door. "Come inside, both of you."

A sense of relief loosens in my chest and I usher Oliver through the door.

We've barely set foot inside when a pair of grey cats run over to Caris and begin rubbing against her legs. She greets them with a bunch of high-pitched baby talk and notices that Oliver watches while she scratches behind their furry ears. "Their names are Brenda and Kelly. Do you like cats?"

I can't stand cats. Mostly because I'm allergic to them. I can already feel a sneeze coming on.

But Oliver is enchanted. He pulls away from me and I let him. He gets on the floor and reaches out a tentative hand. One of the cats sniffs his hand and purrs. He pets her head, so very gently, and the other one gets closer for its fair share of affection. He whispers something to them and when they try to climb into his lap I hear a sound I haven't yet heard; a giggle of laughter.

While Oliver cuddles with the cats, Caris has her phone out. The cracked screen doesn't stop her from texting a mile a minute. I don't need to be a genius to figure out that she's letting my brother know about this surprise visit. She looks up and sees me staring. She's still not completely sure about me but then her eyes land on Oliver crawling around on the floor with the cats and she melts. She sinks down to their level and they have a little cat party while I stand around and wonder if I ought to be explaining myself more thoroughly.

I don't need to wonder about this for very long because right outside there's a sudden shriek of automobile brakes. Caris freezes and looks to me. I understand that an important moment has arrived. I leave Oliver with Caris and her cats and step outside to greet my brother, the man who used to be Jonathan Hempstead and now calls himself Jay Phoenix.

5

RAFE

He charges across the front yard like he's storming the beaches of Normandy. He doesn't stop until he's standing three feet from my chest. I can't get over the sight of him. While we were growing up we didn't really look alike but now anyone would guess that we're brothers. He's a big motherfucker, broad through the chest and with arms that would qualify as lethal weapons. He's almost as big as me. But not quite.

"Jonathan," I say and somehow I can't quite believe it's him.

He stares at me. His eyes are narrowed, his jaw set. He's so tense that if I so much as flinch he'll probably throw a punch. "It's Jay now."

"Right. Jay."

He doesn't relax. "What the hell are you doing here, Rafe? How did you find me? Where's Caris?" He's panicked all of a sudden, looking around as if maybe I've stuffed his girl into one of the clay pots.

"I'm right here." That's her behind me in the doorway. She squeezes around me and he immediately pulls her safely to his side like I might eat her.

I should have rehearsed what I want to say. *Gee whiz, little brother, it's been a minute,* doesn't quite cut it.

Caris is the one who breaks the tension. "Jay, you have a nephew. His name is Oliver. He's inside, playing with Brenda and Kelly."

A wrinkle appears between Jay's brows. He's not expecting this news.

"I should have called first," I say.

My brother sighs. "Yeah, you should have called first."

"I thought you'd tell me not to come here."

He neither confirms nor denies the idea. "Why *did* you come here?"

I can't sum up the last three days in a sentence or two. "I'll tell you if you let me."

Another voice catches my attention. "Hey, I'm Shane."

I have no clue where this other guy came from. Is he a neighbor? Maybe this is what happens in cookie cutter suburban neighborhoods; if a stranger shows up then everyone on the block runs over to say hello.

"Rafe," I reply.

"And this is Oliver," Caris says because the kid has left the company of the cats and walked outside.

I watch my brother's face as he lays eyes on his nephew. The anger drains away and he glances at me, then back to Oliver. He even lets Caris leave his side and go to the boy. She points to the flowers in the pots and tells him they are called petunias.

Oliver is unimpressed. "I want to see the cats again," he says.

"Let's all go see the cats," Shane suggests. I still have no idea who the hell he is.

Caris leads Oliver inside and Shane follows. Jay remains where he is, not yet trusting me enough to turn his back. I take the hint and walk through the door next, knowing he's right on my heels.

Cat Party, Part 2 is already playing out in the living room. The sequel involves little pink balls that make a jingling noise when they roll and Oliver laughs again as the two cats chase their toys. Caris is down on the floor with them and Jay bumps me with his elbow as he enters the room. We eye one another.

Meanwhile, Shane makes himself at home on the sofa. At this

point I'm guessing he's someone Jay and Caris are close to instead of some random neighborly dude.

My brother and I stand mere inches apart and watch my son roll around on the floor.

"Where's his mother?" Jay asks.

I cough once and keep my voice low. "Dead."

He's startled and he takes a good long look at me. "Sorry."

When there's so much explaining to do it's tough to know where to begin. I don't really want to spill my guts in front of Oliver. If I could breathe easier I could probably think more clearly but my sinuses have begun to swell. I sneeze three times in a row and everyone stops to stare at me.

"It's the cats." I rub my eyes, which are now watering. I must look like I'm crying.

Jay snorts. "That's right. You're allergic to cats." He jerks his head. "Let's go out back."

Oliver picks up one of the cat toys and laughs again as the animals jump on him. I see that Shane is paying careful attention to me as I leave the room. His eyes shift to Jay and whatever passes between them prompts a nod from Shane.

The backyard is home to more clay pots and a shallow strip of grass. There's a wooden picnic table with four chairs and Jay takes a seat. He watches while I do the same.

"Who's your bodyguard?" I ask.

"Shane is my best friend. He's more than that. He's a brother to me."

Ouch.

I can read his real meaning. He considers Shane to be far more of a real brother than I am. So be it. I'm not here for me.

Jay crosses his arms. He's no longer scowling but he's not looking real friendly either. "Caris remembers you from Arcana."

"I'm sure she does." I pause. "She knows that I never hurt old lady Chapel, right?"

"She does know that."

"Kind of weird how shit works, huh? You guys ending up together after everything that's gone on between our two families."

He looks away. "I guess."

"And you're getting married."

He turns his head back to me and lifts an eyebrow. "And you're a dad."

"It's a long story."

Jay shrugs. "I'm not in a hurry to get anywhere right now. Tell it."

I tell him a little bit about Dana. I try to keep my language as clean as possible even though it's not my style. Dana was just an unhappy woman in search of some dirty thrills. At the time I was glad to supply them. There was never supposed to be more to it than that.

Jay leans forward in his chair when I get to the part where Dana didn't want me to play a role in our son's life. "And so you just walked away?" There's some disgust in his voice.

"Thought I was doing him a favor. I mean, shit, I was twenty years old and had just served a few months of time for assault. I didn't even have a regular job. She had a rich husband waiting in the wings and said he'd take care of her and the baby. I wasn't exactly stellar father material."

"And now you are?"

I don't think he's trying to be mean. It's a fair question. "I'm trying. The guy Oliver thought was his father doesn't want anything to do with him, said if I didn't take the kid then he'd get turned over to the state. I don't know what might happen to Oliver, getting shuffled through the system with no one to look out for him."

Jay inhales sharply and I'm surprised to see he has gone ashen. Something I said produced this reaction.

"You don't want to know what might happen to him, Rafe." There's a hard edge to his voice. His right hand is clenched. This is personal to him.

I choose my words carefully. "Did something happen to *you*?"

He nods. "Me and Shane. There are plenty of good people out there trying to do something decent for kids in need. But there are also some evil fuckers trying to do something else. Luck of the draw, I guess. We drew a shitty card."

I am genuinely sad to hear that he's been through some rough times. During our brief phone call he'd mentioned that our mother had abandoned him. I know the feeling. It fucking sucks. Now that I've got Oliver in my care I don't ever plan to let him feel like that.

We look at each other in silence, me and my brother, each of us with our own memories. Bad ones. Worse ones. Maybe a few half forgotten good ones imbedded deep. I couldn't have been all bad. Still, I was no picnic to live with.

"I was a messed up kid," I say.

He nods. "You sure were." He blows out a breath. "But that's all you were. A kid."

"I'm sorry."

He mulls that over. He shifts in his chair and lays his hands on the table. They are big hands, calloused, hard working. "You don't know what the hell you're doing, do you, Rafe?"

No point in denying the obvious. "Nope. I'm flying by the seat of my pants. There will come a time when I'll need to explain to Oliver who I am, this petty ass criminal who's been in and out of lockup. And I want to do right by him." I think for a second and decide to be brutally honest. "I don't think I'm a good guy. Maybe you are. At any rate I shouldn't be the only thing he knows of family."

His jaw works. He's still not sold on what to do about this sudden invasion of family members into his life. "So you plan to stay in Hutton?"

"Hoping to. A former boss hooked me up with a construction job about twenty miles from here. I haven't had any time to go apartment hunting but there's got to be something around."

The conversation is interrupted because the sliding glass doors open and Oliver leaps out. He's clutching something messy in his right hand and there's chocolate on his cheek.

Caris is right behind him and she smiles at the sight of us. "I gave him a chocolate chip cookie, Rafe. I hope that's all right."

It's a weird thing to be asked for permission for someone else to have a cookie. "That's just fine."

Caris follows my son to the far side of the yard, where he's discovered a mound of dirt. He stomps all over it while still holding his cookie. Jay watches every step Caris takes and from the look on his face it's clear the boy is crazy in love. Huh. I wonder what that's like. Some of us just aren't built for finding out.

Shane must have become lonesome in the house with just the cats for company. He's a thin, wiry guy. He's got to be my brother's age but he could pass for a high school kid if he wanted to. He wears a blue shirt that says 'Ruby's Bakery'. He sinks into one of the remaining chairs and gives me a grin.

"Your kid's awesome. He's got a lot of energy."

"Tell me about it. After just three days of chasing him I'm exhausted."

Shane looks confused. Jay takes it upon himself to explain, which I don't mind. After all, Shane is a *brother* to him.

"Rafe just met his son a few days ago. Oliver's mother died and his stepdad refused to be his guardian. Rafe took custody of Oliver rather than allowing him to become a ward of the state."

The last words are delivered in a hard tone and Shane catches on. The two of them exchange a grim look, which I suppose has to do with whatever they suffered together.

Jay nods in my direction now. "You'll have some trouble finding a place to live in Hutton right now. The university is about to resume classes and with all the college students pouring into town there's not going to be anything left."

Not great news. I've already given up my place in Houston. Plus I've promised I'll be at work at the new job site next week. I'm also beginning to realize what a colossal chore I've set for myself; not only do I need to find a decent place to live where there's no gunshots echoing at night and no heroin addicts haunting the stairs but I've got to figure out a childcare situation for Oliver. The term 'biting off more than you can chew' comes to mind.

"I'll figure it out," I grumble and look over to where my son continues to stomp on the dirt.

"You wouldn't be able to stay here, not with your cat allergy."

"I'm not asking to."

My brother rolls his eyes and then fixes his gaze on Caris and Oliver. "But maybe Oliver could stay for a few days. You know, until you figure a few things out. I'll be around and Caris is crazy about kids."

It's good of him to make the offer. And for a second I'm tempted to take him up on it. Ever since I left Kevin Walsh's office the crushing weight of sheer responsibility has been choking my peace of mind and destroying my sleep. It's possible that crashing in a motel room somewhere for a few days would give me a chance to breathe and figure shit out.

Except...

Except I made a promise.

The day we met, when I was still reeling from my new obligations and Oliver would hardly look at me, I made him a promise. After a long, confusing day he was finally exhausted and I let him have my bed to sleep in. He kept his eyes closed and his face turned when I sat on the edge of the bed but he wasn't asleep. He heard what I had to say. I promised my son that from now on it was going to be him and me. He's already lost more than anyone should have to lose. I have to be the person he can count on. If I break my first promise to him then he'll have no reason to trust any other ones I make.

"I appreciate it, but he stays with me."

Jay cocks his head and I could swear he seems mildly impressed. It's probably crossed his mind that I was just here to dump the kid in his lap and then take off. I'm prepared to prove differently.

Shane clears his throat. "I might have a solution."

Even Jay is puzzled. "You do?"

"The apartment."

"Thought you had tenants lined up for that."

He shrugs. "They flaked." Shane explains the situation to me. "I own a house just a few miles from here and it's split into two separate units. My girlfriend and I live in one. The other one is currently empty. There were supposed to be a couple of Lana's friends moving in but they decided to live in one of the Greek houses. I'll knock money off the rent since you're Jay's brother. It's furnished, has two bedrooms. You can stay there as long as you need to."

I shoot a glance at my brother. He's staring at his best friend and his expression is difficult to read. I get the impression he's not thrilled with this arrangement. Still, I'd be a fool to turn it down.

The words 'thank you' don't come easily to me. "Thank you, Shane. And I accept."

Oliver is done playing in the dirt. Cookie remnants stick to his hand and he bounds over to claim the last patio chair. Caris slides into Jay's lap and he wraps his arms around her. Oliver is happier than I have seen him yet and I deliver the good news.

"Guess what? We've got ourselves an apartment."

His face puckers. His hair is a wild mess. It didn't occur to me to comb it today. "I want to stay here," he complains.

"Well, we won't be far from here."

"Just three miles," Shane assures him.

Oliver is not convinced. "But I like it here."

Caris talks to him gently. "You can come over whenever you want, Oliver. Brenda and Kelly would love to see you."

He's thinking. "Will there be cats at the new apartment?"

"Afraid not," I tell him. "I'm allergic to cats."

His jaw sets. "Maybe you don't have to be there."

Okay, that stings a little. I know it'll take time for the boy to see me as a parent but life will be easier once he stops thinking I'm some kind of monster.

"Oliver, this will work out just great. We'll be living there together."

He swings his legs, his feet far from touching the floor. "I went to the bathroom."

I stand up. "You need to go to the bathroom?"

"No. I *went* to the bathroom."

"You went to the bathroom just now?"

"Yup."

"In the chair?"

He grins. "Yup."

"Fuck." I've got to stop saying that.

Caris saves the day. I'm extremely grateful when she takes Oliver inside to clean him up while I search through the truck for one of his little suitcases so I can get him something to wear that's not covered in piss and chocolate. Caris even gives him a bubble bath and as I stand in the living room, listening to the echo of his happy laugher, I'm struck again by how much the kid must miss his mother.

Jay approaches and while he's in a much better frame of mind than he was when he stormed the front lawn, he's still wary.

"I might be stepping over a line, Rafe, but are you sure you can handle this?"

"What?"

"Parenthood. You'll need to stay out of trouble."

I'm not sure about anything.

"I'll do my best."

Shane is in the living room, actively searching the couch cushions. "Jay, you see my phone?"

"No. Did you have it on you earlier?"

"Not sure. More than likely I left it at the bakery again. I was going to text Lana to give her a heads up that we've rented the apartment and we'll be home in a little while."

Jay tosses him a set of keys. "Maybe it's in the truck."

Shane rattles the keys. "Be right back."

Jay waits until Shane is out of earshot to comment. "He's got the biggest heart in Texas."

"Yeah, it was cool as hell to offer up his place to some guy who just walked in off the street."

Jay doesn't blink. "I'm just saying, if you fuck him over in any way, you'll have me to answer to."

I meet my brother's eye. "I have no doubt."

The moment of tension is broken when Oliver runs into the room. He's clean and combed and I have to admit he is pretty cute.

"I threw his clothes in the washer," Caris tells me as she takes her fiancé's arm.

"I owe you one." I can't stop myself from yawning. I've probably cobbled together less than six hours of sleep over the last three days. Shane mentioned the apartment has two bedrooms and is already furnished. The prospect of getting a full night's rest on a bed doesn't sound half bad.

Shane did not find his phone in the truck. He shrugs good naturedly. "Doesn't matter. Lana won't have a problem with you taking the apartment. She'll be glad she doesn't need to look for new tenants." He takes a look around at all of us. "Should we go? I can ride with Rafe and show him the way."

Jay nods. "See you there."

Oliver is unhappy. "I don't want to leave."

I take his hand and lead him out to the truck. "Everything's going to work out great, Oliver. You'll see."

I hope to god I'm telling the truth.

6

IZZY

The apartment is beyond perfect. There's way more space than I need and the small kitchen suits me just fine because I don't even like to cook. The furniture is mismatched and has seen better days but I'm sure not going to complain about that.

Lana insists on helping me haul some of my suitcases inside and then suggests leaving the rest for Shane. I had no intention of turning her boyfriend into my personal moving service but she claims he won't mind and besides, she wants to go swimming. She offers to lend me a suit if mine is buried in my luggage but luckily I know exactly where my favorite bikini is. It's white with pink polka dots and the cups contain some added padding to help disguise the fact that my breasts 'could be helluva lot bigger' as a certain lame ass ex boyfriend said in a parting line.

Lana is already swimming around while I linger by the edge, tying my hair into a knot.

"We'll invite some people over tomorrow," she promises as she treads water. "I forgot to ask if you're in a relationship."

"No boyfriend at the moment." I hop into water that's cool and delightful and reaches my chest. "Just a long and storied list of temporary mistakes."

"No worries. I know a ton of people. And you're hot. These Hutton boys will be breaking the door down."

I have no intention of boyfriend hunting anytime soon. In fact, I've begun to think that boyfriends might be overrated. I hate being cynical about love but I've been disappointed too many times.

Lana has dumped a couple of inflatable rafts into the pool. I climb on one and close my eyes. I've inherited my mother's excessive paleness along with her thick curtain of bright red hair so I should be wearing sunscreen. Hopefully it's late enough in the day that it won't matter.

There's a splash and then Lana's voice. "Hey, baby. Did you just get home?"

When my eyes open I see her climbing out of the pool and into the embrace of the guy who must be Shane. He's got the kind of baby-faced looks that girls go crazy for and he wraps her in a hug even though she's dripping and must be getting his blue shirt soaking wet.

I don't dwell on Shane for more than a few seconds because he's not the only one here. A man stands in the shade of the patio over-hang and holds the hand of a solemn little boy. This guy looks nothing like Shane. He's built like a Mack Truck. And, astonishingly, I recognize him. He and the little boy were the ones eating at Greasy June's this afternoon. What a coincidence that he turns out to be a friend of Shane's. At least that's my guess. There's no other reason for him to be standing around in the backyard with his kid. Hutton must be a smaller town than it seems.

His eyes lock on me and the corner of his mouth tilts up. He remembers me for sure and while I'm not naked as I lie here on this pool raft, when his eyes skim over my body I feel as if I am.

My attention shifts because something is going on between Lana and Shane. She has her hands on her hips and she's arguing with him. Shane gestures to the man and boy and then listens to his girl-friend as she points at me. He throws me a rather sheepish look.

In the middle of all this, new people are arriving, a guy and a girl. The girl is a cute blonde with glasses and I'm sure I haven't seen her before. But the man whose hand she's holding bears a strong resemblance to the tattooed demigod who remains in the shadows. Lana approaches them and exchanges a few words with the girl, who looks at me and then puts her hand over her mouth. Voices clash as different people begin talking at once and I still have no clue what's going on but the time has come to leave the pool and find out because Lana is gesturing in my direction a whole lot.

It's not until I'm standing on the cement that I realize I failed to bring a towel outside. I stand there dripping for a few seconds and no one notices, not even the tattoo king, who is now speaking to the newly arrived couple.

I square my shoulders and resolve to be dignified in my wet polka dots even though I suffer from a slight wedgie.

"Hi." I wave, not at anyone in particular.

I don't have a loud voice. No one hears me.

However, in all the confusion the little boy has escaped the grasp of the tattoo king. He stands at the edge of the pool and peers into the water.

"Hello." I crouch down beside him because instinct tells me not to leave a child unattended beside the water. "I'm Izzy."

He looks at me. He really is adorable, with thick black hair and big blue eyes. He's wearing a different shirt than he was wearing earlier today.

"Do you live here?" he asks.

"I do live here. I just moved in today."

He bobs his head and inches closer to the water. "I live here too."

That seems unlikely. Lana told me she lives here alone with Shane. He must be confused. Perhaps this house looks like his house. He's leaning over now, in danger of pitching headfirst into the pool. He's making me nervous.

I put my hand out in case he falls. "Do you know how to swim?"

He doesn't answer the question. He smiles at me. "I'm Oliver."

I would have to be cold blooded not to smile back. "Hi, Oliver. Is that your dad over there?"

Oliver glances at the tattoo king, who has yet to notice that his child is no longer beside him. Oliver makes a face. "Yeah, I guess."

That's kind of a strange answer. He's examining me now and chewing on his lower lip. He seems to be troubled about something.

"You have hair like my mom," he says softly.

"Will your mother be coming over today too?"

"No." He plops down on his rear end in a miserable heap. "She died."

Judging from the sudden tears in his eyes, the grief must be relatively fresh.

"Oh Oliver, I'm so sorry. I'm sure you miss her very much."

He sighs. It's a man-sized sigh from a little boy and it breaks my heart.

"Oliver!"

The boy's father has finally noticed that he's hovering by the edge of the pool and talking to a stranger.

"Hey." He crouches down and drops a hand on the kid's shoulder. "Don't run off like that."

Oliver shoves the man's hand away. "I didn't run."

The guy looks at his son. He looks at the pool. Then he finally gets around to looking at me.

"I was just keeping Oliver company," I say because he seems annoyed. There's something unsettling about being within four feet of him. He's big and he's hot and he could likely crush metal objects in his meaty hands. But more than that, he radiates unpredictability. Maybe it's the hard glint in his blue eyes or the way the muscles in his forearms flex, like he's silently coiling his strength in preparation for a fight. He makes me think of a bear that's just been let out of a cage.

"I'm Izzy," I add because he's obviously the kind of person who needs to be prodded on matters of courtesy.

"Rafe," he replies.

Oliver kicks off his right shoe. "I wanna go swimming now."

"No, not right now." Rafe stands and takes the boy's hand. "Come on."

Oliver wrenches away. "I WANNA GO SWIMMING!" He backs up and tilts his head back to deliver an accusing glare at his father. "Did you even pack my floatie arms?"

Rafe is confused. "Your what arms?"

"My FLOATIE arms!"

"I don't know what that is but I'll get you some."

I decide to help him out. "Rafe, I think he means flotation arms. It's a device that helps children stay afloat before they know how to swim."

The guy gives me a flat stare. I'm not sure he understands what I just said. Perhaps he's not all that bright.

"When I was in high school I taught swim classes at the local community center," I explain. "And the kids would-"

He cuts me off. "So you're the girl who was planning on living here."

I don't like the sound of that. "Uh, yeah."

He makes a noise that sounds like a mixture of a grunt and a laugh. "Better get over there then."

I get to my feet. I really wish I had a towel. Even though Rafe isn't openly leering at me, I feel as if I'm somehow at a disadvantage. But this feeling might have nothing to do with what I'm wearing.

Oliver has dashed back to the patio. He climbs into a cushioned chair, crosses his arms and frowns at the pool from a distance.

Whatever Lana is in the process of explaining she's very animated about it. The other girl, the one with the glasses, throws a sympathetic look my way.

Rafe bends over to retrieve his son's abandoned shoe.

I'd like to know what I'm dealing with before I go wading into the fray.

"Do you know what's going on?" I ask him.

"Yeah."

"Would you kindly share your information?"

He's starting to walk away but I hear him plainly. "Apparently we've rented the same apartment."

And that's exactly what I was afraid of.

I've signed no lease. I have no legal claim on the apartment.

I just can't freaking believe this.

When did I begin having such shitty luck? Have I cracked a mirror or accidentally walked under a ladder?

Maybe it's Texas. Texas must hate me.

I can't think of another explanation for the fact that I seem to have lost two apartments in one day.

Supposedly there's not a single available apartment in Hutton. Either I can beg to rent someone's sofa or I can set the 'asserting my adulthood' goals aside and ask my dad to place another phone call to Lou.

I'm already feeling defeated before I make the short trek from the pool to the patio to hear what I already know.

7

———

IZZY

Only a few sentences are required to sort out who's who and what we're all doing here. Jay is Shane's best friend and Rafe's brother. Caris is Lana's best friend and Jay's fiancé. I already knew that Oliver is Rafe's son but I'm stunned to hear that he has only met the boy a few days earlier, following the sudden death of Oliver's mother.

And yes, Shane has already offered the apartment to Rafe when Rafe showed up in Hutton with Oliver and no place to live.

Once everyone has been introduced and the situation has become awfully, depressingly clear, Jay suggests moving the discussion inside. Caris takes the initiative to volunteer to keep Oliver occupied on the patio so he doesn't have to hear the rest of us argue.

Lana offers me a towel and a quick hug. "I'm so sorry, Izzy. We'll figure this out."

I hope she's right.

At least now I have a towel to wrap around my body but I don't want to sit on the furniture and possibly get it wet so I stand against the wall in Lana's living room. Everyone else takes a seat except Rafe, who leans against the opposite wall. The arrangement makes it seem as if Rafe and I are about to enter hand to hand combat while a team of spectators watch.

"I'm sure there's a way we can solve this," Shane announces. He does look quite miserable. He was just trying to be a nice guy and do a favor for his buddy's brother. It's an unfortunate quirk of chance that Lana offered the empty apartment to me the same hour Shane offered it to Rafe. Apparently it's out of the question for Rafe to stay at Jay's place because Jay and Caris have two cats. And the guy who looks like he bench presses tractors in his spare time is allergic to cats.

"There aren't really a lot of housing options in Hutton right now," Jay reminds everyone in the room.

Lana sits beside her boyfriend. "Does Rafe really need to stay right here in town? He's not a student, is he? I bet he could find a place in Gaitor and it's only about twenty miles from here."

"Not a great area," Shane tells her gently and takes her hand. "Wouldn't be a good place for Oliver."

"Oh." Lana slumps into the sofa. "Maybe Izzy could stay over here on this side with us."

This is my cue to speak up. "Lana, you're a doll but I can't do that. You guys are used to having your own space. Plus didn't you tell me that the second bedroom is now filled with equipment for Shane's bakery?"

She sighs. "It is."

"The apartment has two bedrooms," says Shane. "Maybe until something else comes along, Izzy could take one bedroom and Rafe and Oliver could have the other one."

Lana objects before I do. "That's a terrible idea for Izzy. From the little I've heard about Rafe he sounds like a violent disaster."

I look to Jay to see if he's going to jump in and defend his brother. He doesn't.

Rafe defends himself. "Nobody needs to be afraid of me, least of all some helpless college girl."

Helpless??

Lana sniffs. "I'm not so sure."

He glowers. "Look, the only time I touch a woman is when she's begging for a fuck."

Gasps all around. One of them comes from me.

Jay is furious. "Rafe," he growls.

"What?" Rafe fires back. "The kid's not even in the room and I don't have a lot of patience for being accused of shit I'd never do."

"No one accused you," I point out. "You are making a fool out of yourself for nothing."

He yawns. "Fine, I'll swear on my left nut that I won't touch a hair on your virginal little head."

"I am NOT a virgin!" I shout this far louder than I should have.

Everyone stares.

I bite my lip.

Rafe laughs out loud.

Jay glares at his brother so hard I wouldn't be shocked to see Rafe get smacked.

Yeah, Rafe's an asshole all right. I've met plenty of assholes. A lot of girls find them inexplicably fascinating but I'm not one to be tempted by some grouchy prick, no matter how hot he looks. Ordinarily I would have no trouble cutting him down and turning my back. Rafe can go sleep in a dumpster for all I care and I'm sure Lana is on my side.

Yet the image of sad eyed little Oliver haunts me.

"You have hair like my mom. She's dead."

The poor child has been through hell and he's now stuck with this clueless tyrant. Oliver needs a home. He needs stability. He needs to be surrounded by people who will care about him when his nightmare of a father drops the ball. If ever there was a time in my life when I had the opportunity to step up and make a difference this is it.

"All right," I say. "I'll take one bedroom and you can have the other. I can be an adult and stay out of your way if you can do the same and stay out of mine."

If Rafe is surprised he doesn't show it. "Works for me."

Lana is less enthusiastic. "Izzy, are you sure?"

No. But I am my father's daughter. I should be capable of meeting any challenge. And I am not *helpless*.

Rafe is watching me. He actually does look exhausted. He's unshaven and there are circles under his eyes. He's not having a great day either. And despite the fact that he has some likeability issues, I feel a little bit sorry for him.

"I'm sure," I say.

Rafe dips his head in a nod, perhaps a gesture of respect or just because he doesn't feel like talking about this anymore. He starts heading for the door. "Gonna go unload my truck."

Lana pokes her boyfriend in the side. "Izzy still has some boxes in her car that need to be moved."

Shane rises from the couch. "I'm on it." He's cheerful now, relieved that the situation has resolved itself.

Jay appears less cheerful. He has a hand on his face, running his thumb across his chin. "He'll behave himself," he says to me.

I would feel better if there was more confidence in his tone. I hand my keys over to Shane so he and Jay can go outside to do some heavy lifting.

"Oh my god." Lana is on her feet and remains quite distressed. "I'm so sorry about all this. I had no idea. And Izzy, if you don't feel comfortable-"

"It's all right." I hook my arm through hers and squeeze. "I'll have my own room so I can close the door when Rafe gets on my nerves. Besides, the kid is awesome. This will be fun."

I'm trying to sound as upbeat as possible so she doesn't feel bad. Maybe it really will be fun. Despite his eye catching looks, Rafe is certainly not my romantic ideal so no worries about that kind of tension.

She pulls me toward the back patio. "Let's go see what Caris and Oliver are up to."

Before I leave the living room my eye is caught by something through the open front door. Rafe is carrying a trio of boxes stacked on top of one another. They are not big boxes but they are heavy. I know they are heavy because they are mine. They are filled with hand weights and hardcover books. Why is he carrying my boxes?

"Where do you want these?" he asks when he reaches the living room. He sounds bored, as if he's simply ferrying mounds of cotton. I try real hard not to be impressed by the sight of him balancing all three boxes with no effort when I'm aware that I would hardly be able to drag one of them across the floor.

I open up the connecting door between the two units. "I already started setting up in the first bedroom on the left. If that's a problem I'm sure we can negotiate."

He grumbles something. I think it's "I don't care" but there might have been a "fuck" thrown into the mix. I watch him stroll away with my boxes. I wish he didn't have such a nice ass. It's shapely and muscular and looks fantastic in his worn jeans. I make a private vow to myself never to notice this again.

Out in the backyard, Caris is showing Oliver pictures of her cats on her phone. She smiles and urges me to sit beside her on the patio sofa. Within a minute I get the impression that she's very sweet and very friendly. I'm pleased to think that she'll be another friend.

"Let's order pizza," Lana suggests as she skims the surface of the pool with a bug net. "I'm starving."

"Pizza sounds marvelous," I agree. "My treat for everyone. What do you think, Oliver? You like pizza?"

He nods. "With peppers."

"You mean pepperoni?"

"No. Peppers."

Caris objects, saying that I shouldn't be paying when it's my first day in town, but I'm determined and I win this fight.

Jay and Shane join us before the pizza shows up but Rafe doesn't. He pokes his head into the backyard a few times to see if Oliver is all right and he says nothing. Oliver takes no notice of his father's absence. He enjoys being the center of attention and he's a really bright little boy. As twilight settles he begins yawning a lot and chooses my shoulder as a place to rest his head when he dozes off.

Jay rises and goes inside, presumably to speak to Rafe, but he isn't gone long. Upon his return he collects Caris and the two of them say quiet goodbyes. Before he goes, Jay murmurs something in Shane's ear, prompting Shane to glance at Oliver and nod. I've already concluded that Jay and Rafe do not have a close relationship and I assume he's telling Shane to look out for the boy.

Lana moves to Shane's lap and looks at the sleeping Oliver. "He's precious."

"He is," I agree in a whisper. "But my arm is asleep and I'm afraid to move."

This isn't a problem for long because Rafe returns to the backyard. He stares at his son for a few seconds before lifting Oliver's small body in his arms. His hand brushes my arm in the process and the tingling thrill that results is both involuntary and unwanted.

"Have some pizza," I tell him, extending the proverbial olive branch. "There's plenty."

He shakes his head and looks to Shane and Lana. "Hey, thanks again for everything."

"Sure, man," Shane replies. Lana tilts her head and a small smile curves her lips as she observes the way Rafe cradles Oliver with care, the way one would carry a tiny baby. Rafe and I likely won't be great friends but he can't be completely awful. If he mouths off again I'm more than capable of firing back. He says not a word to me before disappearing with Oliver.

The night descends rapidly but I don't especially want to go inside. Lana and Shane are couples goals. I enjoy being in their company. Also, I have little desire to confront the overwhelming chore of unpacking all those boxes and suitcases. But eventually the long day catches up to me and I stifle a yawn. There's still some pizza left and I push the leftovers on Lana and Shane. I'm also still wearing Lana's towel and I insist on washing the thing before returning it.

"You're stubborn," she laughs. "I like it."

"I'll see you guys tomorrow. Is it okay if I go in through your place? I don't know if the side door is unlocked."

"Sure." Lana snuggles in her boyfriend's lap and her eyes are closed. "Good night, Izzy."

Before I twist the knob of the door that connects the two housing units together I listen for a moment. I'm hoping Rafe decided to turn in early. I'm too tired to deal with him. I crack open the door slowly, trying not to make any noise. I ease my head through the opening and take a look.

Rafe waves from the sofa. "What's up?"

I hope I keep my face from grimacing and step all the way in, closing the door behind me. "I thought you might be asleep."

"You mean you were hoping I would be asleep."

No point in lying. "Yes."

He thinks this is funny. I notice now that there's a blanket thrown across the sofa. And I also notice that Rafe is not wearing a shirt. Earlier today I wondered if he had ink on his chest. I don't need to wonder anymore. I'd have to get closer to see details but he has multiple chest tattoos and they are mismatched, all certainly drawn by different artists at different times. And Holy Toledo, the guy is ripped. Beyond ripped. Shredded. I'll give him that. His body should be enshrined in marble. Still, shredded marble or not, I'd rather not have a conversation with him right now.

Rafe stands and crosses his arms. "I want to talk to you."

I try not to sigh. "Can it wait until tomorrow? I'm exhausted."

"Too exhausted to spare a minute?"

"I can spare a minute." I lean against the counter. Someone, probably Rafe, has placed one of my boxes on the counter, the one I cleverly labeled 'Kitchen Crap'. Perhaps he's trying to atone for his earlier bad attitude.

He stays where he is by the sofa but he's frowning. "It's about what your friend said in there."

"You mean Lana?"

"Yeah, her. She said I was dangerous. I don't know what she's heard from Caris and Jay but it sounds like she knows that I have a record."

"I see." So Rafe has a criminal record. I'm not exactly shocked. "What did you do?"

"Nothing lately. But I've been convicted of some small time shit.

Drug deals, club fights. I meant it when I said I don't ever hurt women. I don't. You have nothing to fear from me but feel free to run a background check if you want details on my rap sheet. My last name is Hempstead and I've lived in Texas all my life."

It's an unexpected moment of candor. "Thanks for telling me. I might conduct that background check. But you don't scare me, Rafe."

He chuckles. "No?"

My eyes, traitors that they are, wander over his muscled arms. "No."

He cocks his head. "You don't scare me either."

"I'm glad we are mutually unafraid. Is Oliver asleep?"

"Yeah, he never woke up. I just let him stay in his clothes."

I point to the couch. "What's with the blanket?"

He glances behind him and then turns back to me. "I thought the kid should have his own room."

"So you're going to sleep on the couch?"

"Unless you have a problem with that."

"And if I do?"

"Tough shit."

I snort out a laugh. And I manage to lose my grip on the towel. It falls to my waist and gives Rafe a view of my polka dot bikini top. He doesn't stare. He doesn't have any reaction at all. He starts moving the sofa cushions to fold out the bed feature. I start walking to my room and I look once over my shoulder, wondering if I should say good night or something equally friendly. Rafe is already reaching for the light. A second later the room plunges into darkness.

I'm really not afraid of Rafe. He's gruff and irritating but I like to think I can read people pretty well and I don't get any frightening feedback from him.

However, after thinking about it for a minute, I decide to press the lock on my bedroom door.

Just in case.

8

RAFE

My face dives between soft thighs just after I'm offered a giant plate of bacon.

There's nothing weird about the scene because it's a dream. A female voice clearly says, *"Now how does that taste?"*

I open my eyes and instantly realize there's a boner the size of North America in my shorts. I sit up on the couch and cover my face with my hands for a few seconds in the hopes of scrubbing the images from my head. I don't know what time it is but it's early and I'm still not caught up on my sleep.

"I didn't mean to wake you," Izzy calls from the kitchen, which is mere steps away. Her hair is coiled on top of her head and she wears this silky looking robe thing that's patterned with pink flowers. After only three days of sharing an apartment with Isabella Gentry I've discovered two things:

1. She talks constantly.
2. She's a morning person in the most annoying way.

Oh, and there's a third thing I've discovered too.

I can make myself come really fucking hard when I imagine plowing her tight body while I beat off in the shower.

I'm doing my best to get cured of this new habit.

Izzy would be a prime piece of ass for sure but she's my roommate and so she's off limits. I think I even made a promise to that effect, something about swearing I'd never touch one hair on her virginal little head. She got mad when I said that. Screamed to the whole room that she's not a virgin. As if that matters. Just because she's been fucked before doesn't mean she's been fucked right. I snort out some laughter when I imagine the look on her face if she could read my thoughts right now.

"What are you laughing at?" she asks.

She's staring at me. So is Oliver. He's sitting at the table and chewing with his mouth open.

"Funny dream," I grumble, although I have a small problem. Scratch that; it's actually a big problem. So big it'll be waving hello with a will of its own if I stand up. With effort I clear my mind. I think of prison; the never ending noise and the stench of shit mixed with bleach. That flattens my hard on in seconds.

My sweat pants are draped over the back of the sofa and I discreetly yank them on over my boxers before standing.

"There's extra bacon," Izzy says. She's sitting down and scrolling through a tablet now. "It's over by the microwave."

That explains why the apartment smells like a sausage factory.

"Nah, I'm good," I say and search around the immediate area for a shirt. I could have sworn that I left one lying around before I turned in last night.

I can't find it now so I just fold the bed back up and figure Izzy will have to suffer through the sight of my bare chest.

"Oliver says he's never had bacon before." Izzy uses her thumb to swipe at her screen and then flashes a smile at my son, who's happily invested in his breakfast of cereal with a side of bacon.

"Is that right?" I feel as if I'm intruding on their cozy little breakfast scene. It's weird sharing a place with a girl. But that pales in comparison to getting adapted to fatherhood.

Things have been a little bit better since our arrival in Hutton. Oliver and I haven't had a real breakthrough yet but he doesn't glare at me as much and hasn't kicked me in forty-eight hours so that's something. As for my brother, I don't have any issues with thinking of Jonathan as Jay. He and Caris have been over here a lot. Caris is terrific. She tries to be a buffer between Jay and me, like some kindly adult who wants two warring neighborhood kids to be friends. I'm willing, even if I'm no good at being the friendly type. I just really don't know what to say to him. If I thought it would do any good, I'd start every day with an apology for being a shitty brother when we were kids. I am honestly grateful for all the help he's given us. And he clearly has a soft spot for Oliver. He brings a little present for the kid every time he shows up.

Then there's Izzy. She's all right. Oliver loves her and she's great with him. I just hope I have enough willpower to resist temptation. Even when it's sitting right in front of me, bare legs crossed, robe slipping from one shoulder, hair in a sexy heap that's dying to be grabbed by my fist and pulled.

STOP!

I don't want my dick to get hard again right now. Because then I'll have to think about prison once more in order to tame the beast and that's not the way I want to start the day.

Instead of picturing Izzy naked, I decide to make some coffee and try to engage my son in a conversation.

"What have you got there, Oliver?"

He stuffs another piece of bacon in his mouth. "Food."

"No, I was talking about the book."

He touches the colorful illustrated children's book that sits on the table in front of him. "Yeah, it's a book."

"Want me to read it to you?"

This time a heaping spoonful of cereal disappears into his mouth and he chews a whole bunch before answering.

"I can read it myself."

I sigh and wish for the coffee to finish brewing more quickly. The coffee maker is Izzy's, one of those fancy machines with a bunch of buttons and seventeen gourmet settings. She takes pity on my struggle.

"Press the button on the left," she says.

I do as she says. The machine makes a weird noise.

"No." She sets her tablet down and stands up. She's over here in two steps because the kitchen area is tiny. "The other button on the left."

Apparently I'm not quick enough to suit her because she sighs and reaches over to press it herself. The machine immediately beings to purr again.

"See?" She grins and crosses her arms. "Easy."

The hell it is. I used to have my own coffee maker. It had a single on/off button and no one needed to take a freaking class in order to operate it. The glass pitcher broke somewhere during the move and I haven't had a chance to buy a replacement yet.

Izzy is still looking at me. She's standing close, close enough to see the freckles sprinkled across the bridge of her cute nose and smell her shampoo.

"Lana had an idea," she says. "She suggested that she and I could take Oliver to the mall for some back to school shopping since he starts kindergarten tomorrow. Maybe it would give you a chance to get a few things done. Like unpacking." She surveys the scattered boxes and bags and wrinkles her nose. "The living room is practically a fire hazard."

My brain cells are not alert enough to handle this flood of information. But I look around and notice that all the boxes of random shit and garbage bags filled with clothes belong to me. In my defense, I'm always messy. Usually there's not anyone around to care. And since I got here I've been spending all my time just keeping up with Oliver. Caris helped me get him registered for school and it's true that his first day of kindergarten is tomorrow. The idea that he'd need school supplies had not yet occurred to me.

While these thoughts tumble through my head, Izzy continues to talk. "Do you know what size shoe he is? I suppose it doesn't matter. We'll have him measured at the store. And he says he wants a backpack with cats on it. We can get him lunch too since we'll probably be gone for a while. Oliver doesn't have any food allergies, does he?"

"Food allergies?" I scratch my head. I look at the kid, who chews on another bacon slice and turns the pages of his book with greasy fingers. "Not that I know of."

She pours a mug of coffee. It's hers, a hot pink giant of a thing that's almost wide enough to be a soup bowl and has the word 'SASSY' painted on the front. She hands it to me, which is nice because I don't know where the hell my own simple black coffee mug is. I just hope that drinking from this one doesn't make me grow a vagina.

There's a slight frown on her face now and her hands land on her hips. "So it's fine if we take Oliver to the mall?"

Oliver is listening to the conversation more than he appears to be. "I wanna go to the mall."

The coffee is hot enough to burn my throat but I swallow a few big mouthfuls anyway. There are only two chairs at the table and Izzy had been sitting in the second one before I interrupted their breakfast by waking up. I don't want to take her spot so I just lean against the counter.

"I can take you to the mall, buddy," I offer. I'm trying to sound all chipper but my voice comes out like ragged gravel.

His lower lip juts out. "I wanna go with Izzy."

I shouldn't feel hurt by that. He and Izzy have definitely bonded these last few days, which is cool but also makes me feel guilty. I never had any plans to turn her into a live in babysitter.

"Oliver," she says with sweetness. "Remember we talked about table manners. Now use your napkin."

He wipes his mouth with a paper napkin and throws an angelic smile in her direction. Who am I to deny the kid a fun trip with his new favorite person? Sure, I could insist on taking him myself but it's a safe bet he'd fight me every step of the way and then no one would have a good time. Besides, I should figure out how to store my crap so that no one breaks their neck walking to the kitchen.

I locate my wallet where I left it on an end table and pull out a wad of cash. I drop it next to Izzy's plate.

"That should cover whatever he needs."

She peers at the cash with a dainty frown. "Rafe, I really have more than enough to pay for everything. Oliver's trip to the mall is my treat. Besides, I know you don't have a lot of resources and I'm sure you could use the money to pay for other things."

She says this so grandly, like a queen giving out favors to her subjects. I don't know what her deal is or how she has money to burn. She's a full time student, just moved here from Arizona, and has said nothing about getting a job. Yet she drives an Escalade and owns a ton of designer accessories that even my uneducated eye can see cost a pretty penny. She reminds me of the rich girls who go slumming for cheap thrills and dirty fucks in places like Spit, the downbeat bar where I met Dana Walsh.

But my son adores her and I really do owe her for all the time she's been spending with him. I'll bite my tongue this time.

That doesn't mean I'm going to let the money comment go by. I may not be bathing in riches but I have enough to pay for my own kid's backpack and shoes. Plus, there's only so much I'm willing to be indebted to Izzy Gentry.

"Use the money," I tell her in a tone that warns the issue is settled.

We lock eyes. Seconds pass.

"I'll bring back your change," she says, lifting her chin so she can keep staring me down.

But I have a gift for staying focused without a single blink and I can outlast her.

Izzy breaks eye contact first. I'm not sure but I think she's blushing. She puts her dishes in the dishwasher and leaves the room. A few seconds later I hear the shower switch on.

Oliver continues to page through his book.

I gulp my coffee and set the SASSY mug down. "Oliver, would you read a few pages to me?"

He closes the back cover. "I just finished."

Now that Izzy is gone I figure there's no reason why I can't take her chair. She's left her tablet on the table and it's open to the last thing she was looking at. She was reading one of those digital books and the title is listed on the top of the screen.

In The Duke's Bed (A Naughty Nobility Story)

That's funny. In her spare time Izzy likes to imagine fucking a duke. Somehow I'm not surprised.

Oliver is in the process of crushing the remnants in his cereal bowl with the back of his spoon.

I forget about Izzy's duke and spend a minute struggling with the task of finding something to say to my own kid. I wish there was a book I could buy, something with a catchy title like '*How To Speak To Children*'. I also wish I hadn't missed every important moment in his first five years.

I clear my throat. "So you're off to kindergarten tomorrow."

He quits smashing his cereal and his eyes lift. "Do I have to go?"

I don't know. Does he? I think so. Kids are supposed to go to school.

"It'll be fun," I assure him. I try to recall my own kindergarten days and draw a blank.

He makes a face and slumps in his chair. My new job begins tomorrow and luckily the school offers before and after school daycare. I feel bad that he'll need to be there for so many hours but I spoke to the teacher who runs the daycare program and she made it sound like a ton of fun. They have snacks and they watch movies and they run around on the playground. That all sounds better for the kid than hanging around the apartment.

"Oliver." I reach out and touch his arm. It's so small, like the rest of him. "You know if there's ever anything you want to talk about, you can talk to me, right?"

He frowns. "Like what?"

I search for the right words. I ought to spend some time writing out a script so I'll have some handy sentences to spit out. "Just any feelings you might be having. Or if you have any questions about me." I hesitate to say the last sentence but I know it should be said. "You can also talk about your mom if you want."

He jumps off the chair and collects his book, holding it to his chest. "I'm going to my room."

"Hold on, I'll pick out some clothes for you."

"I know what I want to wear."

"Did you brush your teeth yet?"

"Nope." He disappears and slams the door to his bedroom, leaving me alone in the kitchen and wondering how to help a grieving child feel better.

I was older than Oliver when I lost my dad. He was drunk and he was driving. The police were chasing him and he slammed into a tree. My little brother cried a lot in the days that followed but I don't remember crying. I remember being in the backyard and feeling like my chest was going to bust open if I didn't do something. So I did something. I punched the side of a half rotten woodshed over and over until my knuckles were bleeding and stuck with a bunch of painful wood splinters. My mother was irate and dragged me off to the doctor for a tetanus shot. On the car ride she looked at me in the rearview mirror and it was the first time I realized she didn't like me much.

"You'll live up the Hempstead name all right. You're just like them, Rafe."

When Kevin Walsh took it upon himself to rearrange all of Oliver's paperwork and insert me into his birth certificate, he also switched Oliver's last name from Walsh to Hempstead. I signed him up for school as Oliver Hempstead and I'm not sure Oliver understood that when I told him about it.

Fuck. It's not fair that a little boy has to deal with so many of these adult issues.

When Oliver emerges from his room he's wearing red shorts and an orange shirt. Far be it from me to argue with his fashion choices.

There's a knock at the door connecting our apartment with Shane and Lana's place. I have found my shirt and take the time to yank it over my head before opening the door to find Lana on the other side. She's warmed to me quite a bit since the day we met but I wouldn't call us friends.

However, she has no such reservations about Oliver.

"Lana!" he yells and jumps into her arms when she opens them.

Meanwhile, I had told him he could call me Rafe if he didn't want to call me Dad but he still just refers to me as some variation of 'Hey, you'.

Izzy appears with perfect hair and makeup, her light pink sundress making her look like an advertisement for summer picnics. A lot of female squealing ensues as she and Lana fuss over Oliver and I wonder how long my head can take the noise before a migraine blooms.

"Say goodbye to your dad," Izzy tells Oliver when she takes his hand on her way out the door.

He turns just long enough to glance at me. "Bye."

"Bye, Oliver. See you later."

He nods and tries to drag Izzy outside.

She tosses a stunning length of long red hair aside and faces me. "I'll have him back by three."

"Great."

Her eyes sweep over the living room. "And you'll be hard at work unpacking, right?"

Instead of answering I just cross my arms and stare at her. Lord, she's fucking pretty. Bossy and prissy as hell, but the things I want to do to that little pink sundress should be illegal.

She thinks I'm just being a dick by standing there in silence so she rolls her eyes and follows Oliver and Lana out the door.

The apartment rings with the silence of their absence. This is the first time since the moment I walked into Kevin Walsh's office that I am actually alone. I celebrate this by searching up some amateur porn on my phone and then heading for the shower to jerk off. And as much as I try to keep my mind focused on the hot scenes I just watched I can't stop thinking about flipping Izzy Gentry's pink dress over her head and bending her into some crazy positions. In my head I come in her mouth and then for real I come on my hand. Fantasy Izzy swallows like a good girl and I lean my head against the shower tiles with a thick groan.

I'm in a better mood after that release and I'm pretty sure I can keep my thoughts clean for the rest of the day. After throwing a load of laundry in the wash I begin pawing through the carelessly packed boxes and random garbage bags. It's not like I had loads of time to pack my life up and I ended up leaving a lot of things behind in Houston but I guess if I haven't missed them yet then I'm not going to. The clothes that can be hung up are placed in the closet in Oliver's room because there's no other empty closet I can take. One of these days I'll buy a separate dresser but for now I take the top two drawers of the one in his room.

When Kevin Walsh gave my son to me I was also handed two suitcases and a small sealed box, like *'Here are your Oliver accessories'*. He said Dana's personal effects would be placed in a storage unit that would be paid for until Oliver was old enough to decide what he wanted to do with everything.

As I stand in my son's room it makes me sad to look at those two lonely little suitcases lying in front of the bed. They are mostly full of clothes and a few stuffed animals and books. I unload the clothes into the bottom dresser drawer, set the stuffed animals on the bed and the books on top of the dresser to cheer the place up a little.

Suddenly I'm mad. He should have more than this. Dana was the type who would have given her kid anything he wanted. Walsh likely just couldn't be bothered packing it all up.

I stow the suitcases beneath the bed and reach for the lone box that is still sealed with packing tape. When I open it the first thing I see is a yellow baby book with a picture of a teddy bear. Underneath that there's a framed photo of Oliver and his mother. The picture must have been taken on his first birthday because he's about to smash a fist through a cake with a big number one stuck in the middle. For days I've been struggling to recall the details of Dana's face and I stare at the photo. She's laughing and she's holding her baby, our baby. She looks happy.

With care I set the photo on top of the dresser beside a stuffed giraffe. I leave everything else in the box and store it on a shelf in the closet. Someday Oliver will want to go through the contents. Maybe he'll even want to show them to me.

Now that all the unpacking is done the living room looks less like an episode of one of those hoarding shows. And then, because I shouldn't be such a slob now that I'm a dad, I clean the surface of every piece of furniture in sight before moving on to scrub the kitchen and clean the bathroom. When I discover a mop that's been propped up inside the tiny coat closet I take that as a sign to mop the entire floor.

All in all, the place looks very satisfactory by the time Izzy and Oliver return. Izzy's loaded down with a bunch of shopping bags and I wonder how much stuff is required to begin kindergarten. Oliver whizzes right past me while shouting that he's going to change into his bathing suit.

Izzy sets the bags on the kitchen table.

"How was shopping?" I look down into one of the bags and see a green backpack covered with cat cartoons.

"Oh, we had a great time. Your son is a natural shopper. He didn't complain once. He is the happy new owner of a backpack, a lunch bag with a matching water bottle, markers, pencils, glue sticks, new sneakers, and because he's such a gifted little reader I encouraged him to pick out some new books. We had lunch in the food court and Oliver ate a turkey sandwich. When he asked for potato chips I talked him into an apple. He likes apples. Did you know that? Anyway, Lana and I told him we'd take him swimming in the pool. Is that all right?"

I'm not sure if I'm supposed to respond at this point or if she just needs to breathe before she keeps talking. I take a chance and say, "Fine by me."

She walks around, inspecting all the newly cleaned corners of the apartment. "This is much better. You did a great job in here, Rafe."

"Yeah, maybe I can get a position as a maid if my other job doesn't work out."

It's a joke. At least, I mean it as a joke. But Izzy gives me a funny look so apparently I need to work on my delivery.

She's already en route to her bedroom. "Would you like to come swimming too?"

"Think I'll sit this one out." I can't remember the last time I dipped a toe into a pool.

When everyone is suited up and in the backyard I decide to go out and observe my son having fun. Oliver withstands getting slathered with sunscreen and is so excited about his swim date he even throws a smile my way. This makes me double down on my appreciation for Izzy. I'll try to keep the apartment neater from now on.

I'll also try to stop making her suck my dick inside my head.

Izzy and Lana toss around a giant yellow beach ball with Oliver while I stay on the shaded patio. I have to grin at the sight of him having the time of his life, paddling around the pool with the swim vest that keeps him afloat. Another gift from Izzy.

Shane sits in the shade with me for a little while, just shooting the shit. He's a genuine guy and could probably befriend a rattlesnake with no trouble. After a while he decides it's too hot to stay out of the water so he jumps in and lifts his girlfriend in the air, much to Lana's squealing delight.

Jay and Caris stop by because they want to wish Oliver good luck for his first day of kindergarten. Jay delivers a nod of greeting and then wanders off to talk to Shane while Caris sits beside me in a patio chair.

"Here." She sets a grocery bag on the table. "I brought you some boxes of cheese sticks, fruit snacks and granola bars in case you're short on things to pack for Oliver's lunch this week."

That's right. He'll be eating lunch at school. Izzy mentioned buying him a lunch bag. Somehow it hadn't sunk in that I'd need to pack it with food every day. Maybe I should carry a notebook around so I can keep lists of all the small but important chores that come with caring for a child. So far I'm not very good at figuring these things out on my own.

"Thank you," I say to Caris. She's using her shirt to clean her glasses and she gives me a smile before turning her attention to the fun and games going on in the pool.

"Yay Oliver!" Izzy claps when he catches the beach ball. He throws it up in the air and Jay's so busy talking to Shane that he doesn't notice anything until the ball hits him in the head. He laughs and tosses the ball back into the pool.

"Jay's crazy about his nephew," Caris says, grinning as she watches my brother.

"I'm glad." I'm also watching my brother. He and I have yet to have a lengthy conversation alone and I feel like we should.

This is not the time, though.

"Did you guys set a date?" I ask Caris.

She holds out her left hand, admiring her engagement ring. "We're thinking about May. We're planning on having the wedding at the butterfly conservatory here in Hutton. It's a special place for us and it'll be beautiful in the spring."

When I look at her I can still see the skinny girl who ran all over Arcana with her friend Jonathan Hempstead. I broke into her house once. Well, her aunt's house. That's where she lived the summer she stayed in Arcana. It was just a thing that I did, just for the pure hell of it, just because I was bored and enjoyed being a creepy asshole. It's a big reason why the cops picked me up when Varina Chapel was attacked. I'm sure that Caris remembers all of this.

"How is your family?" I ask her. This not a topic I've touched on yet. Her mother was orphaned when Billy Hempstead went on his murder spree.

She doesn't mind answering the question. "My parents are great. They are currently on a Caribbean cruise." Her face then falls and she stares at her hands. "Aunt Vay died six months ago."

Aunt Vay. That's Varina Chapel. "I'm sorry to hear that." And I am sorry. That woman never did wrong by me. She wasn't even conscious when the cops decided I must have been the one who assaulted her. I was cuffed and thrown in a cell so fast my head spun.

Caris is still troubled. She's twisting her ring around on her finger and biting her lip. "Rafe, I should tell you something. I'm the one who told the police you'd broken into our house and that you'd been sleeping in our shed."

I'd only been sleeping in their shed because my mother had kicked me out and I hadn't figured out a plan yet.

Caris is nearly tearful as she looks at me. "It's my fault you were arrested."

"Nah." I feel the urge to pat her shoulder but that would probably be too much. "It's not your fault. Everyone was looking for reason to collar me for something, being the grandson of Billy Hempstead. My dad was no prize either. But your folks had the worst of it after what my grandfather did."

She looks at Jay. And then she looks at me. "Didn't Jay tell you?"

"About what?"

"I don't think your grandfather murdered my grandparents, Rafe. There was another man, a drifter and known killer, who confessed to killing Richard and Nancy a few years ago. He's dead now but he knew details. And he was in Arcana at the time. "

Hearing this is so startling that I don't even have anything to say. All my life I've known that I was the grandson of a hated killer. No one can understand what that's like, to have everyone look at you as if evil runs in your veins. It was what messed up my father. It messed me up too. Finding out that maybe it was never true tilts the world on its axis.

My head spins. How much of a difference would this have made in our lives? There's no telling. We might have grown up like regular kids, if not for a lie that spanned generations.

My brother could have found the time to tell me all this himself by now. I can't explain why he didn't.

"Rafe?" Caris looks worried.

"You shouldn't let him know that you told me," I say to her.

She's puzzled. "Why?"

"Just don't."

She doesn't agree but she doesn't argue either.

The latest developments are still running through my mind when

Jay calls to Caris that they should get going. He's got to go pick up some materials for tomorrow's jobsite.

"You have a fabulous first day, sweetheart," Caris says, blowing Oliver a kiss. Jay bends down close to the side of the pool and offers a high five, which Oliver gladly responds to. Jay grins and roughs up the kid's hair before taking Caris's hand and walking toward the back gate.

"You got everything you need?" he asks me on his way out.

"Yup," is my one word answer.

He pauses to look at me, probably hearing the clip in my tone. But an instant later he keeps walking.

Leaning back in the chair, I close my eyes. I'm not a big lover of alcohol, not anymore, but I sure wouldn't turn down a bottle right now.

The echoes in my head are ten years old; the din of Friday night football in small town Texas, the chants of the roaring crowd.

KILL-ER! KILL-ER! KILL-ER!

My eyes are still closed when I sense a shadow has fallen nearby and I open them to find a dripping wet beautiful girl in a bikini. She's displeased with me. I know the signs by now. Her hands are on her hips and her pouty lips are pressed together.

"How can I help you, Izzy?"

She's in the mood to pass out lectures. "I was just thinking that since you're not doing anything maybe you should go in the pool with your son."

Oliver stands on the side of the pool, takes a running jump and leaps in, causing a small tidal wave. Lana is right there to make sure he stays afloat. She and Shane cheer.

"Did Oliver say he wants me in there?"

"No," she admits. "But it's probably a better use of your time than sitting over here by yourself and glaring at the patio cushions."

"You know what, Isabella Gentry?" I stand up and stretch. "Every once in a while you should just really mind your own fucking business."

Too late I realize Oliver has climbed out of the pool again. He's also taken a few steps in our direction, probably because he wants Izzy to watch him jump. In any case, he's well within earshot of what I just said.

Izzy's really pissed now. She snatches her towel and stalks into the house. That's bad enough but when I catch the expression on Oliver's face I feel even worse.

As far as he's concerned, I'm the shittiest person in the world.

9
____

IZZY

y father was born in a small prison town in the desert. His mother was an immigrant from Mexico and his father was a Gentry; a scandalous local family whose ranks were filled ruffians and criminals. They both died long before I was born but he always spoke of his parents with affection.

My mother's story is different. Her father was a powerful bishop in an insular religious community on the northern Arizona border. Her mother was one of his many wives. I never met them either but that's mostly because my mom never wanted to see them again after they forced her to marry an old man when she was just sixteen years old. After stories about the cult became public, thanks to my brave Aunt Promise, my mother was rescued and for the first time in her life she was allowed to live normally.

Anyone who meets the two of them would quickly notice that they are very different. Deck Gentry is big and fierce and can easily intimidate anyone if he wants to. Jenny Gentry is gentle and sweet and will give anyone a hug if they look as if they need one.

I'm lucky to be their daughter and I love them both very much.

It's always been just the three of us, although my extended family is huge. When I was around five or six I became obsessed with having a brother or sister. All of my many cousins had siblings. I was the lone only child. I would write down this wish on Christmas lists. I would beg for the gift of a sibling for my birthday. Then I would cry when I never received one.

My dad always laughed at me and said he'd already scored the best kid in the world on his first try. He didn't feel like he could do any better.

Just last year I learned the truth. My mother had suffered three miscarriages. One before I was born and two after. And this time I cried to know that while I pleaded for a sibling she was in agony over the children she'd lost.

While I watch the early morning shadows shift on the ceiling above my bed I think about last night's conversation with my parents. After a long first week of classes and coming home every day to the company of sullen Rafe Hempstead I was feeling a little homesick.

My mother wanted all the fun details. Did I like the professors in the graduate program? Have I made lots of friends? Have I met any guys worth mentioning?

My dad, on the other hand, wanted to remind me that if anyone gives me any trouble then he's only a phone call away. I know he meant Rafe. He just about hit the ceiling when I came clean about my living arrangements. Only the soothing interference of my mother and my explanation about Oliver calmed him down. Of course he looked into Rafe's criminal history. What he found was exactly as Rafe said. When Rafe was young he had a few drug offenses. He got into some fights. His last conviction was for assault and according to the case details he hit a man who was trying to strangle the bartender. That was five years ago. His probation expired recently and lately he's stayed out of trouble.

My father is all for rehabilitation and second chances but I'm not sure he's as generous with those traits when it comes to his only daughter. I wouldn't be surprised if Deck Gentry has an alternative means of checking up on Rafe to make sure he's maintaining his status as a law abiding citizen. For Oliver's sake I hope that he is.

Rafe, of course, is completely oblivious to the fact that he's been the source of all this parental anxiety. All week he's been up before the crack of dawn, drops Oliver off at the school's early daycare, picks Oliver up after work and falls asleep on his couch bed before ten. We've barely spoken since last Sunday when he told me to mind my own fucking business when I tried to prod him off his brooding patio throne.

Remembering this brings a sigh of aggravation.

Fuck Rafe Hempstead.

Not literally.

No way.

If being barked at by an irritable jerk got me hot then I'd be all over Rafe's dick.

Instead, I'm going to focus on the things that are important, the things that make me happy. Like school. And my new circle of friends. Especially Oliver.

A smile rolls over my face as I remember how excited he was yesterday to show me the picture he drew in school of a pair of grey cats. Then he grew serious and asked me if cats know how to brush their teeth. He is too adorable for words. And he is the star of our little social clique. Lana and Shane are thrilled by every little thing he does. Caris and Jay are completely devoted to him. I don't know them as well as I've come to know Lana and Shane but I like them. Caris is a total sweetheart. Jay is kind of a quiet fellow, although he is light years ahead of Rafe when it comes to basic pleasantness.

I'm not sure what the deal is between the two brothers. Lana has told me a little, about how they grew up in a small town here in Texas and they didn't have an easy time. They had not seen one another in years when Rafe showed up here in Hutton with Oliver. I can't imagine that, how someone could have a sibling out in the world and not see him for years. If I had a sister I'm sure I would be in her face every single blessed day.

The seconds tick by and the light grows brighter and I know that I won't be getting any more sleep. Last night I made a pledge to myself that I would take the rare step of sleeping in today but that's not happening.

Sitting up, I reach for the phone I left charging on my desk and instead my fingers bump into Lou's candy dish. The root beer barrels were finished days ago but yesterday I poured a bag of Reese's Pieces in there. Chewing on a handful of these seems like a fine way to greet the morning and I shove them into my mouth before hopping out of bed.

The tile floor is cold and I stuff my feet into my pink fuzzy slippers while looking around for my favorite robe, a decadent washable silk that I bought last year while on a long weekend trip to New York City. Typically I sleep braless in a tank top and I'd rather not shuffle into Rafe's territory with my nipples announcing their existence.

Upon cracking open the door I find the apartment to be silent and dark. Oliver's door is still closed and when I pause outside it I hear nothing except the whir of the sound machine I loaned him when he complained about having trouble sleeping in his new bedroom.

He never talks about his mother. Neither does Rafe. There's a photo on Oliver's dresser and I know she has to be the woman pictured with baby Oliver. She's quite a bit older than I was expecting and her hair is indeed red. In the photo she looks classy and prosperous and frankly I can't imagine how her relationship with Rafe would have started.

There's enough light in the living room for me to see Rafe is still asleep on the sofa bed. Even though I feel the urge to kick him now and then I have to admit his decision to give Oliver the bedroom and make do with the sofa was a selfless one. He doesn't look particularly comfortable sleeping atop the covers with one leg hanging off the edge of the noticeably lumpy mattress.

He snores once and rolls over. Despising Rafe Hempstead would be far easier if he wasn't such a hot stack of bricks. The boy is freaking *built*. And I can never quite stop myself from admiring the sight of him all laid out in nothing but his black boxer shorts.

Then I'm reminded of the fact that I have no need to drool over Rafe Hempstead.

I have a date tonight. His name is Grant and he's a second year law school student. We met at the Student Union coffee shop when I accidentally grabbed his non fat latte with caramel drizzle. He looks like a younger version of the hot Irish doctor from Grey's Anatomy and he gallantly pulled out a chair when he invited me to sit down for a chat.

While my thoughts dwell on Grant, I'm trying to be quiet as I program the coffee maker. It now sits beside its more modest counterpart, a simple machine purchased by Rafe this week when he ran out of patience with mine.

I choose the bold setting and begin brewing. The rustling and a creak of bedsprings at my back warns that I have not been quiet enough. Rafe is awake. There is a high likelihood he will say nothing to me so I don't bother to turn around. He yawns loudly, walks down the hall and disappears into the bathroom. There haven't been too many times when he and I are alone, with no Oliver cushion. I don't really want to be alone with him right now.

I'm planning to just take my mug and a box of cereal to my bedroom but Rafe returns within thirty seconds. He flips all the blinds open, fills his coffee pitcher with water from the tap and then just dumps a bunch of grounds into the filter compartment without measuring before walking away to fold up the sofa bed.

I take a sip from my mug. "Good morning, Rafe," I say in a sugar sweet voice that sounds like bullshit. Because it is. But since I'm already interacting with him I abandon the idea of scurrying to my room with a box of cereal and decide that I'd rather sit at the table.

"Morning," he grumbles, his back to me while he fixes the couch cushions.

Someone left a plate littered with some crumbs at the table. I'm about to get irritated and then I remember that I'm the one who left it there yesterday evening when I ate a Pop Tart before bed.

Rafe has already thrown a pair of sweats on over his boxers and pulled on a wrinkled t-shirt. At least he's marginally considerate in some minor ways.

"Is it all right if I take Oliver to visit Caris and Jay this morning?" I ask him. "He's been asking to see their cats again and Caris said I could bring him by if you didn't have other plans for him."

He stretches one thick arm across his chest, brings his other arm up underneath and pulls with a wince. "Yeah, he'd like that."

He repeats the same move again and seems to be in a little bit of pain.

I take another sip of coffee. "Did you hurt yourself?"

"No. Just had a long week of moving heavy shit."

"Do you like your new job?"

From the look he gives me it's obvious he thinks the question is stupid. "It's a job. It pays money."

"Yes, most of them do." I make an effort not to scowl. The guy sure doesn't make a conversation easy. "By the way, I won't be home this evening. I'm going out."

My statement doesn't appear to register with him in any way. I try to explain.

"I have a date. I just brought it up in case Oliver asks you where I am."

He shrugs and returns to the kitchen so he can lean against the counter in all his space consuming masculine glory. "That didn't take long. Who is he?"

Do I detect a twinge of jealousy?

"Just a nice guy that I met over at HSU. He's a law school student and his family's in the oil business. I just met him so there's not much to tell, other than we both enjoy drinking non fat lattes with caramel drizzle."

Rafe coughs on his laugh. "Yeah, I can picture him. Probably wears two hundred dollar cologne and folds his underwear."

I feel like I ought to be defending Grant. "Most people fold their underwear, Rafe. And there's no crime in having good taste. After all, he took an interest in *me*, didn't he?"

Rafe runs his knuckles across the dark bristles shading his lower jaw. "I get the feeling you're waiting for some flattery."

"I don't need to fish for compliments. I know I have a pretty face."

"And not at all conceited."

"No. I can candidly admit that while my face catches attention my body is mediocre. My hips are bony, my boobs are too small and alas, I'll never have Kardashian level curves no matter how many hot yoga classes I suffer through."

Rafe has lost interest and now he stares at the coffee machine. Watching liquid drip into the glass carafe is apparently more stimulating than having a conversation with me. Just as well. As my own words echo in my head a sense of mortification creeps in because I am deliberating boobs and hot yoga with Rafe Hempstead. I don't want Rafe Hempstead to consider the size of my boobs. At least I don't think I do.

I stand up and take the dirty plate to the sink. The longer the silence drags on the more awkward the moment becomes. I switch on the faucet. Rafe yawns. The coffee machine belches.

Rafe finishes his yawn. "Who the hell lied to you?"

I switch the water off. "What?"

He doesn't elaborate right away. He casually fills his mug to the brim with coffee, takes a seat at the table and folds his arms across his broad chest. A chest with muscles impressive enough to strain the cotton fabric of his white t-shirt. Not that I'm staring.

Rafe looks me up and down. "Who the hell lied to you and said you have a mediocre body?"

"An ex boyfriend. His name was Felipe. He worked in a tea shop. It doesn't matter. I can see my reflection in the mirror and I'm capable of honesty. I didn't say I was ugly. I've never seen anyone recoil in horror when I put on a bikini."

I should stop talking. My forehead feels hot. Rafe continues to evaluate me.

"No, Izzy. No one will recoil in horror." He laughs. There's always an unpredictable factor to his laughter. Rafe's laughter is a needle cruising the surface of a balloon. It's sharp and can destroy if that's the kind of mood he's in. Rafe also doesn't care if his response is appropriate or not so one never knows what will follow his outbursts.

When he's finished laughing he cocks his head to the side. I brace myself for an insult. I can take it. I'll insult him right back. Like, how much muscle does he need? He must spend half his life pumping weights. His muscles are obscene. And enough with the rakish scruff on his jaw that he never quite gets around to shaving completely. I mean, have a beard, or don't have a beard. Choose one!

Rafe decides to speak again. "No one will recoil in horror because you're fucking beautiful, you dumbass. *Fuck.* You know what I would do to you? I would suck those tits raw. I would eat your pussy so good you'd scream. I would ride that hot little ass until I owned it."

OH. MY. GOD.

There must be a fitting response to his explicit declaration but I can't find it to save my life.

I can't move. I've stopped breathing. My heart thumps in my chest.

And I am so fucking turned on I might sink to my knees right here and now.

Lust wars with common sense.

I can't want him that way.

It's out of the question.

Despite the fact that thinking about getting my core rocked to pieces by the rough moves of Rafe Hempstead makes me want to come on the spot, he can never know.

That's right. Hooking up with him would be a disaster.

Common sense wins.

"Gotta go," are the brilliant words that come out of my mouth before I abandon Rafe, my coffee and little shards of my pride as I run to my room, lock the door and use my favorite extra large vibrator to get myself off in a hurry so that I won't be tempted to test Rafe's intentions.

10

—————

RAFE

Know what happens when I start running my mouth before being properly caffeinated?

I tell my uptight roommate that I want to eat her pussy until she screams.

Maybe I wanted to shock her. Maybe I'd been unknowingly injected with a truth serum. Or maybe it fucking bugged me to hear that she doesn't understand how drop dead gorgeous she is. And this Felipe guy from the tea shop is suspect as shit if he told her otherwise.

I meant every word I said.

That doesn't change the fact that I shouldn't have said it.

She practically choked on her own tongue before she ran away from me. I know I should apologize to her but then I figure that would just make things worse.

Besides, less than a minute after she closes the door to her bedroom, Oliver wakes up. He shuffles into the kitchen barefoot in his blue summer pajamas that have pictures of baseballs and frogs all over them. With one hand he rubs his eyes and with the other he carries a stuffed cat by the tail.

"I want a grape jelly sandwich for lunch." He takes a seat at the kitchen table and dumps his cat on the surface.

"Not a problem," I assure him. "But lunch isn't for hours. What do you want for breakfast?"

He thinks for a minute. "I want Izzy's granola cereal."

"Ah, we can't just take Izzy's cereal, buddy. How about some corn-flakes? I'll get you some granola cereal, whatever that is, when I go to the store later."

He pouts. "Izzy said I could have her cereal anytime I want."

The sensible thing to do would be to just walk over to Izzy's door, knock on it and ask if Oliver can have some of her cereal. Unfortunately, I can't do that right now, not mere moments after I told her I want to suck her tits raw.

Anyway, I have no reason to believe Oliver isn't telling the truth. And if Izzy has a problem with the fact that some of her cereal is missing I'll buy her more. I really do need to go to the grocery store today.

Inside the tiny six shelf closet that serves as a pantry I find the green box called Granola Glee and pour a big bowl of it for Oliver. While he digs in I slide into the chair across from him and reconnect with my cup of coffee.

I watch my son eat and then pick up the stuffed cat. "What's this guy's name?"

He chews and swallows. Takes another spoonful. Chews and swallows. He hasn't said much about school this week. His teacher says he's doing just fine but she's got a classroom full of kids so unless he's causing trouble she wouldn't have a reason to pay him special attention. I wish I didn't have to get him up so early and take to him to the morning daycare program but it can't be helped. Construction work begins early.

The stuffed cat stares at me with green plastic eyes. I set it down.

"His name is Cliff." Oliver takes another spoonful of cereal.

"Cliff." I grin. "That's a good name. Do you want some juice?"

He shrugs. I decide to take that as a yes and pour him a glass of orange juice. He won't call me 'Dad' or anything that sounds like it but I believe he's at least getting used to me. I'll take it.

After breakfast Oliver wants to watch some cartoon about talking space ships so I haul out my laptop, eventually find it on a streaming service and set him up on the couch. I've been doing a decent job of keeping my area picked up. Not having any real privacy continues to suck but I won't complain. We're in a good place and Oliver is surrounded by people who care for him.

The next time I see Izzy she's showered and dressed and ready to take Oliver to their cat play date. She behaves as if nothing had gone awry this morning, as if nobody has mentioned riding a hot ass or sucking tits. I have no problem with pretending the same.

Oliver is happy to let Izzy help him get ready and he has his clothes on and his teeth brushed in minutes. He's all smiles as he follows Izzy to the door. At the last minute he darts back to the couch, snaps up Cliff, and pushes the rather musty smelling stuffed animal into my lap.

"Take care of Cliff," he orders.

Being commanded to take care of the stuffed cat actually makes me happy. It's the biggest vote of confidence I've received so far from Oliver.

When they're gone I hold up Cliff and stare him in the eye. "Don't you go running off on me. I don't want to look bad."

Listen to that. I'm talking to a stuffed cat in an empty room. Things in my world have sure changed in a hurry. I set Cliff on a couch pillow where he won't be disturbed.

I have every intention of showering without jerking off to thoughts of Izzy. But I fail. In fact I've become a little too addicted to my shower time masturbation ritual starring one unsuspecting Isabella Gentry. Although, thanks to my outburst today, it's possible she suspects I've had a few thoughts about her. More than a few.

Fuck.

Oh well. Too late now. I shoot a thick load down the drain while imagining my cock having a field day with a doggy style rough ride while my hands are all tangled up in her hair as I enjoy the view of her sexy back.

I should feel guilty about this and I do. I also know I'll be doing the same thing tomorrow or maybe even later today.

Going grocery shopping is way down on the bottom tier of things I enjoy doing, between getting a tooth drilled at the dentist and cleaning the toilet. Yet I have to make sure a growing boy has something better to eat than fast food and potato chips so I do the responsible thing. I use my phone to make a list and then I visit a food store the size of a football stadium. I fill a cart with bags of colorful produce along with plenty of milk, eggs and various food items that promise the contents are 'organic' and 'all natural'. I'll cook some spaghetti for Oliver's dinner tonight. Even I can't fuck that up. I'll even make plenty of extra in case Izzy wants to join us.

Then I remember that Izzy won't be around for dinner because Izzy has a date with some law school prick who likes caramel drizzle. I sort of hate him already. Even more than that, I hate the thought that his over-educated hands are going to be all over her. I hate it so much that I don't pay attention to where I'm going and accidentally push the cart into a tower of Ritz crackers.

The grocery store trip takes forever because the brightly lit aisles are endless and because I spend at least fifteen minutes conducting online research on the merits of whole wheat pasta versus chickpea pasta. Plus I search everywhere for another box of Izzy's granola cereal until I finally give up and ask some kid who's wearing a red smock. He doesn't know so he asks another kid in a red smock. That kid doesn't know either and asks a fortyish woman who wears a manager badge. Ms. Manager knows and she is delighted to show me. While I'm debating whether or not I'm supposed to give her a tip she wanders off. I dump four boxes of Granola Glee in the cart and head for the checkout line.

Shane is out in the front yard when I return and he's cheerful as always when I roll up to the curb. He wants to help bring in the groceries and I let him even though I don't need any help. Lana is apparently off having lunch with some friends so he hangs around while I'm unpacking and I'm glad for the company. Shane is impossible not to like and I can appreciate why he and my brother have been best friends for so many years.

Shane is still here when Izzy and Oliver arrive home. Oliver is the proud owner of a new pool toy that shoots water eight feet up in the air and he wants to go swimming.

"I can take you swimming," I say and he looks to me in surprise because I've never gone in the pool here.

Shane thinks this is a great idea. "Let's all go in the pool! I'm sweating like a pig. Those summer temps are really hanging on." He looks over to where Izzy stands silently beside the kitchen table. "How about it, Izzy? You in the mood for a round of pool volleyball?"

She looks in my direction. Our eyes meet and I can't read the look on her face. We break eye contact at the same time.

Izzy smiles at Shane. "No, thanks for the invite but I've got some school work to do before I go out tonight." She beckons to Oliver and bends down to his level. She quietly says something to him and he laughs, throws his arms around her for a hug and then dashes off to his room to change into his swimsuit.

This reminds me that I actually do not own a swimsuit. I decide no one will arrest me if I swim in a pair of gym shorts.

After a week of punishing hard labor under the hot sun, my muscles sure aren't complaining about the soothing feel of the pool water. Oliver paddles around in his little swim vest, Shane floats on a pool raft, and I keep shooting water in the air with the aid of the new toy Oliver received from Jay.

"Again!" Oliver squeals after getting showered with another spray of water.

I grin, refill the pump for another round and let the water fly. Out of the corner of my eye I notice a flash of red hair and when I glance that way I expect to see Izzy looking at Oliver but instead she's looking at me. She's not smiling and she doesn't stay. She shifts her gaze, calls out some encouragement to Oliver and disappears once more. I don't see her again for hours, not until I'm waiting for water to boil so I can cook the spaghetti.

She parades into the kitchen looking picture perfect and outra-geously fuckable in a dark blue dress that flares out just above her knees. Her hair is done up in some complicated twist. A string of pearls hangs around her neck and the strappy black high heels on her feet are probably going to haunt me later. She's sophisticated and sexy and untouchable.

She twirls. "Going for the Breakfast at Tiffany's look."

I'm not sure what that is. An old song I think. "Hmmph," is my response.

Izzy waves to Oliver and then leaves for her date with her fancy caramel drizzle lawyer. The word lawyer leaves a bad taste in my mouth, reminds me of Kevin Walsh. Mr. Oil Business Lawyer will probably take her out for a wine tasting and maybe a ride in his private plane or whatever the hell people in that moneyed stratos-phere do for fun.

Oliver makes a mess eating his spaghetti but that's fine. He's in a good mood and he's talking to me a lot more than he usually talks to me. Some tomato sauce somehow lands on Cliff the cat so I make a big production out of cleaning the thing's matted fur off with soap and water before I give Oliver a bath. After he's cleaned and combed and dressed in his comfortable pj's he hauls out a stack of coloring books and crayons. He is pleased when I join him and we pass a pleasant hour trying to color inside the lines. At one point he grabs my book and peers down at the picture of a cartoon animal – a possum or something – in a princess gown. I've given it red hair for some reason.

"That looks good," my son says.

I never knew praise from a five-year-old could be so exciting. I feel like someone just handed me a Pulitzer. A short time later he begins yawning and for once he doesn't push me away when lead him to bed and tuck him in. I switch on the sound machine at his bedside. Izzy gave him the sound machine. She said she never used it anyway.

Oliver shuts his eyes and rolls to his side with Cliff, still damp, in the crook of his arm. "I wanna listen to the beach," he says, keeping his eyes shut.

The sound of crashing waves and the calls of seagulls fill the room when I switch to the beach setting. Oliver snuggles deeper into his blankets.

"Like the beach in Florida with Mommy," he whispers and falls asleep.

I'm kneeling beside the bed and I remain there, just watching him for a few minutes. This is the first time he's ever mentioned his mother to me at all. He must have been referring to a trip that Dana took him on. I touch his soft cheek and my heart hurts in a way it's never hurt before.

I'm not sure if I've ever truly loved anyone in my life but I love this kid without reservation. I'd open my own goddamn arteries for him.

Switching off the light, I close the door to his room and return to the kitchen to clean up the splashes of spaghetti sauce that landed on the floor and the walls. I want to get this done before Izzy comes home and looks around at the mess with that sour face she makes when she's annoyed about something.

While I scrub sauce from the floor grout I conduct some mental math, trying to figure out when I last got fucked. Five months? Six months? Before I got the call about Oliver I was in a two job spiral that left me with little spare time. And if we're talking about a real decent screw instead of an ordinary, *'Yeah, go ahead and suck my dick'* type of situation then it's been a lot longer. This must be the reason why I can't stop myself from mentally banging my roommate. Izzy's hot as shit and she's right in front of me every day. But no matter how often I send her to her knees in my head I won't be doing anything about it in real time.

What I need is an hour alone with some quality porn. Starring girls who look nothing like Isabella Gentry.

While mulling this over, it occurs to me to wonder if Izzy watches porn. Somehow I can't picture it. If I had to guess I'd say she likely prefers missionary style with the lights off and likes the wild times to be confined to the pages of *Dukes With Big Dicks* or whatever it was she was reading on her tablet last week.

I glance at the stove clock and wonder if this is what she's doing right now with Mr. Oil Business Lawyer. Like maybe after the wine tasting and plane ride he carried her into his mansion (because in my head he owns a mansion) to go play some bouncy games on his California King-sized bed.

Once again I realize how much I despise Mr. Oil Business Lawyer. Amazing how I can hate a guy without even knowing his name or face.

But apparently I'm wrong because about eight seconds after these thoughts cross my mind I hear the key in the lock and then Izzy walks in. She definitely doesn't look like a girl who's just been bounced around. Her hair is still in place and her pearls are on straight. Now I'm hoping he tried to get it up and couldn't.

She's holding a boxy silver purse in one hand and a bottle of wine in the other.

"Oliver must be asleep," she says and she sets the wine bottle down. "It would be a lot louder in here if he wasn't."

"He's asleep." I move to the sink and wring the water from the sponge I was using to clean with. "How was your date?"

She's searching through the kitchen drawers. "Perfect. Grant is a prince. He took me to the fondue place up by the university. His sister is a sommelier and upon her recommendation he ordered this unbelievable Chianti at dinner. Seriously, it was sinful. And I made such a fuss about it that he presented me with an entire bottle. But you know what? I'm starting to think I left my electric wine bottle opener at my parents' house. I haven't seen it since I left Arizona. Do you have a corkscrew?"

She waits for me to answer. Her look turns to impatience as I say nothing. I'm still wondering what the hell a sommelier is.

"He bought you a bottle of wine?"

"Yes. I just told you that. Do you have a corkscrew or not?"

I laugh. "He bought you an expensive bottle of wine and then you had him take you home after dinner?"

There's a wrinkle of confusion between her brows. "I don't know what you're getting at, Rafe."

"What I'm getting at is that *Grant* was definitely planning for a different outcome."

She looks at the bottle of wine. She looks at me. She's clearly still confused.

"What's that supposed to mean?"

"Never mind." I feel around in my pockets for my keys. I'm not going to be the one to enlighten Izzy Gentry and dash her schoolgirl belief that Grant is just a gallant guy who hands out expensive gifts for the sheer hell of it instead of because he's hoping to get his cock rubbed.

The key to my truck is long enough to twist deep into the bottle's cork and with some effort I manage to pull out the cork in one piece.

It's not lost on me that she's fascinated, her eyes fixed on the muscles of my lower arms. The tip of her tongue sneaks out and licks her upper lip.

I hand the wine bottle over and she snaps out of her trance. She takes it by the neck and removes a couple of goblet style glasses from the cabinet.

"Would you like some?"

"I'll pass, thanks."

She pours herself a glass and takes a ladylike sip. "Flawless."

If I roll my eyes any harder over all the pretention in the room then they'll probably fall out of my head. So instead I spray down the counter with lemon scented cleaner. Izzy glares at me when I accidentally spray her arm while she has her glass raised to her lips.

"So are you seeing this guy again?" I have to struggle to keep my voice even.

"Grant invited me to a cheese tasting on Thursday evening."

"Yeah, I'm sure he wants you to taste a lot of things."

She's annoyed. "What, are you jealous?"

"Not even a little bit."

"Could have fooled me."

"Is that hard to do?"

Her eyes narrow. She sniffs. I'm aware that right now I'm being a prick and I can't help it. I'm just pissed. I'm not even pissed at her. I'm pissed that my kid is hurting and I don't know how to help him. I'm pissed that this Grant jerk exists and can turn the head of a girl like Izzy. I'm pissed that I want a good soul cleansing fuck fest and can't have it.

So there. I'm an asshole.

Izzy agrees. Her cheeks are flushed with wrath. This only makes her look sexier. "You really excel at being an asshole, Rafe."

Suddenly I'm tired. I shouldn't have started this conversation in the first place. The less I talk to Izzy Gentry the better off we'll both be. "I know I'm an asshole. What are you gonna do about it? Throw your wine at me?"

And then she does. She actually throws her fucking wine in my face. Or at least she tries to. The flick of her wrist comes up short when I rear back and the wine splashes on the floor, leaving her standing there with a stupid empty glass and a puzzled expression. *That should have worked,* her pretty eyes say. *Why is this jackass not covered in my wine backwash?*

There's no effort required to pluck the glass out of her hand. I toss it in the sink, where it promptly shatters.

"Hey," she complains. "That was Waterford crystal, you dick."

I chuckle and close in, aware that I'm hard and getting harder. "Now that I'm thinking about it, that just might be your problem, Isabella."

Her eyes flash. Her lips pout. In another second she'll be stamping her heels on the tile. "What the hell are you talking about?"

"This." I run a hand low, over the shape of my cock. She can see the rigid outline through my pants. I know she can. She sucks in a corner of her lip and jerks her head to force her eyes away. I take this opportunity to taunt her. "You don't know how to handle one, do you?"

"You're disgusting."

I laugh at her again. "You wish you thought so."

I'm surprised when she lashes out with sudden ferocity. She

pushes her palms to my chest and shoves me backwards. At least, she tries to. She doesn't have much of a prayer of moving me anywhere I don't want to go but I like the effort. Feeling her hands on me makes good things happen to my cock. Even if she *is* trying to push me through the nearest window.

"What are you guys doing?"

Oliver is standing in the hallway. He's sleepy eyed and confused over the sight of us wrestling in the kitchen. Izzy drops her hands from my chest and takes a huge step backwards.

She rises to the moment more quickly than I do. "Oliver, hi. I just got home and I was helping your dad clean the kitchen."

He makes a face. "I heard something break."

"That was my fault," I say and start to walk over. "Sorry we woke you, buddy. Let's go back to bed."

He maneuvers away from me. "I want Izzy to tuck me in now."

Of course he prefers Izzy. She's nicer than I am.

"All right. Get some sleep, Oliver."

Izzy takes his hand and brings him to his room. She's back less than a minute later and goes straight to the sink, picking out the pieces of broken glass.

"I'll do that," I offer.

She shakes her head. "I'll do it."

"Sorry about your Waterford crystal. I'll get you another one."

Izzy sighs. "I don't really like the style of those glasses anyway."

"And I'm sorry that I'm an asshole."

She sniffs out a laugh and tosses the glass pieces in the trash. "You can't help it. In your case it's a natural talent."

Izzy wipes her hands on a dishtowel and turns to face me. I swear she gets prettier every time I look at her.

I jerk my head toward the living room. "I'll be going to my couch now."

She nods, picks up the bottle of wine and sticks it in the fridge. I know nothing of wine so I can't guess whether an open bottle will be any good tomorrow. What a shame if Grant's present goes to waste.

There I go again with my asshole talents.

I know she's still standing there in the kitchen when I begin folding out the couch bed for my nightly nap. A minute later her heels start clicking in the direction of her room and then they abruptly stop.

"Hey, Rafe?"

I turn around with a pillow in my hand.

She smiles sweetly. "I just want you know that I've never met a dick I can't handle."

That's all she wants to say. Without another glance she walks to her room and shuts the door. Quietly, so Oliver won't be awakened a second time.

11

IZZY

Lana has mixed pina coladas to celebrate the first official day of autumn. I fail to see what one has to do with the other but I'm not going to turn down a cool drink and a relaxing chat with girlfriends on a weekday afternoon. Caris is here too and she's brimming with excitement over her wedding plans.

"We meet with the planner this weekend. Lana, did Shane tell you he's making our cake?"

"Are you kidding?" Lana sets down her drink and becomes animated. "He's become obsessed with wedding cake design. Last night it took him ten minutes to notice that I was strutting around the bedroom naked because his eyes were glued to the phone screen as he scrolled through Pinterest photos. When I started performing high kicks he finally looked up but only to ask my opinion on buttercream versus fondant."

I raise my glass. "Definitely buttercream. Tell him I am available as a taste tester when he begins making prototypes."

"Will do."

Caris smiles at me. "What time does Oliver get home? I've got a roast beef in the slow cooker that I need to go deal with soon but I was hoping to see him."

I check the time on my phone. "Rafe picks him up right after work and usually they come straight home. In fact they should be home by now. Why don't you text him?"

"Who, Rafe?" Caris shakes her head. "I don't want to bother him. He and I aren't really on the texting buddy level. He doesn't even text back and forth with Jay."

"No?" Lana is surprised. "I thought they were getting along better the last few weeks."

Caris sips her drink and then frowns. "They don't fight. It's not like that. It's kind of a perpetual state of suspicion, at least on Jay's part. I don't feel comfortable telling him he shouldn't feel that way. I know Rafe was a bully when they were growing up in Arcana. I remember what Rafe was like and I sure wouldn't have wanted him as a brother back then. But people change. And I wish Jay would give his brother more of a chance."

"That's because you're an angel." Lana smiles at her best friend. The conversation shifts to talk about the wedding dress. Caris plans to go shopping next month when her mother visits and of course Lana, as the maid of honor, will be accompanying her.

"Will you come too, Izzy?" Caris asks me. "You have outstanding taste so I could use the input and besides, it'll be fun."

I'm surprised and happy to be included. Wedding dresses are my secret obsession. I have no plans to walk down the aisle soon but when I do I'll be wearing a strapless ball gown with yards of pleated tulle for a real full skirt look. Vera Wang in particular carries my dream of a wedding dress and I hope it's still available when my time comes. Not that I'm in any hurry. Finding the right groom is a little bit more important than finding the right dress and I'm not even close to that. I've had plenty of boyfriends. Never once did I imagine standing beside any of them in my Vera Wang dream dress. I have yet to feel the consuming, almost desperate level of passion that I read about in my romance novels. And I'm not just talking about sex. Good sex isn't that hard to come by. But I've never known what it's like to be so into a guy that I can't catch my breath. I want to feel that way.

I'm jarred out of my daydreams of dresses and romance when Lana winks and then reaches over to slap me playfully on the thigh.

"How are things going with Grant? Come on, spill the tea."

"Grant is wonderful. He wants to take me on a trip to Santa Fe next weekend."

Caris tilts her head. "You don't sound thrilled."

"Well, I have a couple of big papers to write so I don't know."

I stick my face in my drink so that I don't need to elaborate. Grant really is wonderful. Over the last three weeks we've been out eight times. I know we're reaching a point where sex is going to be on the table, especially if I take this trip with him next weekend. Aside from some ordinary kissing and the night at the sushi bar when the back of his hand accidentally brushed against my right boob while reaching for the soy sauce, we haven't done anything. And he apologized for the boob brush. Profusely.

Really, I should be more excited about Grant.

Grant is nice. Grant is handsome. Grant is destined for success and comes from a powerful family. More than anything, Grant is polite. If Grant wore a cape he would surely use it to cover puddles or any other messes that might lie in my path. Grant is swoon worthy, chivalry in the flesh. There is nothing on earth wrong with Grant.

No, there is something wrong with me.

Because, alas, I don't spend my time thinking about the upstanding young man who has made it clear he will treat me like a queen if I give him the opportunity. Nope. In fact I tend to forget all about him until he calls or texts.

There is a man who invades my dreams and my vibrator sessions. But he's not Grant. He's nothing like Grant. He's crude and disrespectful and inconsistent. And I'm appalled by the fact that there are times when I want him so much I can hardly stand it.

"You're blushing," Lana points out. "Is there something you're not telling us?"

Why, yes. Yes, there is. I'm not telling them that secretly I am lusting after my infuriating, oversexed barbarian of a roommate.

"Rafe," says Caris and for a horrifying split second I'm sure I've uttered my last thought out loud.

But Caris is only responding to the fact that Rafe has stuck his head out the door to peer into the backyard. She waves to him. He's still wearing his orange construction vest and somehow he manages to make it look hot. What a jerk.

Oliver shoves his father aside and comes careening into the backyard. I freeze when he runs a little too close to the edge of the pool but then he bounds over to the patio and takes a leap, landing on the seat beside me.

He is so full of five-year-old energy that he makes the furniture shake and he nearly knocks the drink out of my hand. I don't mind. A few minutes with Oliver would put even the starchiest grump in a great mood.

Speaking of grumps...

Rafe has stepped outside and stands on the edge of the patio. Lately we've been coexisting without a problem. I'm aware that it's an uneasy truce, mostly made possible by the presence of Oliver. I really love living in the same house as Oliver. Being an only child, the large home I lived in with my parents was always quiet when I was growing up, unless my cousins were visiting, which they often did. But as soon as they left there would be this silent void in every room and a feeling of loneliness would set in.

"Caris," says Rafe. "I hate to ask this, but would you be able to watch Oliver for a little while? I had to leave work early to go to a meeting at his school and now I need to go back to help clean up the job site."

"I can watch him," I say before Caris has a chance to answer. She mentioned she wanted to get home and have dinner with Jay so it would make more sense for me to look after Oliver. I'm not doing anything and besides, I live here.

A slight frown shadows his face. "You sure?"

I don't know why it's even a question. I've spent plenty of time with Oliver and I think I come across as a responsible person. Leaving him in my care for an hour or two shouldn't be a problem.

"Of course. I'll even make him dinner."

Oliver bounces on the seat some more. "We'll color pictures, Izzy. Did you see my new coloring book? I got it from him."

'Him' is Rafe. I know this because it's the only way I ever hear Oliver refer to his father.

If this bothers Rafe right now he doesn't show it. The look of grudging gratitude he flashes my way follows the word, "Thanks."

Then he looks at Oliver and his face changes. I know that look. I've seen it on my own father's face when I catch him watching me. It's love and pride and a touch of worry. It's the look of a caring parent.

This is why it's so difficult to seal Rafe into a box and be done with him. There are times when it's tempting to dismiss him as some brainless brute with no feelings but this would be unfair. Rafe loves Oliver. For weeks I've had a chance to observe the way Rafe interacts with his son. He's patient. Gentle. Never loses his temper despite the obvious evidence that he doesn't have any experience with children.

Thinking of Rafe right after thinking of my father makes me wonder what would happen if the two of them ever met. Then I shudder. I hope I never have to find out. Rafe isn't one to back down and my father isn't a man who tolerates being disrespected. The collision could be epic.

After one last fond look at his son, Rafe promises to return before dark and exits through the back gate.

"Guess what, Oliver?" Lana asks him. "We were talking about Caris's wedding. When Caris marries your uncle she'll be Aunt Caris."

He thinks about this. Then he smiles. "Okay. Can we go swimming?"

"I'm afraid we can't go swimming today. Shane says the chemical levels are way off so he has to have the pool guy come over tomorrow to fix it."

"Where is Shane? Does he have any of those little muffins with the chocolate chips?"

Lana laughs. "I'll text him and make sure he brings some home from the bakery for you."

Oliver is satisfied with his news. Then before I can stop him, he reaches out, picks up my drink and takes a big gulp.

"Oliver, no!" I pry the glass from his little hand.

He's making a face. "That tastes funny."

"That's because it has alcohol. It's not for kids."

"Do you like it?"

"Sure, but I'm an adult."

"So it'll taste good when I'm old?"

"Um." I look to Caris and Lana for help. They're both too busy giggling. "It might. But you shouldn't try to drink it again before that. Stay here with Lana and Caris. I'll go get you a juice box."

When I go inside to grab one of the juice boxes that are kept in the refrigerator, I bring my drink with me, just in case Oliver is tempted to take another sip.

Twenty minutes later Shane shows up and he has with him a paper bag filled with the mythical chocolate chip muffins. Oliver is ready to gobble them all up but I remember how I promised Rafe I'd make sure he ate a meal so I hold him off with a compromise that he can have a muffin after dinner.

Speaking of dinner, I don't really have a plan. I'm not much of a cook. Sometimes I find success with meals that have four ingredients or less but I'm not feeling a lot of inspiration. What I do feel is the weight of responsibility as Oliver looks on from the kitchen table while I search the pantry for something that can be cobbled into a dinner suitable for a little boy.

"You like spaghetti, right, Oliver?"

"I had that yesterday."

I look in the fridge. "How about a grilled cheese sandwich?"

"Why would you grill a sandwich?"

"It's not really grilled. It's just...melted."

He crosses his arms. "Gross."

I close the fridge. "Do you like salad?"

He's thinking. "Like tomato salad with lettuce?"

"Yes. You can put other things in salad too. I like mine with chicken and croutons."

Slowly he nods. "I can eat that."

I did not find any salad fixings in the fridge but a brand new Salad Time just opened up right next to the HSU campus and they deliver. I use my phone to place an order (hooray for modern tech!) and then sit down at the table to color pictures with Oliver as we wait for the food to arrive.

Most of the pages of my coloring book have already been filled in. I'm flipping around and looking for one that hasn't been scribbled on yet. Then I start laughing.

"Is this supposed to be me?" I turn the book around so he can see I'm referring to some kind of furry creature that wears a ball gown. The funny part is that he's given the animal princess loads of bright red hair.

Oliver looks up. "I don't know. That one was colored by him."

Him.

Meaning Rafe.

Rafe decided to add red hair to the thing even though the animal did not have any hair to color in the illustration.

I'm not sure what to make of this, except file it away as evidence that I occupy space in his head. Then again, I already knew that. Rafe outright said he's physically attracted to me, although despite his obscene language he hasn't so much as bumped into me in the hallway. The one time I touched him was when he made me furious after he broke my wine glass and provoked me with a profane comment. In a fit of anger I placed my hands on his rock hard chest and I wasn't thinking straight. All this sexual tension boiled to the surface at once. I was incensed and I wanted to shut him up before he saw through me anymore than he already did.

"You're disgusting."

"You wish you thought so."

My fingers tighten around the waxy crayon and it snaps in half.

Yes. I do wish I thought so. But I don't. And he knows it.

Oliver hasn't noticed the broken crayon. He's examining his hand and rubbing at the knuckles. "This hurts a little."

"Your hand?"

"Uh huh."

"How come, Oliver?"

"Because I used it to hit Aiden Ball."

"Does he go to your school?"

"Yes. He's mean."

"Oliver, you really need to go tell your teacher if someone is being mean to you."

"I did tell her. Right after I hit Aiden I told Ms. Alvarez that I hit him because he's mean."

Rafe mentioned he needed to leave work to go to a meeting at Oliver's school. Oliver's fight must be the reason.

I search for something to tell Oliver. We've all dealt with bullies at some point in our lives. When I was in third grade there was a boy named Griffin Oretto who would constantly call me ugly. He sat behind me in class and would poke me in the back with the sharp point of his pencil until one day I got fed up, grabbed my hardcover history book and smashed his nose in with it. What a big deal that was. My parents were called to the school. His parents were called to the school. Griffin's father was bald and wore a suit and his face was very sweaty. My own father wore a black leather jacket and leaned against the far wall of the principal's office with his arms crossed while Mr. Oretto shouted that his son was 'assaulted without provocation by an emotionally disturbed girl'. The school nurse was brought in and verified that I did have marks on my back that appeared consistent with being poked with a sharp pencil, just as I said. At this point my father summoned Mr. Oretto out to the hallway for a word and when they both returned Mr. Oretto looked pale and even sweatier than before. He declared that his son would write a letter of apology. Then he collected his family and ran from the room.

And my dad?

He looked at me and winked.

That was the moment I realized Deck Gentry could fix anything.

If he were here he'd have words of wisdom for little Oliver. All I can give Oliver is a hug. But he smiles just the same.

Not until the food arrives do I belatedly wonder if I should have also ordered something for Rafe. I don't even know if Rafe likes salads. Oliver and I are still sitting at the table eating when he walks in.

"How much do I owe you?" he asks when I explain that I ordered takeout.

I swallow a mouthful of chicken Caesar salad. "Nothing. It was my idea. I want to pay for it."

He withdraws his wallet anyway, yanks out a ten dollar bill and drops it on the table. There's a bag under his arm and he leaves this on the counter before telling Oliver he's just going to take a quick shower. Oliver nods and keeps eating.

Rafe returns in fifteen minutes. His hair is wet and his face is freshly shaved. I should be used to the sight of him roaming free in his frequent evening attire of a plain white tee and sweats. Typically I'm more of a man-in-a-suit casualty but no designer suit ever did for me what Rafe's five dollar t-shirt does. My hormones don't stand a chance. I cross my legs underneath the table.

Oliver grabs his coloring book, rips out a sheet of paper and holds it up in the air. "I colored this for you."

At first Rafe doesn't realize that Oliver is speaking to him. "That's for me?"

Oliver waves the paper. "Yeah, for you."

Rafe reaches over to accept the piece of paper from his son with as much care as if it were priceless art. "Thank you, Oliver. You did a great job coloring this kitty cat."

Oliver accepts the compliment in stride. "You can't have real cats because they make you sneeze. So I made you one."

For a second I could swear the gruff and mighty Rafe Hempstead is in danger of crying. He stares at the piece of paper for another minute and then moves over to the fridge where he uses a Hutton State University magnet to secure it to the front. He steps back and stares at it some more. It's a moment worth smiling over and I'm grateful to witness it.

I know I'm still smiling when he turns my way. Our eyes lock and an internal earthquake trembles. As looks go, Rafe is perfect. Usually it's his body that captures my attention but right now I'm looking at his lips. I'm wondering how they taste and how he uses his tongue when he kisses. I want to know the answer.

"Well." I stand up. "I've got some schoolwork to do so I'll leave you two gentlemen alone."

He's unpacking the bag he walked in with. There's a frozen pizza roll and a beer. He pops the pizza roll in the microwave and points to the table. "Take your money."

"No." I drop a kiss on the top of Oliver's head.

Rafe shakes his head. "Stubborn," he mutters.

"Terminally."

He smirks.

A sense of forlorn banishment gnaws at me after I close the door to my bedroom. I like being around them. Both of them.

My phone buzzes and I look down to find a brand new text from Grant.

Just wanted to let you know I was thinking about you.

How sweet. I don't want to tell him I was doing the same. I'm not a liar.

While I'm deciding how to respond a second text comes through.

Have you thought about next weekend?

The trip to Santa Fe. Grant's father is part owner of an upscale resort just outside town and the family always has a top floor suite at their disposal. There's a full service spa with all the new age beauty treatments anyone could think of. The resort sits right beside a gorgeous wildlife preserve and everything about it sounds relaxing and ideal. I'm sure it costs a small fortune for the paying guests.

So why is it I keep dwelling on the image of Rafe Hempstead's lips instead of being thrilled that this Prince Charming of a guy wants to whisk me away to a dream getaway?

Let me try to get caught up on my work. I'll let you know when

I see you this weekend.

I really do have a lot of schoolwork and school ought to be my priority since this is the reason I moved to Hutton. So this is not a lie. Just a half lie. Because I could buckle down and get everything finished long before next weekend if I chose to.

I bite the tip of my thumbnail and watch the screen. In a moment Grant's response appears.

Sounds good. Sweet dreams.

I set the phone facedown on my desk and grab a handful of Reese's Pieces from Lou's candy dish. I believe I like these better than root beer barrels now.

For the next two hours I try and fail to stay focused on the pages of dense reading that need to be completed for my Traumatic Brain Injury And Speech class. At the end of this time I close the book and try in vain to recall a single thing I've just learned. Since nothing comes to mind I declare the night a loss and decide to get ready for bed.

The apartment is quiet. Oliver has probably been asleep for a while. Rafe must have given him a bath before bedtime because there is a small puddle of water on the floor and a yellow rubber ducky sits in the middle of the bathmat. I pick up the toy and place it on the edge of the tub before washing my face and brushing my teeth.

When I return to my bedroom I have every intention of changing into my standard comfortable pj's and reading myself to sleep. Yet instead of throwing on a wash-faded tank top and shorts I open the closet. Right in the front hangs a black silk thigh-length nightgown with ivory lace embroidered across the low neckline. I just bought it a few days ago. While I waited on the checkout line I refused to think too hard about why I was buying it. A girl can never have too many sexy nighties, right? And I haven't ruled out sex with Grant. I could bring this along on my romantic weekend with him, if I decide to go.

Or....

I could put it on right now for no particular reason and wander around the apartment.

This is a good idea. This is what I choose to do.

I shiver as I slide the material over my bare skin. It wouldn't look right with a bra and so I don't wear one. I don't need a mirror to tell me I look desirable. I feel confident and excited and crazy sexy. I fluff out my hair and spray on some light perfume, a floral scent with a hint of vanilla that was specially blended for me at my mother's favorite Scottsdale boutique.

Then I leave my bedroom and tiptoe barefoot down the hall. The living room light is on and while the couch bed has been unfolded it is also empty. Rafe's keys are sitting on the counter so he must not have gone far. Oliver's picture hangs in its place of honor on the refrigerator. And the door to the back patio is open.

Usually the backyard lights are left on but someone has switched them off and I can't see where I'm going. With care I make my way along the short flagstone path that leads directly to the patio. The pool lights are still glowing and this is enough for me to see him, just his shape as he hunches forward and stares at the empty pool. He's sitting on the cushioned sofa and he's alone.

With a little throat clearing noise I announce my arrival and he jumps.

"Jesus." He exhales loudly. "You scared the shit out of me."

I sniff the air. "Smells like cigarettes out here."

"Guilty. Needed one of my vices tonight." He reaches for the tall can in front of him and holds it up. "Two of them actually."

I've never seen him drink or smoke. Maybe he stopped for Oliver's sake.

Rafe gulps down his beer and places it back on the table with a clink. My eyes adjust to the dimness. He has shed his t-shirt and sits there bare chested, wearing only his sweatpants.

Rafe hasn't really looked at me too carefully yet and he does this now as I sit beside him with my legs tucked aside.

"What are you doing here?"

"I live here, Rafe. I can use the patio if I want to."

He takes it in, the fact that I'm inches away and wearing something that screams to be noticed. Even if I can't make out the look on his face I can guess what's going through his mind.

"You should go back in the house."

"No. *You* go in the house."

A snort of laughter. He stares out at the pool again and drinks his beer. He doesn't move when I unfold my legs and toy with the hem of my nightie.

"Oliver said he was in a fight today."

Rafe hangs his head. "The other kid was giving him shit about his mom being dead."

"Oh god." That's even worse than I thought it was. "And what happened?"

"Nothing. The school was very understanding. Hell, even the other kid's parents were very understanding. I don't think it'll happen again."

He sounds miserable, defeated. He tenses when I touch his arm, hesitantly at first, running my fingertips over his skin. He feels bad and my heart hurts for him. If I could make him feel better for a few minutes then I want to.

And I also want to just because I *want* him.

"Izzy."

The way he says my name. Like a warning. I don't need to be warned. I don't scare easily.

He watches when I rise to my feet. He doesn't stop me when I sit right back down, this time in his lap. He makes no move when I deliberately slide one nightie strap off my shoulder and allow it to fall.

"You don't want this," he says and he's angry. This shouldn't excite me, his anger, and yet it does.

"Yes I do." I'm touching him, his chest, his shoulders, the elastic waistband of his pants. I'll go to my knees for him. I'll take him in my mouth to make it clear what I'm after. He can't tell me what I do and do not want. I'll be the one telling him.

"Fuck," he hisses and stops me before I get there.

With no effort he lifts me off the ground and returns me to his lap, this time with my back against his chest. And now I can feel him, how hard he is. He's fucking massive and he wraps his arms around me, pinning my own arms in place and keeping me centered as his cock pulses against my ass. If that's the way he wants it then he can have it. I let him know this by rocking my body back and forth to send the message that all he needs to do is pull the fabric away.

Rafe groans, his hot breath next to my ear. "Damn you," he whispers.

"Fuck me," I whisper back, trying to grind on him harder. Who cares if this is nuts? It feels good.

"No." But his hand dives between my legs and he groans again, this time because I've proven that I mean what I say. I didn't wear panties for a reason.

"I want this," I tell him. "You do too, Rafe. That's enough. We don't even have to talk about it tomorrow." Because maybe this way I can get him out of my head. Since he entered my life, Rafe Hempstead has been the itch I've refused to scratch and I'm out of self-control.

With one arm he keeps me in place so that I can't move unless he lets me. With the other he shoves my thighs apart and teases without mercy.

His voice in my ear is low, menacing. "Bullshit." His fingers push inside of me and I gasp. "It won't be enough for you, Izzy. Once you've got my dick you'll demand the rest of me too." He says this but he begins fucking me with his fingers. "You're too goddamn used to having everything you want."

I'm going to come. He knows it. He goes faster and I get wetter. His thumb rolls over the most sensitive inch and I moan. But Rafe's not done telling me off. He just wants to wait for the right moment.

His laughter sounds wicked in my ear. "Isabella Gentry, while you're one sheltered princess who could probably use a few fucking real world lessons, I'm not willing to be the one to break you in."

My teeth grind together. I don't want to come yet but I can't stop. The rising tide is seconds away from overwhelming my senses. "No dick can break me you arrogant bastard."

"I could prove different tonight."

"Then do it."

"You'd hate me." He whispers these words just as I come so hard I have to bite my lip to stop from waking the neighborhood with a shriek. I'm shaking from the spasms and I know that I'm going to feel mortified when all the shattering vibrations pass but I can't seem to make myself care.

Rafe isn't finished. His hand remains between my legs. Now he's going to take something for himself as well. It's just not what I asked for. His pants are still on but he jerks up my nightie so that my bare ass can dry hump his dick. So he'll use me to get off. He just won't fuck me the way I want him to, not even if I beg.

Fine.

If that's the way it's going to be then I want to come again. I roll my head backwards, arch my body and open my legs wider. He sharply sucks in his breath and I don't know if I've surprised him or if he's cursing me out in his head. During all the action my other strap has fallen and my back is against his naked chest. His other arm, the one that was wrapped around me like a vice, is now on my hip so he can guide my movements. Everything about it is hot and everything about it is wrong. I shouldn't have come out here. I'm not going to forgive myself tomorrow.

He's getting close. I know it by the way he stiffens with a fresh moan and I add my fingers to his down in between my legs to get myself there faster. His cock feels so hard against my backside I wouldn't be surprised to see a bruise there in the morning. For the second time I come and with a final string of obscenities Rafe does the same. It seems like this should mean something, bind us together somehow, when we both lose ourselves in the same instant, but I know it won't.

I don't stay there in his arms and he doesn't invite me to. Without looking at him I pull my nightgown back to a decent state and return to the house, ignoring the jellied feel of my legs and the way I tremble inside.

Rafe promised that if we had sex I would end up hating him.

Maybe I would.

Maybe I will anyway.

12

IZZY

Rafe and Oliver are long gone by the time I wake up. Following the little backyard liaison, I showered and then slept soundly until my phone alarm began going off with the sound of birds chirping. Once I read an article stating this was the most emotionally soothing noise to awaken to. I do not feel emotionally soothed.

Today there aren't enough chirping birds on earth to erase the flood of flashbacks from last night. Pulling the covers over my face with a groan does not purge the memory of Rafe's breath in my ear as I came on his hand.

"I'm not going to be the one to break you in."

I throw the covers off my face.

If I think about him anymore I'll just get angry. Rafe Hempstead has no idea what he's talking about. For his information, I have had *all of the sex*. I've been having sex since the summer after my junior year of high school. He flatters himself to think he has some kind of all powerful cock that can conquer any woman it pleases.

Yet something bothers me about the things he said. He was being vulgar, not unusual for him. He succeeded in offending me but I'm not sure that was his goal. Even before I humiliated myself in my lingerie last night he could have had me if he'd ever made a move. He never has, despite the fact that he wants to. I don't think he's in the habit of being a gentleman. Maybe, despite his rough way of showing it, he's trying to be one now.

Rafe doesn't hate me. But he might hate himself.

In an abrupt move I sit up and decide that's enough of dwelling on Rafe Hempstead for now. At some point we'll have to face each other. We live together. He's not going anywhere and neither am I.

My first class of the day is in an hour and I get ready in a hurry so I'll have time to stop somewhere for breakfast. I can think of no place more deserving of my business than Ruby's Bakery, which I think of as Shane's Bakery, though Lana has said he has no intention of changing the name of the place he inherited from his godmother. Shane hooks me up with a pair of cinnamon rolls fresh from the oven and the day improves dramatically.

Outside the weather is pleasant enough to believe that the dry heat of summer will soon be in the past. I'm grateful to have three classes in a row because this leaves me little time to think about anything else. My mother calls just after my last class ends and I'm careful to keep any mention of Rafe out of the conversation. Instead I stick to talking about Oliver. She loves hearing all about the little boy who has captured my heart.

The call doesn't last long because she's running late for the job she took at my Aunt Truly's store when her empty nest status left her feeling bored. I had stopped in a shady spot on the quad so I could talk to my mother in peace and as her voice fades from my ears I look at all the people moving around, most of them students, many younger than I am.

In my family there's no shortage of people who suffer from a troubled past. My mother was raised in an oppressive cult. My father's cousins – triplets Cord, Creed and Chase, suffered horrifying abuse and neglect as children. My own cousin, Thomas, was brutally assaulted in a home invasion and his injuries cost him his major league baseball dreams. They've all endured their journeys and come out stronger on the other side.

But I'm not one of them. Rafe was unnecessarily harsh when he called me a 'sheltered princess'. He also wasn't quite wrong. I've led a charmed life and I have no reason to believe the future will bring anything different. I like to think I'd rise to any challenge but I can't prove it. I also can't guess how different I would be now if I'd been forced to deal with the terrible things that have been experienced and overcome by the people I love.

And now I'm thinking about Rafe. He's never talked to me about his past but Caris has told me enough. He grew up in a small town, branded from birth with the stain of a murderous legacy he had nothing to do with. He was only a teenager when he was kicked out of his home and arrested for a crime he didn't commit. What might that have done to him? What is it still doing to him?

Last night I thought I might hate him after all. Today I'm only sorry for him. And I don't hate him. No, I don't hate him one bit.

My classes are finished for the day but I'm not in a hurry to leave campus. I decide to get a sandwich from a sub shop in the Student Union and eat it at a table close the one where I shared those first lattes with Grant. I don't know if he has classes today. We're not at the point where we've memorized each other's schedules and honestly, I don't even know if he's seeing anyone else or not. I don't think he is but I can't recall the subject ever coming up.

After my sandwich is in ruins I still have little desire to go home, mostly because I have no idea how to deal with Rafe when I see him again. So I do what any brave girl in a similar situation would do. I go hide on the third floor of the library in a comfortable chair and escape into the scandalous fictional exploits of nineteenth century British high society.

By the time I get tired of reading it's after five o'clock. I can't hide in the library all night. Or maybe I could. I haven't seen another person walk by in two hours. With a sigh I get to my feet, collect my belongings and trudge out of the building and all the way to the south lot where my car is parked.

The instant I turn down my street I can see Rafe's truck parked at the curb and my nerves kick into overdrive. I'm being foolish. I don't need to cower and cringe just because Rafe said some harsh words, then finger banged me and turned down my seduction attempt. I'm sure he's done worse. He might not even remember.

Oliver is sitting at the kitchen table with a bowl of macaroni and cheese next to a glass of milk. He brightens when he sees me and runs over for a hug.

"You're late today," he accuses, his arms wrapped around my waist.

Yes, I suppose he's become used to the routine of seeing me when he arrives home.

I give him a squeeze. "I'm sorry, Oliver. How was your day?"

"It was okay." He returns to the table and resumes his attack on his macaroni and cheese.

Rafe is standing next to the sink. He's looking down and cutting up vegetables. He moves some green pepper sticks onto a small plate before giving it to Oliver.

"There's some mac and cheese in the pot if you're interested," he says with no trace of discomfort.

"No thanks. I ate on campus."

He lifts his head. His eyes, always a startling blue, don't focus on me for long. He won't say a word about last night, not with Oliver here. I hope he figures out that I would prefer nothing to be said about it at all. I'm an adult. I can handle rejection without throwing a tantrum.

Rafe washes off the knife he was using and then dries it with a dishtowel. His movements are very slow, halting, like he's preoccupied with something else.

"Well." I cross my arms. "I'll leave you guys to enjoy your dinner. I've got some studying to do this evening." A handy excuse, always ready to be trotted out when you're in school.

Oliver is unhappy. "But I want to show you my new book."

I don't have the heart to disappoint him. "How about this? I'll come see you before bedtime and you can show me your book then."

I just need to get out of this room right now. The skin prickles on my arms, every one of my senses acutely aware of Rafe's proximity.

Oliver is satisfied and smiles before taking gulping sips of his milk.

Rafe stares down at the counter as if there are words to read on the granite pattern. He waits until I'm halfway down the hall.

"Izzy?"

I freeze. If I turn around then he'll see on my face the proof that he was right all along. He was right and I was wrong. His dick wouldn't be enough. I would demand all of him.

I hear his sigh.

Then he says, "I hit the sack so early last night that I forgot to lock the back door. I guess you did too."

He's giving me an out. He's also giving himself one. All I have to do is play along.

"Yeah." I still won't turn around. "I did some studying and then I went straight to bed. I never checked whether the place was locked up."

"I'll make sure it's locked up tonight." His way of saying he's not going to get caught up in a moment of weakness again.

"Then I'm sure it will be." My way of saying that I won't either.

I feel better and worse after this little coded exchange.

Nothing eventful happens this night.

Or the next one.

Or the one after that.

On Saturday Grant takes me out for a group date with some of his old frat brothers and their girlfriends. On the drive to the steakhouse I tell him, "Yes, I can go with you to Santa Fe next weekend." He lights up and reaches for my hand. At the end of the night he walks me to the door and I let him kiss me for longer than usual even though I feel like an awful fraud with his tongue in my mouth while my thoughts drift somewhere else. From now on I'll give Grant my full undivided attention. He deserves it.

It's late and I enter the apartment with care because I assume Oliver, and probably Rafe too, will be sleeping. Instead, I find Oliver hysterically sobbing on the couch while Rafe tries to hold him as he guides a plastic syringe to Oliver's mouth.

"NO!!!" Oliver screams and covers his mouth. His face is blotchy and wet with tears. He's on the verge of hyperventilating.

"Buddy." Rafe's face crumples and his hand wilts in mid air. "You need to take your medicine. It's the only way your ears will get better."

I drop my purse on the floor and run to them "What happened?"

Rafe is panicked, about to begin sobbing himself. He tries to calm a struggling Oliver while explaining. "I tucked him into bed and then he started screaming that his ears hurt. His head felt hot to me and so I took him to urgent care. The doctor said he had double ear infections and he was running a temp of a hundred and one. I was able to pick up his medicine at the twenty-four-hour pharmacy but he says it tastes bad and won't take the whole dose."

I pick up the bottle and recognize the medicine. I've seen it before when I babysat for my cousin Cami's daughter while she recovered from an ear infection. I sniff at the bottle and observe the white chalky consistency. Then I remember something important.

"You can ask the pharmacist to add flavoring so that it will taste better."

Some cautious hope on Rafe's face. "Really?"

"Yes. I'm sure of it. I'll go to the pharmacy and have it done."

"Izzy," Oliver whimpers. Tears continue to roll down his face and his small arms reach for me.

My heart dissolves as I kneel and hug him close. "It's okay, Oliver. We'll have you feeling better in no time."

He continues to cry in my arms. "I want Mommy."

Rafe buries his head in his hands.

Oh, heartbreak in this room. There are no words.

I rub Oliver's back. His little body still feels awful feverish.

"Rafe? Have you given him a pain reliever already? It'll lower his temperature too."

He raises his head and his eyes are red. He dashes to the counter and grabs a white paper bag. "The pharmacist told me to buy this." He withdraws a bottle of children's Tylenol.

"Stay here, Izzy," Oliver begs, clutching my neck.

"I'll go," Rafe says quietly as he watches his son cling to me amid sobs. "I'll go get his medicine fixed." He swallows. "Could you please stay with him?"

"Of course I'll stay with him. And I'll give him the Tylenol. It's cherry flavored so he won't mind the taste. It'll bring down his fever and help with the pain."

Rafe nods. "I won't be gone long." His eyes are still teary but he looks directly at me. "Thanks, Izzy."

Once he's gone it takes a few minutes to get Oliver calmed down enough to agree to take some Tylenol. He won't let go of my neck so I carry him to the kitchen in order to get a glass of water to wash down the medicine. He's deceptively heavy and he holds onto me for dear life. As I coax him to swallow the necessary dose an enormous wave of sadness consumes me, not just for Oliver but for the woman who should be holding him instead of me. The woman who can no longer comfort her baby when he cries and will never see him grow into a man.

Life has never seemed so unfair to me as it does just now.

I carry him back to the couch and find my phone. The tears are beginning to dry on his cheeks as I search for something to entertain him. Bless the Internet for having no shortage of goofy cat videos. I know I have a digital thermometer somewhere but I can feel his fever already starting to cool and he giggles occasionally as he watches the screen with his head on my shoulder. There's a blanket nearby, the one Rafe uses for his bed, and I drape it around Oliver's body.

This is where we are when Rafe returns with the antibiotics for Oliver's ear infection, which has been made more palatable with the addition of bubble gum flavoring. It takes a little bit of convincing to persuade Oliver to give the medicine another try but he's getting sleepy now and he willingly opens his mouth the next time Rafe brings the syringe close.

"Good job, Oliver," I praise him.

He yawns.

Rafe and I were so focused on Oliver that we took no notice of how close we are. His muscled arm brushes my shoulder as he shifts away. I cradle his sleepy child while his blue eyes survey me. There's exhaustion on his face, but also relief. And gratitude.

I wish he had called me. I would have left Grant at the steakhouse and come home immediately if I'd known what was happening. I would go to Oliver anytime he needed me. Not just Oliver. I would go to Rafe anytime he needed me too.

"Fever's down," I whisper.

He nods and scoops his arms under Oliver's body. There's no way to avoid some skin to skin contact between us as we transfer the little boy but there's no thrill involved and I'm sure it's the same for him. Our issues don't matter and everything we do right now is for Oliver's sake.

While Rafe carries his son off to bed I remain on the couch, touched by a half forgotten memory from many years ago. I was probably Oliver's age and I had come down with a wicked case of strep throat. The pain was so bad that I couldn't sleep and my dad stayed up with me all night. We watched Disney princess movies together. I took for granted the amount of unconditional love that surrounded me at all times.

Rafe returns and finds me sitting on the couch. I should probably move. After all, this is his bed. His hand slides through his hair. The longest front strands can now swing over his forehead all the way down to his eyes. When we met his hair was cropped close and I'm sure he hasn't had it cut since he moved here. Perhaps he hasn't had the time.

He sinks down on the couch, close but not too close.

"He'll be all right," I tell Rafe.

If Rafe were anyone else I would reach out a comforting hand but I can't do that, not with him.

He lets his breath out slowly. "I owe you one."

"You owe me nothing. I love Oliver."

Rafe leans back into the couch cushion and gazes at me with those blue eyes that can turn cold or stormy or sexy or humorous, depending on his mood. They are now bleary. Tired. Maybe a little beseeching. "I know you're pissed at me."

I shake my head. "I'm really not."

The twist to his mouth says he knows different but there's something else there as well. Remorse. "I wasn't trying to hurt your feelings that night. You're beautiful, Izzy. You're a good person. I'm glad you're in my life. And in Oliver's life. Honestly, I can't imagine how things would be without you, how we would make it."

This is Rafe at his most vulnerable. I am sure he doesn't let his guard down like this very often. Rafe is saying that he needs a friend more than he needs sex. Perhaps that's what I need too.

"Are we friends, Rafe?" I honestly want to know and I think he'll tell me the truth.

He lifts an eyebrow, plainly worried. "I hope so. Are we?"

Are we?

Rafe tries to be a considerate roommate. He is a good father. Sometimes he can also be a jerk and sometimes I feel an urge to throw objects at his head. Other times I want to jump his bones so badly I can't think clearly. But I like being around him. I care about him. And I believe, despite all our arguments and eye rolling, that he cares about me too.

"Yes, Rafe. We're friends."

He smiles. I don't want my heart to pound but it does. He should smile more often.

We sit side by side in pleasant silence until I rise and stretch, my muscles aching from spending so much time in one spot.

"You should get some sleep," I tell him. "I'll keep my door open in case I hear Oliver crying in the night."

His eyelids are heavy, his voice soft. "Good night, Isabella."

Some vague but persistent ache warns me it's not right to leave him sitting here alone and yet it's what has to happen.

Once I'm in my own bed with the lights turned off and the door open a crack to hear Oliver if he needs me, I can almost imagine that the strange, impassioned, almost furious connection with Rafe had never happened that night in the darkness.

Almost, but not quite.

13

RAFE

"I'll be here in the morning to pick you up. And if you want to come home early, just tell your Uncle Jay to give me a call."

I'm crouched down at his level and he doesn't answer. He's looking at the cats, eager to get back to playing with them.

"Can I have a hug?" I ask my son and he comes to me willingly. He gives me hugs now even though he has never called me 'Dad'. I won't push him. I'll just be grateful for the hugs.

He runs back to the other side of the room where there's a complex tower structure complete with ramps and carpeted stairs, all for the benefit of two pampered cats.

"We'll take good care of him," Caris says. She's got her arms wrapped around my brother and she's smiling. "I'll make sure to give him his medicine before bed tonight. You said his ears aren't hurting anymore, right?"

"He hasn't complained about it lately." I watch as Oliver rings a bell in one of the cat towers. One of the animals bats at it playfully and Oliver laughs. "He's just got a few more days left of the antibiotics."

Jay is watching Oliver with a grin. Then he looks my way and his grin fades a little. "So what have you got planned tonight?"

"Sleep." I yawn. "Maybe I'll watch a movie if I'm feeling really crazy."

"You should go have fun," Caris urges.

Really, I wouldn't know what kind of fun to chase. I could go haunt the college bars. There are plenty of them around here. I could set my sights on some pretty, adventurous girl and enjoy a few hours of excitement. I could even take her home. It's not like anyone else will be there tonight. Caris and Jay invited Oliver for a sleepover and he was all over the idea, especially since it meant he could play with their cats to his heart's content.

And as for Izzy...

Izzy is at home getting ready for a weekend trip to Santa Fe with that guy she's seeing. Grant. I want to puke every time she utters his name, although I think I'm pretty good at keeping my gag reflex in check. She has no idea.

Caris leaves Jay's side to go sit on the floor next to Oliver. Leaving him behind feels wrong and not because he won't be cared for. Caris and Jay are great with him. I've just grown used to having him with me. If I get up in the middle of the night to check on him, as I often do, he won't be there sleeping in his bed. I'll miss him.

"See you in the morning, Oliver."

He waves but doesn't turn around. "Bye."

Jay follows me outside to my truck. It's kind of awkward. We should have learned how to deal with each other by now after all these weeks but somehow that never quite happens. I'm still waiting for him to tell me the news that Caris shared about our grandfather but he and I never talk about Arcana. We don't really talk about anything except Oliver.

Jay clears his throat. "Caris told me he's been having a tough time at school, that he's been in some fights."

"Yeah." I lean against my truck, my heart sinking as I think about being summoned to Oliver's school again today. This time he wound up scuffling with a different kid because the boy told him that his picture was stupid. "The school thinks he needs some counseling."

Jay nods. "Maybe that would help. Oliver's been through more than any kid should have to take."

"I know. And I know he misses his mom every day."

"Of course he does."

Exhaling thickly, I focus on a crack in the sidewalk and try to put words to my fears for my son. "I don't want him to be all about his anger. The way I was. You remember. I was a tornado in school, destroying anyone who gambled on hassling me. It's not a good way to start life. At least not the kind of life that I want for him."

Jay doesn't argue. He's thoughtful, perhaps looking through the window of his memories into the past. "People gave you a hard time because we were Hempsteads. They thought the stories their parents told them made us easy targets because we were just the town trash. I'll tell you one thing, though. They didn't come after me as much because you blazed such an ass kicking trail."

I snort out loud. "That's one way of putting it." If a world record for playground fights has ever been established then I'm sure I'd have it beat. I used to fight more often than I'd write my name.

Jay is now paying attention to the approach of a man with two little boys. They've all got baseball gloves on and they're probably heading for the grassy park at the end of Jay's street. The man gives Jay a smile of greeting as they pass so he must be a neighbor.

And I'm waiting.

I'm waiting for him to say something else about our shared history, about our name. Well, *my* name since he decided to change his. I'm waiting for him to tell me what he knows about whether or not our grandfather was the murdering bastard we've always believed him to be. He might be aware that Caris already told me. Yet I still want to hear the story from him.

Jay watches as the man and his sons move farther away. Then he takes a step toward the house. "I should get back inside. I told Caris I'd throw some burgers on the grill." He pauses. "Do you want one?"

"Thanks but I'm trying to go vegetarian."

"Really?"

"Hell no. But I think I'll get on home just the same. I'll call in the morning before I swing by to pick him up."

"Sure." Jay backs up and stuffs his hands in his pockets. "Have a good night."

That's unlikely. This would be the perfect occasion to buy a couple of bottles with the sole purpose of getting bombed. I was never really an epic drinker. I would go out and toss a few shots back and have some beers now and then but getting crocked off my ass wasn't something I did all that often. Since arriving in Hutton the only time I've touched alcohol was the night I bought a single beer and drank it alone on the back patio. I would have stayed out there alone if not for Izzy. Even though it's been a few weeks and we've mended our differences about what happened that night I'm still conflicted. About her. About me.

Part of the problem is that I've seen the kind of guy Izzy gets attached to. The kind who gets haircuts named for Hollywood actors and creams his pants over the latest two thousand dollar tech accessory. I don't have anything in common with a guy like that, the kind she wants. I assumed we both understood that without needing to say so out loud.

Then she had to go marching outside in her sex goddess clothes. I was tempted to give her what she wanted.

But I didn't. Because...

She's Izzy.

She comforts my kid when he's sick and she shares her favorite cereal and she asks me questions like she cares about what I think.

She's my friend.

I've never had many friends.

And I've never had a female friend but I think you're not supposed to bend them over the patio table and fuck them like the fate of your cock is at stake.

That's what I wanted to do.

That's what Izzy wanted me to do.

That's what I almost did.

What I actually did was bad enough. I fingered her in my lap and rubbed by dick on her until I came. I did feel like a piece of shit afterwards. But not as bad as I would have felt if I'd taken her up on her offer.

Since then we've dealt with the fallout. She forgives me. She's still my friend. There shouldn't be any problem. Except when I think about her taking off this weekend with that Grant fuckhead my chest wants to cave in.

So that's why I might get trashed and treat myself to the best porn I can find. I won't have to worry about my brain getting messed up and doing something stupid, like screwing my pretty roommate. There's no danger of that tonight. She won't even be home.

And there goes my chest, feeling all hollow again.

When I get to the house there's a part of me hoping that she's already left. Seeing her march out the door and into his arms is going to be torture. But she's still here. I can hear music coming from her bedroom as I take a seat on the couch. The song is an old one, a U2 song I think. I hear the lyrics 'with or without you' and then Izzy begins singing along.

Pulling my wallet out, I withdraw the card I was given by the school psychologist. The card says Grief Counseling For Children and I've already left a voicemail at the number listed. When I look at the words I try to imagine what kind of soul crushing work is involved in dealing with sad kids every day. Yet I'm glad someone does it. It means I can have hope that my son will receive help before he turns into this furious monster looking to shred anyone who gets too close. Before he turns into me.

"Hey, I didn't hear you come in." Izzy wheels her suitcase into the room and pushes the handle down. She looks off the charts hot with her hair flowing in red waves halfway down her back, her black dress short yet tasteful and made of some kind of stretchy material that molds to her sexy body.

She smiles at me with no clue that she's naked in my head. "Was Oliver excited for his sleepover?"

I rip my eyes away from shapely legs that are capped with black patent heels. "Yeah, he helped pack his bag himself. I bet he'll try to sneak at least one of Caris's cats in there when I show up tomorrow to bring him home."

She laughs. Not every woman looks even better when she laughs but Izzy does. She's beyond radiant. I want to bury myself in her in the worst way.

"What time's your flight?" I ask her as she fusses with the strap of her silver watch.

"In exactly two hours. Grant should be here any minute."

Ah, yes. Grant. The guy who has all the manners money can buy. He's on the golden path to success and he knows how to behave. He's the duke she's been pining for. He's what she really deserves. He's not some ex-criminal head case being chased by his demons.

"You have a good time this weekend." I was trying to fake some enthusiasm and failed. My voice sounds flat and half dead.

She notices and takes a step in my direction. "How did the meeting go at Oliver's school?"

"As well as it could I guess. I got handed a card for a grief counselor. It's Friday so they were already gone when I called. I left a message." With a sigh I run a hand through my hair and remember the kind expressions of the well meaning people at Oliver's school. "The school psychologist thinks the reason he keeps lashing out in anger has everything to do with Dana's death."

Izzy sits on the arm of the sofa and gives me the most sympathetic look in the world. I wish she wouldn't do that. It just makes me think about how she's all that I want and can't have.

"He doesn't talk about her," Izzy says. "Not really."

"I know. I've tried to get him to talk but he shuts down."

"You don't talk about her either."

I blow out a breath and remember the night a woman edged close to me at a crappy bar that I wasn't even legally old enough to be in. *"I'm Dana and I'm buying. What are you drinking?"*

It's true that I don't talk about her. I don't feel like I ever really knew her.

"We weren't exactly together. We just had a thing for a few months. It was sex and nothing else. Dana was married and she was a lot older than I was. I didn't take it seriously and neither did she. She thought she couldn't have kids. Then she tells me that she's pregnant and it's mine. The next day I had to report to serve five months in lockup after an assault conviction. The whole time I was in there I never heard from her at all. So the minute I get out I look her up. She says she's having a boy but she and her husband are going to raise him. I'm not invited to be part of his life and at the time I think that's best."

Izzy is quiet. She's looking at me so intently and I want her to understand the way it was. The way it *is*. I want her to understand me.

"I was twenty. I was a fuck up. Dana had money and she was going to give him a nice life. A family. It didn't work out that way. But despite everything that went down between me and her I think she was a good mother. I know that losing her will always be a hole in Oliver's life that I'll never be able to fill. I'll do the best I can. But in my bad moments I'm afraid he'll end up like me."

"Rafe." She reaches out to touch my shoulder and then pulls back. She bites her lip and folds her hands in her lap.

"Look," I tell her. "I don't mean to bring you down. I'm not looking for pity."

"I'm not offering you any. But you are *not* a villain and someone should tell you so. I watch you every day. I see you killing yourself trying to do the best you can for Oliver. You've made some mistakes. Who hasn't? Sometimes I want to scream at you in frustration. But you're a decent guy. You deserve to be happy. You shouldn't doubt that."

I've never wanted to kiss anyone as badly as I want to kiss her right now.

All the push and pull between us that's been raging since the day we met comes down to this moment. I have to ask her a question. And I don't know what I'm going to do when she answers it.

"Do you think *you'll* be happy, Izzy? With him?"

"Grant?" A shadow on her brow. "We haven't known each other for very long. I enjoy his company but I don't really see us being this insanely devoted couple like Lana and Shane. Or like Caris and Jay. I hope I'll have a relationship like that someday. Like my parents do." She sighs. "But then again, maybe not everybody gets that."

I think we could have that, Izzy.

The doorbell rings. She slides off the arm of the couch. She extends the handle of her rolling suitcase.

"That's Grant." She looks at me and cocks her head. "You call me if you need to talk. And you think about what I said."

If this moment goes then she goes.

I'll sit here all weekend, picturing her with him and wanting to punch myself in the face for being a fucking coward.

It takes only a second to decide. I stand up and cross the room in two long strides. This is a risk. A far bigger risk is that I might lose her forever if I let her walk out.

She's already reaching for the doorknob when I grab her wrist. There's no time for her to react before my other arm circles her waist and pulls her in. My mouth takes possession of hers without hesitation, without apology. It's fierce and it's intense, the way I kiss her, and I drop her wrist so I can tangle my hand in her hair. She's startled only for an instant before pressing right into me. She's been hungry for this, a part of her waiting for it to happen. A low moan rolls out of her throat and her body arches against mine. I want her feel me, feel how hard I am.

We're close enough to the wall that I can back her right into it and I do. Her legs fly up around my waist and I push between them while our mouths devour each other.

The doorbell rings again.

Fucking Grant.

Her dress gets shoved up over her hips and she moves her body in rhythm, pulsing, grinding. If she wants me to take her right here against the wall then I will. Grant can come in and watch if he wants.

Isabella Gentry.

I'll give her anything.

Everything.

I'll give her me.

She kisses me back and hungrily pulls at my pants. Her legs open wider, circling my waist. She's so eager to ride my cock that she's practically whimpering.

And then she stops.

She jumps down, cups her hand over her mouth and backs away. Her eyes close, she takes a shuddering breath and she shakes her head twice. Then she walks right out the door, wheeling her suitcase behind her.

Well.

Shit.

She's gone.

And now I really am alone in an empty apartment, muttering the word 'FUCK' over and over because I'm a fool.

Worse, I'm a fool with a hard dick and nowhere to put it.

Worse yet, I don't know how to treat the only woman who has ever really meant something to me.

I return to the couch and stare at the ceiling. Mostly because I have nothing else to do. The ceiling offers no advice. The ceiling doesn't care that Izzy is lost to me, in the arms of a guy who kicks my ass on paper even if he could never kick my ass in real life. Minutes pass, every one of them worse than the last one.

The door is flung open. Izzy and her suitcase have returned. Her face is flushed and she's not smiling, not even a little bit. She's downright furious.

She shuts the door, kicks her heels off in a temper and throws them in a corner before stalking over to the couch.

"What. The. Fuck. Was. THAT?" She gestures wildly. Her eyes flash with so much rage that I wonder if she's thinking about kicking me in the balls.

"So is the trip to Santa Fe off?" I really want to know but the question just makes her madder.

"Dammit Rafe!" She doesn't kick me in the balls but she does swat at my knee.

Then she flops down on the couch, crosses her arms over her chest and glares. "What game are you playing?"

"None."

"Bullshit. You don't want me but you don't want anyone else to have me either? Is that it?"

That's what she thinks?

I guess I can't blame her.

She threw herself at me once and I pushed her away.

Maybe I've got one more chance to get this right. If I blow it this time I can't count on her giving me another one.

"Isabella."

She keeps her arms crossed, unwilling to give an inch. "I told Grant I couldn't go with him this weekend. Or any other weekend." She uncrosses her arms but only because she wants to pound on the couch with her fists. "I'm such a fucking idiot!"

"Izzy."

She's still smoldering but she's also blinking back tears. She doesn't flinch or move away when I get closer. I cup her chin in my palm and her lip quivers.

"Rafe. *Why?* Why didn't you just let me go?"

"Because." My thumb brushes her lip. "I want you more than I want to keep breathing."

Her eyes widen. The anger drains away. She's shocked.

"You said I'd hate you," she reminds me.

"And sometimes you might. God knows I'm easy to hate."

"Do you want to be hated?"

"No." I shake my head for emphasis. "Especially not by you."

She's thinking. Her face is still in my hand. She's not pulling away. Her posture loosens. She takes my hand and kisses the inside of my palm. Then she suddenly swings one leg over to straddle my lap. She wants to look at me eye to eye. She has a command to deliver.

"Then don't let me. Don't let me hate you, Rafe Hempstead."

My hands slide under her dress and up her soft thighs to grip her hips and move her closer. I'm so fucking hard that my pants are about to bust open but for the first time in my life I'm on a level that's about more than sex.

Not that I have no plans to fuck her six ways to Sunday before the next sunrise. She'll be lucky if she's able to walk straight tomorrow.

We'll get to that.

After this.

"Izzy, I want to be everything you want."

She reaches down, grabs the hem of her dress and slowly pulls it over her head. Then she braces her palms on my shoulders and leans in to press her forehead to mine.

"Rafe. You already are," she whispers.

This next kiss is not as fierce as the last one. When my mouth claims hers it's not a demand. It's a promise. But we're both too sexed up to sit here making out on the couch for very long. After so many weeks of holding back instead of giving in the damn is about to break. Fuck, I'm going to enjoy the look on her face when my cock invades her. No mental porn while jerking off in the shower can beat reality. I already know how easy it is to make her come. Now there's nothing holding me back. This girl is in for a hell of a ride. She's about to get owned in every sense and she's going to love every blessed filthy second.

My fingers twist her bra open and with two moves it's gone, somewhere on the floor. Her tits are perfect and I get my mouth on one, sucking the tenderness of her skin while she threads her fingers through my hair and tries to rub into me any way she can.

"My god, you feel so good." She's riding my zipper, almost gasping because she's so close to her limit.

I take my mouth off her tits and seize a handful of her hair. "I didn't tell you that you could come yet."

Her lips tilt up and her eyes are full of fire. Yeah, she likes this, playing rough. I figured she would. She flicks the snap of my jeans open. "As if I need your fucking permission to come."

She tugs on the zipper. I tighten the fist in her hair. My cock is freed and meets her palm. She inhales sharply as she gets a load of what she's dealing with.

"You gonna be able to take all that, princess?" I have to admit I'm having some trouble staying in the game now that she's squeezing and stroking.

She smiles with fake innocence. "Call me a princess again and I'll make you pay."

I've had enough. "Now you're just daring me."

"Yes. What are you going to do about it?"

I stand straight up with her legs around my waist. We're going to her bedroom. I want her on her back this time, the first time. Izzy sucks on my neck throughout the short trip. Her bed is large and firm and I lay her down in the middle where I can take a minute to admire her. She's beyond gorgeous. She's Venus. She's perfect. She's even more perfect after I get rid of her panties. If she's mad that I've torn them in two to get them off then that's too bad. I'm sure she forgives me the instant my tongue goes to work between her legs. She moans my name and arches her back to give me better access. I've imagined this a hundred times; my face between her thighs, my mouth doing the job of fucking her so good that she's losing control.

But I can't watch her from here and I want to watch.

She writhes around and gets frustrated when I pull away.

"Rafe, I *need* you," she complains, trying to pull me back in.

"Don't worry." I yank my shirt off with so much force I hear a rip. "You'll get me."

She'll have her chance to be in charge. If directing traffic is something that gets her hot then she can navigate me to her heart's content. Right after I finish blowing her mind.

My pants come off. My boxers follow.

FUCK!

I don't have a condom. I haven't been carrying them around since I moved to Hutton because I wasn't expecting to get a chance to use any.

Izzy reads the mood. She dives into her nightstand and plucks a handful of foil wrapped squares out. I snatch one and scatter the others. We'll use them all before we leave this room again. I can get a condom on quicker than a bolt of lightning can strike. It's a handy talent when patience is running low.

She bends her knees and hooks them around my hips.

I push her knees apart even wider and tease her wet center with the tip of my cock. "Look at me, Izzy."

She breathes hard, her beautiful bare tits rising and falling, nipples standing at attention. Her eyes, heavy with lust, flicker to my face. She's ready.

At first I'm careful with her. She's tight and on the slim side and I'm far from small. We can test out her appetite for rougher action later. When I ease my way inside, her body stretches and her head rolls back. The low groan comes from me. She feels too fucking exquisite. Holding out is going to be tough. I pump once and she clutches me. Twice and she bites her lip. Slow and deep it is. I'll take us both right to the fucking frenzied edge and we'll jump together.

"Rafe." Her body shakes. Her nails dig into my forearms.

I grin down at her. This is exactly what I wanted. To see her face when it happens. "Now you can come, princess."

Her eyes fly open with a glint of defiance. She wants to rebel but she's too close. I'm pumping faster and she doesn't stand a chance. She knows it. Her muscles stiffen and she squeezes her eyes shut. The noise she makes is perfect porn and I'm ruthless as she comes apart.

I've got her.

She's mine.

Never have I seen a girl come so hard or for so long. It's obscene beyond belief and I can't hold on anymore. With one more colossal thrust I fill the condom and keep pushing until I've got nothing left. My heart nearly pounds right out of my chest as the waves crash. There's a full minute when I can't catch a good breath because I'm so blown to smithereens.

I've learned something new today.

I've learned that this girl is the best goddamn screw I'll ever have. Maybe it's because I've spent so much time wanting her or because we connect in a way that's far deeper than anything I've had before. Whatever the case, I'm all hers.

We're both sweaty and breathing hard. I'm totally spent for now but I don't want to crush her with my weight so I drop a kiss between her breasts and roll to my side.

Izzy's hand is over her eyes and she breathes out a laugh. "Holy shit. Rafe. That was…"

"Just the beginning," I tell her and prop myself up on one elbow. My other hand roams over her tits, her belly, her thighs. I won't need much time to get hard again. Shit's going to get creative before I'm ready to take a nap.

Izzy cracks one eye open and looks at me. Then she abruptly rolls on top of me and it's cute the way she tries to pin me down, holding my arms on the bed, her face hovering inches away while strands of her hair tickle my skin. She's not joking, though. She's very serious.

"It's *us* from now on, right?"

She says it as if she's afraid of the answer, like she has some doubt about whether we'll just go back to being plain old roommates tomorrow or maybe thinking I'm looking for a friends with benefits situation.

I respond by kissing her. Gently. Tenderly. She softens and releases her hold on my arms. I wrap them around her body while we kiss on and on. I'm giving her the answer she needs with my mouth until she breaks away and rests her cheek against my chest. Then I stroke her hair and hold her close and give her the answer out loud, just in case she still has a sliver of doubt.

"It's us from now on, Izzy. I swear."

14

IZZY

Rafe sighs in his sleep. It's a happy sound. I'm sure he doesn't realize he does it every now and then as I burrow closer to his body in the darkness.

The mild light of an autumn morning filters in through the slits of the window blinds and I'm wide awake beside a sleeping mountain of muscle but I have no desire to move. Rafe's arms are around me and he shifts ever so slightly, enough for me to feel something else that often happens in his sleep. He gets hard. I smile at the sensation of his swollen dick against my hip and my body responds. I want him again.

It's been two weeks.

And oh my sweet heavenly stars, what a two weeks.

I've never been with a guy like Rafe. He's wild. Nothing is off limits. Nothing is too weird to try. If I said I wanted to wear a rubber chicken butt plug while he licks mayonnaise from my tits then he'd be into it.

Rafe makes me feel bold and daring in a way no one else ever has. Lately I've had trouble sitting through class lectures because my mind would prefer to indulge in erotic flashbacks.

It has to be said.

The guy has the stamina of ten bulls.

But he's so much more than that. Rafe comes across as rough around the edges and he is. There's also a deep well of loyalty and courage inside of him. I watch the way he is with his son and marvel at his capacity for patience. Every time he shows this tender side of unselfish devotion he claims a little bit more real estate in my heart. At this point he nearly owns the whole thing.

It's happened.

Finally.

I'm in love.

I'm also completely, utterly, devastatingly infatuated.

I'm reminded of this by the familiar vague ache between my legs and I reach down to touch myself. A pleasant soreness greets my probing fingers. I can't get enough of him. I'm tempted to wake him right now and take what I want. Instead I push two fingers into my own soft center and suppress my moan. In my mind it's him inside me. His tongue, his cock, his fingers. I've had them all and I'll have them again. I'm so wet for him and my fingers slide deeper. I'm trying to stay still as I fuck my own hand but perhaps Rafe can read my mind in his dreams. His hand slips between my legs and pulls my hand away in order to replace it with his own. One finger. Two fingers. I need more. I open wider and grip his elbow while I rock my hips. I have no shame. I'll use his hand to get off while he's still half asleep.

The orgasm comes for me with a vengeance and I welcome it. Rafe knows me by now. He's aware that I can come more than once and it's not long before the second wave sweeps me away. His hand stays put until the last spasm subsides and now his blue eyes peer at me with intensity.

He wants something in return.

I pull the sheets away and move lower, an effort he encourages by pushing his fingers into my hair. After all of last night's fun I can still taste myself on his cock and this makes me feel powerful. The connection between us, it's not ordinary. I should know. I've been searching for it for a long time.

Rafe moans, "Fucking hell, baby," when I suck him in deep. I won't lie. I'm damn good at sucking dick. I'll even swallow and he curses up an unholy storm when I do.

Then I tuck the blankets around him once more because I can tell he's still tired and will drift off again. His eyes are already closed when he grabs my hand and kisses the tender underside of my wrist.

"Izzy," he whispers and falls asleep.

I'm smiling as I shrug into my robe and tiptoe across the hall to the shower. Before I close the bathroom door I listen to make sure there's no sound from Oliver but typically he sleeps late on Saturdays. When I get out of the shower I'll have to wake Rafe. He likes to be back on the sofa bed before Oliver gets up. We've been careful not to show physical affection in front of Oliver but I know sooner or later it'll become clear that Rafe and I aren't just platonic friends.

The hot shower is luxurious after a strenuous night filled with sexual acrobatics. After toweling off I throw on a t-shirt and soft shorts because it's time to be not-so-sexy. Last night after some rousing sixty-nine action Rafe and I held each other and talked about our plans for today. We decided to do something Oliver would enjoy. I mentioned the butterfly conservatory where Jay and Caris are going to be married. Rafe liked the idea.

I open the door to the bathroom and a shriek nearly rips out of my throat. I'm not expecting Oliver to be standing right there.

He hops from foot to foot. "I have to pee," he announces and runs past me into the bathroom.

The instant the door is closed I dash to the bedroom and try to haul Rafe out of bed by one thick arm.

"He's awake," I hiss and that does it.

Rafe leaps out of bed with impressive speed, throws on the boxers that were tossed on the floor last night and pulls me against his chest, kissing me hard. Without a word he races to the living room and jumps in the sofa bed just as Oliver emerges from the bathroom.

"Did you wash your hands?" I ask Oliver as I follow him down the hall.

"Uh huh." He stops and stares at the sight of his father stirring on the sofa.

Rafe sits up and pretends to wipe the sleep from his eyes. "Morning, buddy." He grins at his son. When Oliver takes a seat at the table, Rafe stands behind him and winks at me.

My heart skips. My muscles quake.

Oliver gets excited when I offer to make blueberry pancakes for breakfast. I'm no expert chef but I know how to add water to pancake mix and throw in some blueberries. Rafe starts the coffee machine. Lately I've grown used to using his simple coffee maker because it's more sensible not to waste a whole pot of coffee and because he's right; all the buttons on my machine are a pain in the ass to deal with.

While I'm measuring out ingredients, Rafe pours some coffee into my SASSY mug and adds some cream and sugar. It's not for him. He takes his coffee black. It's for me. He hands over the mug and I'm not sure what it means when a guy takes care to fix your cup of coffee exactly the way you like it before he even thinks about pouring his own but I'm seriously on the verge of swooning into the pancake batter.

Rafe yawns, downs his coffee like it's water and announces he's going to take a shower.

"Your pancakes will be ready when you get out," I call as I flip the first two on the griddle.

Meanwhile, Oliver has invited his favorite stuffed cat to the table. "Cliff wants a pancake too."

"Of course Cliff can have a pancake. Hey Oliver, do you want to go see a whole lot of butterflies today?"

He thinks about it. "Maybe."

"It'll be fun," I promise as I retrieve the maple syrup from the pantry. "I've been wanting to go to the butterfly conservatory since I moved here."

I hear him muttering something so I turn around.

"Were you talking to me?"

Oliver shakes his head. "I was telling Cliff that you're my dad's girlfriend."

I nearly drop the spatula. I should have guessed that Oliver might catch on to the fact that Rafe and I are together. That's not the shocker. That's not why my breath catches and tears well up in my eyes.

My dad.

It's the first time he's ever called Rafe anything other than 'He' or 'Him'. With all my might I wish Rafe had heard those words. However, if Oliver said them once he'll say them again.

Oliver doesn't even notice that anything unusual has happened. He grins up at me when I give him a plate of pancakes and he looks so much like a mini Rafe. Before he takes a bite of his food he 'feeds' some to the stuffed Cliff. I kiss the top of his head. I absolutely love this child.

"He really said that?" Rafe is incredulous when I pull him into my bedroom to break the news.

"He did. He said 'my dad'."

Rafe sinks down on the bed. He runs a hand through his wet hair and looks dumbfounded. Then a smile creeps across his face. "I'll be damned."

I take a seat in his lap and slide my arms around him. "You're not damned. You're a dad. You're also liberated from the sofa. Oliver already knows that I'm your girlfriend."

The sound of the word makes me freeze. I tossed it off so casually. We've both acknowledged that this is anything but casual. Yet I've never used that word before.

Rafe, however, seems unfazed. He's poking around the neckline of my shirt. "So be a good girlfriend and show me your tits."

I nibble his neck. "No X-rated games during kindergarten waking hours."

He pouts and tries to push his hand inside my shorts.

Giggling, I climb off his lap. "Get dressed you beast."

After a cozy breakfast, just the three of us, Rafe insists on being the one to clear the table.

"Sit down," he orders. "You cooked. I'll clean up."

Who would have thought such gallant manners were hiding in Rafe Hempstead?

Oliver wants to wear the new shirt sent to him by my mother. It's black and has a picture of a bulldog. He looks adorable and the shirt reminds me that I haven't spilled the beans to my folks about my relationship upgrade.

The conservatory isn't open yet and in the meantime Oliver wants to go to the playground located at the elementary school a few blocks away. Rafe jumps at the chance to take him and although I'm invited to go along I decide to remain here. The two of them should have some father/son alone time and besides, I need to give my parents a call and explain myself.

Choosing which parent to call is a no brainer. It's not that I don't want to talk to my dad but Jenny Gentry is by far the softer touch. My dad's default position is to dislike any boyfriend of mine and usually I'm not bothered by this. Rafe is different. I want him to like Rafe.

My mother picks up on the second ring. "Izzy! Sweetheart, I was just thinking about you. I'm putting together another care package. Which of my homemade jams is your favorite?"

She's an angel. Whenever I think about striving to be a better person I ask myself what my mother would do.

"Hi, Mama. Oliver loves the shirt you sent. He's wearing it today. And I love all of your jams but if you have some extra jars of strawberry in search of a home, ship them out to Texas."

"Will do. I'm in the backyard right now, watching your father build some new garden beds for me. It's a nice view. He should go shirtless more often."

"Gross." I gag. "Please talk about something else." I understand that my parents have always shared a dynamic physical relationship but that doesn't mean I want to hear about it. *EVER.*

She laughs. "So what's new? You've been dodging my calls."

"No, I have not. I've just been...busy." My face flames at the memory of what exactly I've been busily doing.

She knows me too well. "What's he like? This reason you've been so busy? Wait, is it that law student you mentioned a few weeks ago?"

"No." I take a deep breath. "He's Rafe."

"Your roommate? I thought you said he was…what was it?" She searches for the exact quote. "The embodiment of oblivious, exasperating masculinity."

"Yeah. Well. Sometimes he is." I pause. "I'm crazy about him."

"And you're living together." She says this slowly, catching on that this isn't just a fling.

I'm eager to sell Rafe's good qualities. "He's wonderful, Mama. He's such a good dad to Oliver. And we have so much fun together." I search for the right word that describes what being with Rafe does to me. "I get breathless when I'm with him."

She's quiet for a moment. When she does speak I can tell she's smiling. "For you to think so, Isabella, he must be pretty damn incredible."

I'm glad to have her vote of confidence but still I chew my lip. "Do you think Daddy will be so agreeable?"

Peals of laughter. "Not a chance."

We chat for a few more minutes, about school and about Oliver. She makes me promise to send some photos when we visit the butterflies later. After the phone call ends I feel loved and contented.

And slightly worried.

For the first time I'm glad that my folks are two states away. My dad's a fair man and he's a good man. But he's also fanatically overprotective of his only child and I could easily imagine him trying to push Rafe's buttons the first chance he gets. It's a good thing they won't be meeting anytime soon. I need some time to ease them both into the reality of *that* explosive introduction.

While I'm mulling over the inevitability of Deck Gentry's clash with Rafe Hempstead there's a knock at the connecting door that separates our place from Lana and Shane's. I run over and throw the door open, expecting to see Lana, but Lana isn't the one knocking. No, it's Jay.

"Hey, Izzy. How are you?"

Whenever we run into each other he's always super polite, almost bashful. He must know about my relationship with his brother. I couldn't keep a secret like that from Lana and I know she's told Caris.

"Hi, Jay." I step back. "Come in."

He looks around as he crosses the threshold. "I swung by to lend Shane some tools and figured I'd say hello."

"Rafe just took Oliver to the playground. They'll be back soon if you want to wait. Or you could find them there. It's two blocks away at the elementary school."

The look on his face is best described as uncertain. It's kind of strange. We live in an era where people text each other with constant regularity. Why wouldn't Jay have just sent his brother a message to let him know he'd be around this morning?

I'm aware that there is some unsettled business between the Hempstead brothers. Jay isn't the only one who is wary about making an effort. Rafe told me he's been waiting for Jay to approach him about that fact that their grandfather was likely innocent of the murders that tarnished the Hempstead name for generations and had a terrible impact on the brothers as they grew up in their small town. When I told Rafe he should just take the initiative and open up a dialogue he muttered something and changed the subject.

Stubborn as hell, the both of them.

The resemblance between the brothers strikes me anew as I watch Jay stand uncomfortably in the living room. Maybe this will be the day when they both overcome whatever's been holding them back. Jay dislikes his own history so much he changed his name. Rafe is part of that history.

And Rafe? His struggles with regret are never going to be resolved if he doesn't acknowledge them.

"Would you like some coffee?" I ask Jay, hoping the invite will prompt him to stick around.

He notices Oliver's stuffed cat sitting in a kitchen chair and smiles. But then he shakes his head. "Nah, I should get going."

I try not to sigh. "I'll tell him you stopped by. Maybe you guys could make some plans for tonight."

He's suddenly in a hurry to get out of here. "I'm sure you guys have got plans of your own. Tell the kid his Uncle Jay says hi. Take care, Izzy."

Less than ten minutes after Jay runs out the door, Rafe and Oliver return. Rafe isn't surprised to hear his brother was here and I try to downplay the fact that Jay didn't let him know he was stopping by. If Rafe is bothered then he doesn't let it show. He's in a good mood and Oliver is now extremely excited about our impending trip to see the butterflies.

We pack up some snacks and arrive at the conservatory just as it opens. The butterfly conservatory is magical. I feel as if I am in some sort of mystic fairyland as we walk through the lush grounds while colorful wings flutter all around us. Being here would have been enchanting under any circumstances but observing Oliver's sheer wonder makes it far more special. Rafe and I hold hands as the little boy capers in front of us, needing a few times to be gently admonished about not leaving our sight.

"Look at this one, Izzy! It's got green and orange and blue wings."

Rafe puts his hand on Oliver's shoulder as we all crouch down for a closer look at the insect that has paused to appreciate a bright yellow flower.

"That one's my favorite, " Rafe says.

Oliver doesn't comment but when we leave the butterfly to its leisure and resume our walk he takes Rafe's other hand.

After we have finished enjoying the butterflies, Rafe suggests going out to eat at Greasy June's. The plan sounds perfect to me, not just because I love their food but because being there reminds me of a late summer afternoon when I first laid eyes on the two people who have already become my world. The girl who was sitting there all alone and fretting about where she was going to live would never have guessed at the chain of events to come. Life is surprising.

Our server is June, but this isn't the same June who waited on us that first day. Perhaps one must be named June in order to work at Greasy June's. This woman is a generation older, with graying blonde hair, but she's very talkative and she looks familiar. When she mentions that her daughter also works here I understand why.

"Is your daughter also named June?" I ask her.

She beams. "Yes, she is. We are four generations of Junes."

It's nice to think that four generations of women named June exist. The food is excellent and I love that Rafe and I enjoy the kind of vibe where I know he won't care about the sight of me pigging out in front of him.

Oliver doesn't knock over his lemonade this time and he's eager to show us the pictures he colors on the child's menu. I'm shoving the last of my French fries in my mouth when my phone dings with an incoming text. The message is from my father.

And it's rather jarring.

Clear your schedule next weekend, kid. Your mom and I are coming for a visit.

Rafe takes note of my expression. "Something wrong?"

I toss my phone in my purse. "Not at all."

There are a few fries remaining on Rafe's plate. I steal one of them. Then I decide that I might as well tell him what his future holds.

"It's just that you're going to be meeting the formidable Deck Gentry a little sooner than you thought."

15

RAFE

Izzy is dusting the living room for the third time today. She's turned into a housekeeping cyclone in preparation for her parents' arrival, which is happening within the hour. They flew into the little regional airport but didn't want to be picked up. Izzy said her dad would rent a car because he's not the type to accept favors, only grant them. Like he's a sultan. Or The Godfather. Wonderful. Can't wait to meet him.

I'm supposed to be helping her clean but there's only so much sense in sweeping the nonexistent crumbs off the floor yet again. So I just stand around with my broom and watch my girlfriend's ass when she bends to feather dust the lower shelf of the coffee table. She's wearing one of her *'I'm A Fifties Housewife'* type of dresses and I'm digging it. I make a mental note to invite this dress along the next time we're having a little role playing session. She can be the bored, sexually frustrated suburban housewife. I'll be the television repairman. Or something. It doesn't matter. Once Housewife Izzy gets a load of me with a hammer in hand and my shirt off she'll be flipping that flouncy skirt up over her head and begging to get drilled by the biggest power tool I've got. And I'm a hard working guy who wants to satisfy my best customer so I open my belt and...

"RAFE!"

She's caught me slacking and now she's indignant, hands on her hips, probably guessing that I was thinking about something dirty.

"Sorry, I got tired," I say and sweep the broom back and forth.

She still watches me. Her eyes drop down to my pants. She can see that I'm hard. Her lower lip gets sucked in. She touches the pearls around her neck. "You're obviously not tired."

I rub my crotch. "No, but if you want a pearl necklace with a different look you can have one. Turns out I keep them in stock."

She swishes the feather duster and bats her eyes. "What a generous offer, Mr. Hempstead."

The broom gets dropped on the floor. She squeals when I run over there and grab her up in my arms. No need to worry about Oliver hearing. Lana and Shane took him to the playground because he was bored with watching us clean.

Izzy wiggles loose and struts away from me. "I can't let you mess up my makeup."

Then, because she's the most spectacularly filthy-minded girl in the world, she bends over the kitchen counter and pulls her dress all the way up over her ass. She's wearing a black thong.

Fuck yeah.

Izzy throws me a look over her shoulder. "Well?"

No further encouragement required. My zipper's down and my dick is free.

"Hard," she orders, gripping the counter. "You need to be quick."

I fucking love this girl.

The thong gets pushed aside and my dick gets buried. She bears down and pushes back. *Fuck. Fuck. Fuck.* I can be quick.

DING DONG.

I hate that doorbell.

When I'm done here I'm going to murder that doorbell.

But now Izzy's in a panic. She's shooing me away and frantically pushing down her dress. She can't have a dick inside of her when her parents are right there on the other side of the door. It's just not okay.

She's busy smoothing down her hair, adjusting her pearls and putting a non-sex look on her face. She's about to move to the door because the bell keeps ringing when she turns to inspect me. Then she gasps and points. I glance down. My dick waves at me. He's not very happy about this interruption but nothing can be done. I zip up and buckle my belt. Izzy nods with relief that I am now presentable, gives her hair one final pat and opens the door.

"There she is!" The woman who tackles Izzy with a hug could be picked out of any crowd. She's got the same red hair, the same beautiful smile. She's clearly overjoyed to be reunited with her child and she gives Izzy the longest, most loving look before slipping an arm around her daughter's waist.

Then a shadow falls and Izzy shouts, "Daddy!" She throws her arms around her father's neck and he holds her tight.

"Hey, kid." He kisses her cheek.

She laughs and takes a step back. She is thrilled that they are here. I make a private vow to be on my best behavior. I know she really wants them to like me and vice versa.

Her mother is the one to notice me first. She approaches with her hand out.

"You've got to be Rafe," she says. "I'm Jenny. I'm so excited to meet you."

"Nice to meet you too," I say and I really mean it.

Jenny looks at her husband. She raises an eyebrow.

Izzy grabs my hand and drags me forward. "Daddy, this is Rafe Hempstead. My boyfriend." There's an edge to the way she says the last two words, like she's giving me her protection or something. Protection from what? I don't know.

Deck Gentry is not what I expected. I assumed I'd be meeting some pinched, balding suit. This guy looks like he just rolled off the Bad Boy Biker assembly line. He's big and he's muscled and his black hair is a little gray around the temples but I have no doubt he's a force to be reckoned with.

Deck shakes my hand. More accurately, he crushes my hand, or at least tries to.

"Glad to meet you," Deck says although the flash in his dark eyes don't match his words.

I look him straight in the eye without blinking. "Glad to meet you too."

Our standoff doesn't last more than three seconds because Oliver returns home. Lana and Shane say gracious hellos to Izzy's parents but they seem eager to get out of the way. Maybe they can sense all the stress in the room.

At least Oliver is happy. Jenny has brought a shopping bag full of presents, all for him. Izzy gets her big heart from her mother; Jenny instantly treats Oliver like he's the most important person she's ever met. Even Deck cracks a smile when my son sticks his hand out for a grave handshake, just like I taught him.

Izzy shows her parents around the apartment. I would have liked to sit the tour out but Oliver pulls at me to join the group.

"And this is *my* room," Oliver announces proudly as he stands before the open door of his bedroom.

Izzy gives him a little hug. "Oliver worked hard to get his room neat for your visit."

Jenny pokes her head inside. "What a nice room, Oliver!"

Deck, on the other hand, has decided to fuck with me. "So where's *your* room?" he wants to know with a deadpan expression.

I keep a straight face. "The living room sofa pulls out into a bed. I sleep there."

But Oliver rats me out. "No, you don't. You sleep with Izzy now."

Thanks, son.

Jenny breaks the tension by laughing out loud. Deck is visibly less amused. Izzy is mortified, looking from her dad to me and back again like she's bracing for one of us to charge.

"Oliver." Jenny holds out her hand. "I'd love to see all of your toys. Can you show me?"

He's delighted for the chance. Izzy shoots me another worried glance before following her mother into Oliver's room where I can hear Cliff the stuffed cat being introduced.

Oliver's room isn't the largest of spaces and it would get pretty crowded if we all stuffed ourselves in there. I decide this is a good time to take a walk to the kitchen. I'll clean something. Or whatever.

What I don't count on is that Deck has decided to follow me.

I spray the counter and wipe it down with a dishcloth. I can feel his eyes on my back from a few feet away. I'm glad he has no idea that I was fucking his daughter on this very counter the moment he rang the doorbell.

This is not a good thing to think about right now. My dick gets hard.

Deck stays where he is while I fold the damp dishtowel. He watches every move and now I've had enough so I toss the towel down and level him with a stare.

If this guy wasn't Izzy's dad then I'd make him aware that I don't appreciate being looked up and down like he thinks I ought to be cut from the team.

Since he *is* Izzy's dad I just stare back at him and wait out the appraisal.

In the end Deck Gentry smirks with a shake of the head. "I should have known."

There's a lot of meaning packed into that sentence. I'm just not clear on what it is. "What?"

He takes a step closer and holds my gaze. When he can't make me flinch he manages a grudging nod. "I should have known that *my* daughter, a girl with the world at her feet, would choose…"

He trails off and gestures to me in a manner that betrays a hint of disgust. Maybe more than a hint.

"YOU."

I don't get it. He says this like he knows me. We've never met before. All he knows is what his daughter has told him and Izzy's been in a fever to get her dad to like me. She wouldn't say anything negative.

The corner of his mouth turns up, a signal that he can guess what I'm thinking and finds my confusion entertaining.

Yeah, I don't get this at all. But I'm pretty sure I don't like it.

"Hey Deck, just so we can avoid any misunderstanding, why don't you tell me exactly what kind of man you think I am?"

He rolls his eyes as if I'm a bad tempered child. "Settle down. You'll just say something stupid."

"Maybe. But I'm confident that my ass can handle whatever stupid shit comes out of my mouth so let's have it."

He suddenly laughs. It's not a mean kind of laughter but I get the feeling that some men have good reason to be afraid of the sound. When he's tired of laughing he grins at me. "Okay. You've got some spirit. That's not a bad thing. Just don't go pointing it in the wrong direction."

What does the guy think he is, a fucking fortune cookie? This must be his thing, handing out non specific pieces of wisdom that can be taken any number of ways. I don't even know what he's talking about.

But Izzy worships her father. There's nothing to be gained by challenging him.

"Ha. Yeah. Thanks for the advice."

He's not fooled. "You'll treat her right."

I'm aware this is not a request. It's also not something that needs to be said. I'm nuts about Izzy. I've never been knocked on my ass by anyone like this. I'd break my own thumbs before I did her wrong.

"Every day." I'm being completely honest right now. "For as long as she lets me."

I get the feeling Deck Gentry is a man who is not easily impressed and yet the quick flicker in his dark eyes signals that something deep has shifted.

"All right, Rafe," he says and I suppose that's about as much enthusiasm as I can expect to receive. He doesn't like me but he doesn't hate me either. Good enough.

After Oliver finishes showing off his room he wants to open up his presents. Izzy's mom went on quite a toy store shopping spree. She bought him a dump truck, a complete art set, some modeling clay, a whole series of books about a little boy who's half frog and some stuffed kittens to keep Cliff company. I can almost see her heart dissolve when he runs to her and hugs her as thanks for the gift. He's a little more shy with Deck, offering him a quiet 'thank you' and another handshake.

A well-known pang hits me as my eyes follow my son. Twice a week I've been taking him to therapy sessions in the hopes of helping him deal with the trauma of his mother's death. His therapist's name is Nicole and she's young but he seems to like her. I sit outside in the waiting room with other nervous parents and then at the end of the session she calls me in to talk about whatever progress they've made. So far he's been drawing a lot of pictures. He likes to draw pictures of Izzy. And Cliff. And the pool in the backyard. Sometimes I get included in the pictures too. Nicole told me that once he drew a picture of Dana but then promptly ripped it up into tiny pieces. When she asked him why he did that he became angry and said, "She's gone so she can't have a picture."

I'd take all his pain on myself if I could. I'd take on the pain times ten if it would spare him even a little bit.

While I watch Oliver so closely I kind of lose track of what else is going on in the room. It's only when all eyes are on me that I realize Izzy's been saying my name.

"Sorry, what?"

She moves over to where I'm leaning against the wall and hooks her arm through mine. "My folks are going to go check into their hotel now and they want to take us all out to dinner later. Does that sound good to you?"

"Yeah. Sure. That'd be great." I try to smile.

Oliver crashes his dump truck into the coffee table while Jenny laughs.

Izzy holds my arm closer and rests her head against my shoulder.

Deck is staring right at me and I'm expecting to see some disapproval on his face but there's none to be found. I can't shake the sense that he's far more perceptive than most people and that the whole time I was preoccupied with watching my son, he was watching me.

16

IZZY

There's something surreal about seeing the people you love most, the people who know completely different versions of you, meet each other for the first time. My parents think of me as their little girl, forever a child no matter how old I get. Rafe knows me as his sexy girlfriend, a grown woman he can share his life with. My friends are familiar with both my stubbornness and my soft side.

All of these things are true.

"Something on your mind, baby girl?" My mother winks at me, noting that I've stopped tossing the salad in favor of staring dreamily into space.

"Nothing critical. I was just thinking about how I spent a few sleepless nights worrying about the clash of Rafe and Daddy. I guess I worried for nothing."

She laughs and continues to prettily arrange the chicken in a glass baking dish. Their flight back to Phoenix leaves early tomorrow and tonight my mom offered to cook a homemade dinner for us all. I would have argued that she shouldn't feel obligated to prepare meals when this trip is supposed to be a vacation for her but I know how happy she is being in the kitchen. Besides, someone should get some use out of the oven. Rafe and I use the stovetop often and we're masters of the microwave but anything requiring more persistence is usually off the menu.

At the moment it's just my mom and me. My father ran out to pay a quick visit to a friend because of course he has a friend in Hutton. There's probably an outpost of Deck Gentry's friends in just about every square of land on the world map. And Rafe took Oliver to the store to pick out a new pair of sneakers. I can't imagine what happens on that kindergarten playground but Oliver has already managed to wear out the pair I bought him at the beginning of the school year.

I'm enjoying this brief time alone with my mother. When she cooks she frequently hums to herself and the sound is as old as my memory. As a little girl I spent countless hours in the kitchen of our Arizona home, watching her capable hands shape loaves of bread dough or slice vegetables with impressive speed. After so many years of watching her one might think I'd be a star in the kitchen but that's far from the truth. I lack her serenity and her attention to detail. It's not unusual for me to wander away in order to do something more exciting and then become exasperated when I return to find burned cookies or scorched rice. I've concluded that both my self confidence and the smoke detectors are better served when I keep my kitchen ambitions within reason.

"Time for this to get cooking." She lifts the prepared dish in both hands and I abandon the salad bowl in order to open the oven door so she can slide the chicken right in.

She taps a finger against her chin. "Shoot. I forgot to get some Dijon for the vinaigrette dressing."

I reach for my phone. "Rafe is out and about. I'll ask him to stop at the grocery store and pick some up."

"Oh, no need for that. He's got Oliver with him. We'll just improvise." She begins raiding my pantry. She'll likely be disappointed with what she discovers.

My mother and I are exactly the same height, although right now I have the benefit of a few additional inches thanks to my heels. Now and then people mistake us for sisters and they're not just being polite. She looks young and she stays in shape.

It's decided that plain yellow mustard mixed with honey will be an adequate substitute and she measures out the dressing ingredients from memory while chatting about her latest conversation with Aunt Promise. Then she switches topics and speaks of my cousin Derek's upcoming wedding in December.

"Aunt Stephanie was worried you might not be able to make it now that you're in Texas."

As if there's any danger of that. I'm a Gentry. We don't miss family events like weddings. This truism was ingrained in me from infancy. "Of course I'll be there. My finals end two days before the wedding."

"Any you'll be bringing Rafe, right?"

"I haven't mentioned it to him yet. I guess it depends on whether he can get the time off from work. And then there's Oliver to consider as well."

She whisks ingredients in a bowl with the style of a pro chef. "You know how our family is. Oliver will be more than welcome and there will be other children there. Bring him too. He's already won your dad over completely. Did you see the picture Oliver drew for him? Last night at the hotel Deck kept going on and on about what a delightful child he is."

I believe her when she says this. When it comes to adults outside the family, my father is difficult to impress. Children are a different story. He adores children, always has. "I think a person would have to be missing a heart not to adore Oliver."

"And your dad definitely isn't missing a heart." She stops stirring and her expression becomes sad. "How are Oliver's therapy sessions going?"

"Well, he hasn't been in anymore fights so it's a step in the right direction. He's hopefully learning how to channel his anger into something more positive."

"And he still won't talk about his mother?"

"No, he doesn't really talk about her at all."

She grimaces. "He's so young. It must be hard for him to understand. You said she died very suddenly of a brain aneurysm. Was he at home when it happened?"

"I don't know." I've never thought of the possibility before. I'm not even sure whether Rafe knows the answer to that question. "That would be a terrible memory for him to suffer with."

My mother nods. "People always say that children are resilient and I suppose that's true. But still. Terrible memories leave a scar on the soul, no matter how young you are."

With a sinking sensation I understand that she's speaking from experience. She was only sixteen when her parents forced her to marry one of the religion's elders. And what kind of terrible things might she have witnessed long before that, when she was a young girl living under the brutal thumb of cultist leaders in a place where no outside help was available? My mother's personality is so sunny and upbeat that sometimes I forget what she must have endured. When I think about this now I'm awestruck by her. And there's also a swell of gratitude toward my father. For being her prince. For giving her the kind of happiness that she had every right to expect.

I'm made from them both. This will always and forever be a source of pride.

Once the salad is finished it occurs to me that we don't have a table large enough for us all to sit down. The only solution in sight is the patio table. Shane and Lana aren't even home so there's no reason not to have our little dinner party out there.

I'm in the process of setting the table when Oliver comes sprinting into the backyard, eager to break in his new Batman sneakers.

"Step back from the pool edge," Rafe bellows an instant before he appears from around the corner of the house.

Oliver takes a tiny step backwards but he still leans over the water. Just the other day Lana and I were discussing the need to place a fence around the pool. I make a mental note to bring this up again.

Rafe plants a kiss on my lips then checks out his son's position. "Oliver, come on. Why don't you go get your football? We'll play catch."

Oliver runs inside the house and I hook one finger into Rafe's belt, reeling him in. Being close to him does things to me, always, and now is no exception even with my mother possibly watching from the kitchen window. I tilt my head back in search of a real kiss and he obliges. Rafe knows how to put his whole body into a kiss. While our mouths are locked he lifts me up and slides me down slowly, deliberately, so I'll feel the hard swell of his cock through the layers of my skirt and his jeans. I hear the low sound of my moan and I'm honestly embarrassed for me. Rafe has the power to break down the walls of my common sense with one touch and I love it.

I love *him.*

I just haven't found the courage to say the words yet because I've never said them to anyone except my parents, who of course absolutely do not count.

A pointed cough rips through the scene from ten feet away and this is what finally unravels my tongue from Rafe's.

"You're back." I climb out of Rafe's arms and smile at my dad, who watches us with his arms crossed. I hope I don't have lipstick on my chin.

My father looks like he's deciding whether to be amused or irritated. The poor man. I'm sure he'd much rather cultivate the fantasy that his daughter remains an eternal virgin and right now I am making that very difficult.

"Hey, Deck," Rafe says, cool as can be.

Deck Gentry's dark eyes linger on us for a few seconds and then he gives a little shrug, as if he's saying to himself that for once he has no power here. "Your mother chased me out of the kitchen. She said I was getting in the way."

She does this at home too so he shouldn't be surprised.

"Dinner will be ready soon," I promise him as Oliver returns with boundless energy and a lightweight orange foam football in his hands. He fires it at Rafe and hits him square in the chest. Rafe pretends to be injured.

"Ow! Give the old guy a break and don't throw so hard."

Oliver generously agrees. "Okay. I won't use so much strength next time."

My dad chuckles. He takes a seat on a patio chair while Rafe and Oliver head over to the small grassy plot off to the right of the pool in order to throw the football back and forth.

"Quite a pair," he says to me in reference to the duo of Oliver and Rafe.

"Yes, they are." I'm pleased because it's the first time he's acknowledged out loud that he might actually like Rafe a little bit.

Back in the kitchen, my mother is examining the chicken. She never shoos me out of the kitchen, probably because I don't help myself to samples of the food before it's served or try to dance her around the room instead of letting her stir the sauce. My dad has been known to do these things.

After I add the croutons to the salad I pause by the window and enjoy the sight of Rafe playing with Oliver. Oliver throws the football. Rafe acts like he can't catch it and then he falls on the grass as if the effort has knocked him right over. Oliver shrieks with laughter and jumps on his father, a little roughly, but Rafe doesn't mind. Rafe then rolls over and crouches in a football pose, muscles tight, as if he's waiting for a play to be called. He used to play in high school and Caris told me once that he was really good, one of the team stars in a small town where Friday night football is king. Rafe is definitely built for the sport and I exhale a soft sigh as I watch him.

My mom sneaks up behind me and notices what I'm looking at. She nudges my shoulder. "So he's the one."

I nudge her right back. "It's early. We haven't had any serious talks. Who knows."

But she eyes me with a smirk and notes that I'm blushing. "*I know, Isabella. And so do you.*"

Maybe.

Probably.

Yes.

17

—————

RAFE

As luck would have it I've never yet run into a childcare conflict but when I need to work on a Saturday and Izzy has plans I have to think of a backup idea. My boss has been really good about letting me cut out early to attend Oliver's therapy sessions so I don't feel inclined to say no to him about the Saturday hours.

Izzy is the one who suggests asking Jay and I have to admit it's not a bad suggestion. Izzy's plans involve helping Caris shop for a wedding dress so there's a good chance Jay is free. And it's not like I have a long list of dependable babysitters I can call. Before I can say a word she's texting Caris and asking if Jay can watch Oliver on Saturday.

She gets her answer in seconds. Jay would be thrilled to watch his nephew. That's nice to hear and all but now it seems like I'm too much of a pussy to call my own brother and ask him for a simple favor.

When Saturday comes around Oliver is glad for the chance to hang out with his Uncle Jay for a while. My brother's in an especially good mood today, even extends his smile in my direction when Oliver goes running through the front door on a hunt for Caris's cats.

"We'd be rich if we could bottle that kid's energy," says Jay, still smiling. "You still working on that new apartment complex?"

"Yeah, and we're a little behind. A couple of guys from the crew dropped off the face of the earth this week. Plus there were some inspections that set us behind. We'll be making up the difference at least until some replacements can be hired."

Jay nods. "It's tough to find quality labor that's reliable."

He would know since he has a crew of his own. It's kind of funny that we're both in the same line of work, more or less. I mean, he does mostly custom residential jobs and I'm on the crew of a big commercial project but we both build things.

"How's business?" I ask him.

"Pretty good. We get a lot of jobs from word of mouth and if things keep going this way we'll have more work than we can handle."

I'm proud of him. He truly started with nothing and now he's his own boss, building his own company, about to marry his dream girl. He's the shit in the best way. This is on the tip of my tongue to tell him when Oliver runs over and asks Jay if he can have some breakfast.

"You didn't eat breakfast yet?" Jay asks.

"I did," Oliver answers. "But you might have some even better breakfast."

Jay chuckles. "I'll see what I can find." He nods to me. "I can drop him off later."

"I should be done around two."

"Sounds good."

I check the time on my phone and tell Oliver that he needs to behave himself for his Uncle Jay before I jump in my truck and head to the job site. The October weather is downright perfect and it's not a bad day to be outside moving heavy objects around. When I stop for a break a text rolls in from Izzy, saying that she's about to leave for the wedding dress hunt. I never realized that shopping for a dress is supposed to be a group activity but Lana's going too and Caris's mom even flew in for the occasion. Izzy sends a three second video of herself blowing a kiss. She looks sexy, as always, and I'm about to text back some obscene advice about what she can do with that mouth later on tonight but instead I decide to be a little less of a horndog.

Miss you, babe.

I do miss her. I mean, I just saw her a few hours ago and I'll see her again a few hours from now but Izzy's something else. Where she's concerned, I don't mind letting my softer side show. Turns out I have one after all, a softer side. Izzy Gentry sends my brain in all kinds of new directions. Maybe the overhead sun is harsher than I realized because suddenly I'm thinking about something that would have seemed insane to me six months ago and I laugh out loud.

"You crackin' up over there?" Glavin, another member of the crew, gestures to me with a ham sandwich the size of my forearm. "Laughing to yourself and shit."

"Maybe," I say because I find myself wishing that Izzy was the one picking out her wedding dress today. The thought isn't funny. No, I laughed because the image of Izzy in a wedding dress sounds damn good to me.

By the time we're done with the necessary work and have cleaned up the job site it's two thirty. I've lost track of time and I hope Jay's not pissed that I'm not finished when I said I would be. I shoot him a text, offering to pick Oliver up, but he answers that he still has no problem dropping the kid off. I estimate it'll take me twenty minutes to get home and he answers that he'll meet me at the house.

He pulls up to the curb ten seconds after I do. When Jay opens the rear passenger door my son flies out and barrels straight to me on the front lawn. He collides with my legs.

"I tackled you," he informs me.

"Yeah, you did." I grin.

Jay strolls over at a more relaxed pace while Oliver locates a stick and begins stabbing it into the dirt.

I unlock the front door. "Sorry this took longer than I thought it would."

Jay shrugs. "Not a problem." He follows us into the house. "Hey Oliver, tell your dad we had fun. We played tee ball. Kid's a natural."

Oliver bounces on his toes and drops the stick on the carpet. "I scored a home run."

"That's great, buddy." I keep my hand on Oliver's shoulder and look to Jay. "Any word from the wedding dress spree?"

"I don't think I'm supposed to know anything. Bad luck or whatever."

Oliver tugs at my shirt. "I wanna go swimming."

"Getting a little cool for that." I tweak his nose. "It'll be Halloween in a couple of weeks."

He doesn't give up. "It's not cold."

"How about I'll set you up to watch your spaceship show and then I'll make some dinner? Now say goodbye to Uncle Jay."

My brother grabs up his nephew in a hug and it does my heart good to see so much affection between the two of them. Jay and I might never get to the point where we become the closest of brothers but he loves my kid and that matters more.

Jay ruffles Oliver's hair one last time. "I saw Shane's truck outside so I'm just going to stop in and say hello."

"All right." I feel like we should exchange a handshake or something. "Thanks again for watching him."

He shrugs. "Anytime."

"Later, man."

Jay walks away to go knock on Shane's door.

Oliver has already run to his room and returned with the toy dump truck given to him by Izzy's mom. Cliff the stuffed cat enjoys a prime vantage point on the roof of the cab. "Cliff's going on a trip," he informs me as he pushes the truck around the perimeter of the kitchen table.

I crack a yawn. "That sounds good." I'm tired as hell. Sleep wasn't a priority last night, not with Izzy in a feisty mood and my dick eager to take advantage. I'm paying for the sleepless night now, after so many hours of backbreaking labor. While Oliver takes Cliff on a dump truck vacation around the apartment I sprawl on the couch, keeping one foot on the floor, and cover my face with my arm.

"Are you going to sleep?" Oliver asks.

"Nope." I yawn again.

He pushes the dump truck past the couch and runs over my foot. Now I'm thinking I'll just get takeout tonight. I should call in an order to Greasy June's. Izzy likes their burgers and Oliver's a fan of the chicken nuggets. I'll do that as soon as I get up. I just need a minute to shut my eyes and get a second wind. Should happen any second now.

Oliver chatters to the inanimate Cliff. He promises that Cliff will enjoy his imaginary trip.

"You're going to the beach," Oliver promises. "You are lucky."

There's no happier sound than Oliver at play and my overworked muscles sink into the couch. I'd be glad to sleep here for hours but I can't.

Just another minute.

One more minute.

Sounds fade and blend together. Then an urgent beat, dim at first before rising to a scream.

"OLIVER!"

A searing gasp rips through my chest and I sit straight up. I'm still on the couch and the living room is empty.

The living room is empty.

And something is happening outside, right in the backyard.

I don't think. I just move. After jackknifing off the couch, I nearly take the patio door off its hinges in a desperate rush to get out. There's a terror I can't name and don't want to.

Then I see Oliver and relief is instant, chasing away the worst of that dread. But he's beside the pool and he's wet and he's crying. Jay is there too and Jay is also wet. He kneels next to the water and holds Oliver in his arms.

"It's okay," my brother says, dripping water everywhere and comforting my son. "You're okay."

"What happened?" I run to them and Oliver looks to me, fearful eyes wide, water mixing with his tears. Movement catches my eye and I see Cliff the stuffed cat bobbing in the pool. I reach over and haul the sodden toy out of the water.

Jay states the obvious. "He fell in the pool. I was at Shane's place and noticed him through the window. One second I saw him standing by the pool and the next second I didn't see him at all." Jay shudders and swallows hard. "I just happened to glance outside at exactly that second. If I hadn't…"

If he hadn't.

If he hadn't.

I pull my son to my chest, unable to speak. The panic. The relief. The guilt. They mix together and threaten to engulf.

Shane runs out now and he's got a bundle of towels in his arms. One of them he gives to me and I wrap it around Oliver. Another one he tries to hand to Jay but Jay ignores him. He's scowling at me.

"Where were you, Rafe? Haven't you taught him about water safety?" He doesn't mean to accuse. At least, I don't think he does. He sounds shaken up, terrified. And he's right. I know that Oliver can't swim without his flotation vest. I've told him not to go in the backyard by himself but I never told him why. I never taught him how to get himself out of the pool if he falls in.

Oliver shivers. I wrap the towel around him more tightly and lift him in my arms.

"Where were you?" Jay repeats, a little louder, and now Shane steps between us.

"Take it easy," he says to my brother, throwing him a pleading look. "If this is anyone's fault it's mine. Lana told me to look into putting a fence around the pool and I haven't gotten around to it." Shane turns to me. "Rafe, I'm so sorry. I'll get a contractor here first thing on Monday."

Shane shouldn't feel like he needs to take the heat for this in order to keep peace. Oliver's *my* child. My responsibility. Anything bad that happens to him is on my head.

"It's not your fault," I assure him and then I can't say any more because I'm still too rattled to think properly and because Oliver continues to shiver. I need to get him inside and get him dry.

He sniffles into my neck as I carry to him to his room and search for a clean set of clothes. Usually his independent streak objects to anyone helping him get dressed but right now he cooperates completely as I strip off all of his wet clothes and get him into some dry pajamas. They're flannel and they were another gift from Izzy's parents. It's the warmest thing I've got for him because I haven't yet bought him new clothes for the cooler weather and he's already outgrown much of what he had in his suitcases. I need to get him some warmer clothes. I'll do that tomorrow.

Now that he's warm and dry, Oliver is beginning to perk up. The tears on his cheeks have dried and he tries to wiggle away when I make an effort to towel off his hair. He also needs a haircut. Izzy mentioned this last week and I meant to take him but then forgot. Just like I forgot to pack his lunch on Wednesday and he was in a grumpy mood when I picked him up from school because the cafeteria can only offer cheese sandwiches to kids who don't have any money. I won't forget anything anymore. I won't sleep on the couch in the middle of the afternoon and let him fall into the pool. I won't fuck anything up, not ever again.

The tsunami of blame and the sheer weight of parental responsibility collide and I can't breathe. I want to vomit.

If he hadn't...

I force myself to finish that brutal thought. If Jay hadn't been there then Oliver would have drowned while I slept. And the fault would have been mine.

"You're hugging too hard," Oliver complains as he shoves me away. He's right. I am hugging him too hard.

I release him and try to speak. The sound is nothing more than a croak.

Oliver tilts his head and looks at me. "Where's Cliff?"

"He's right here." Jay is behind us in the doorway of Oliver's bedroom. The stuffed cat is awkwardly held in his right hand.

Oliver brightens and snatches his toy. "He's soaking wet." Oliver then grabs the towel that I'd used to dry him off and wraps Cliff inside. He's heading down the hall and I hear Shane's voice in the living room.

Jay is still dripping with pool water. "You okay?" he asks me.

I won't be able to answer that question without crying or screaming. "I can get you a change of clothes."

"No need." He glances toward the living room where Shane is chatting with Oliver. "I should get going. Unless you want me to stay."

"No, that's all right." I swallow hard. "Thank you, Jonathan."

I've grown used to calling him Jay but sometimes I slip and use his real name, the name he had when we were brothers in Arcana. Right now he doesn't even seem to notice.

"I'll call you guys later," he says and leaves the doorway. I hear him saying goodbye to Oliver and then the front door closes.

In the living room, Oliver seems to have recovered from his terrifying incident and he's now showing Shane the features of his dump truck. Shane listens patiently and then notices I'm in the room.

"I called Lana," he says. "She told Izzy and they're on their way home."

"All right." I need to lean against the refrigerator just to stay upright. It's going to be a long time before I'm able to look at another body of water without feeling absolute dread.

"I'm hungry," Oliver announces suddenly. "What's for dinner?"

Shane moves the dump truck back and forth. "I got a great deal on some T-bone steaks. I bought way too many and they're all sitting in the fridge. When the girls get here I'll grill them up and we can eat at my place."

I manage a weak nod. "That'd be great. Thanks." In the meantime I grab a granola bar from the pantry and offer it to Oliver.

Shane is a godsend. He seems to understand that I don't want to talk and also that I'm thankful for his presence. He keeps Oliver occupied and shows him how to help poor Cliff dry off with the aid of Izzy's hair dryer.

Moments later Izzy busts through the door with fright written on her face. Even though she's been told that Oliver is fine she inspects him carefully and then hugs him close for a long moment before turning to me.

"Rafe?" She touches my cheek and looks into my face. What she finds there brings tears to her eyes and she wraps her arms around me, which I'm grateful for. I bury my face in her soft hair and try to pull myself together.

Caris is here too but she's got her mother with her so they don't stay long. Caris hugs Oliver and she hugs me. Then she hugs Izzy. And Lana and Shane. I guess once she got started she couldn't stop.

Shane cooks us all dinner on the grill while Izzy and Lana help beautify Cliff the cat, who has suffered a rough afternoon. I can't really find much to talk about but Oliver doesn't notice and Lana keeps throwing me sympathetic glances. Izzy holds my hand whenever she's close.

Jay does call to make sure all is well and before the night is over he also sends a text saying that he can come over tomorrow and help put sensors on the doors. These can be picked up at the home improvement store for just a few dollars and this way an alarm will sound if Oliver tries to access the backyard again. I don't know why I didn't think of this solution earlier.

Later on, Izzy finds me in Oliver's room. I'm watching him sleep with his little arm wrapped around his beloved stuffed cat as he breathes evenly through dreams that are hopefully untroubled by what might have been.

If he hadn't....

Izzy prods me to bed and snuggles against me, her cheek on my chest, my arms wrapped around her warm body.

"It's okay," she whispers and once again my throat feels thick with tears over how tragically this day could have ended.

I need to do better. Oliver deserves better.

Izzy falls asleep but I remain awake for a long time, tortured by my worst fears.

18

IZZY

"You need to stand still," I laugh. "Otherwise your whiskers will be crooked."

Oliver obeys for approximately one and a half seconds before twisting his head, trying to see his reflection in the bathroom mirror.

"Can I have more whiskers?" he asks.

"If you give me a chance to draw them." I hold his chin in my palm and then make another attempt with my soft eyeliner pencil.

"At least two more on each side," he says.

It's my first attempt at cat makeup. I've already colored the tip of his nose and drawn a line between his nose and his upper lip. Now I'm working on drawing straight whiskers, which is a more difficult mission than it seems when the canvas is a very active five-year-old boy in a hurry to go trick or treating.

"I was a dinosaur last year," he says. "My face was covered in green makeup and at the end of the night Mommy couldn't get it all off." He sniffs. "It was funny."

With care, I complete the final cat whisker. I'm quiet, waiting for him to say more since he so rarely mentions his mother at all.

But Oliver has already moved on to examining his Halloween

costume. He's trying to stand on tiptoes to see himself in the vanity mirror. I pick him up for a better look. The only cat costume I could find was one that looks more like a tiger but a tiger is indeed a cat and Oliver doesn't seem to mind the distinction.

"I don't even look like me!" he exclaims. Then he jumps out of my arms. "Let's go!"

Oliver nearly collides with Rafe in the hallway.

"Look at you!" Rafe laughs.

"Come on." Oliver begins dragging his father away. "All the candy's gonna be gone."

"Don't forget your pumpkin." I chase after them with the orange plastic pumpkin I bought at the store to hold Oliver's Halloween bounty.

Rafe throws me a grin as he waits hand in hand with Oliver by the door.

"Damn good job on the costume," he says.

"Most of the credit should go to Party City." I hand Oliver his plastic pumpkin and stretch in order to plant a kiss on Rafe's lips. "But I did do the makeup."

Oliver is so excited he can hardly stand still. "Izzy drew my whiskers. Oh wait, I forgot to get Cliff."

He runs to his bedroom, nearly tripping on his long tail.

Rafe's eyes flicker up and down my body. "You haven't told me if you're a good witch or a bad witch."

I fix the pointed hat atop my head. As witch costumes go, this one is rather subdued, but this Halloween outing is a family affair. One cannot take a kindergartener trick or treating while dressed in a corseted bodice with fishnet stockings and stiletto heels. No, such things will be reserved for the after hours party.

My long black gown reaches my ankles but it's form fitting enough to stir some hunger in Rafe's eyes as I pose with my hands on my hips. "A good witch, but only until midnight."

He's interested. "Yeah? What happens at midnight?"

"A costume change. You'll like it."

Rafe exhales and shifts his weight. I don't need to glance down to know that he's getting turned on.

I kiss him once more and grab a warm sweater. Then I decide to bring a sweatshirt for Oliver too, just in case, although his costume should keep him warm despite evening temps that are expected to drop significantly. Rafe, naturally, refuses to wear anything warmer than a regular black t-shirt emblazoned with the Rolling Stones logo. It's absolutely something my dad would wear, although my dad would complete the look with a black leather jacket.

Oliver runs into a problem when he can't fit Cliff in the plastic pumpkin so Rafe agrees to escort the shabby stuffed animal himself. Out in the front yard, Oliver has an audience awaiting him. Shane and Lana have set up a fire pit in the driveway with three giant bags of candy ready to give out to eager visitors. Jay and Caris are here too. They stopped by just to see Oliver in his costume.

Dusk has settled and the street lights flicker on, a signal that trick or treating may commence. I've always loved Halloween. A treasured family photo is a framed shot of three-year-old me dressed in a bumblebee costume that was sewn by my Aunt Truly. Year round it hangs in the hallway between the kitchen and the living room.

Many years have passed since I've gone trick or treating and I'm nearly as excited as Oliver. At age eleven I decided I was too cool to dress up and beg for candy. Since then Halloween has evolved into the adult version of parties and club hopping and orange Jell-O shots. Being with Oliver promises to be way more fun than booze and dancing in a sweaty crowd. Although I have to admit I'm really looking forward to showing his dad my costume change later on, after trick or treat time is over and all little wannabe tigers are in bed.

Lana and Shane are dressed like Danny and Sandy from Grease. Caris wears a Cinderella costume. Jay looks like….Jay. He's wearing jeans and a short sleeve Aerosmith tee. When he stands near Rafe it looks like the two of them got together and agreed to go out as under-stated slackers advertising classic rock bands.

I am positive the matching theme is unintentional. They don't have that kind of rapport. It's not that they argue. They just never progress. Maybe it's my imagination but I could swear that ever since the terrible day when Jay pulled Oliver out of the swimming pool, he and Rafe have seemed more ill at ease with one another than ever. I don't understand. The two brothers have issues, issues that will never be resolved if they don't talk about them. I'm not the only one who has noticed. Caris sees it too.

Lana is helping Oliver pick out some candy and Shane is talking about their early morning flight. They are traveling to Hawaii to visit Lana's parents. Shane even closed the bakery for the week and gave his staff paid time off so they could all take a vacation too.

Caris sidles up to me and subtly gestures to our guys. "Check out the twins."

I laugh. "They are two of a kind. They just don't admit it."

The look Caris gives me is a little sad. "One of these days they'll have a breakthrough. They'll cry and they'll laugh and they'll hug it out."

"Let's help them along. Why don't you two come over for dinner on Friday? I'll cook. I can't promise it'll be good but it will be edible. Most likely. And if not I have plenty of cereal in the pantry as an emergency provision."

She giggles. "We'll be there."

Oliver is ready to move on and find out what kind of candy the neighbors have to offer. Jay and Caris decide to head back to their house in order to give out treats. I'm watching to see if Jay and Rafe say anything to each other before going their separate ways. They don't.

"Happy Halloween, Oliver," Lana calls from the driveway as we walk away.

Once we're away from the house Oliver becomes shy. Most of the other kids we see are in groups and he stays close to Rafe's side. For the first few houses Rafe accompanies him up to the door and then Oliver gets more comfortable and starts running ahead a little more than he should. Every time this happens Rafe tenses and shouts Oliver's name, startling him. Rafe has been nervous about letting his son out of his sight ever since the day Oliver fell in the pool. He's haunted with self blame over what might have happened. I don't know how to help. I just have to hope that as time goes on he'll forgive himself.

Oliver's bucket fills up quickly. The sun is now completely gone and I shiver even with my sweater draped over my shoulders. Perhaps I should run from house to house with the trick or treaters. None of the kids seem affected by the chill at all. Rafe slides an arm around my shoulder and I huddle against his warmth.

We reach a house with a makeshift cemetery in the front yard. A fog machine blows fake smoke over the headstones and spooky music plays. It's a popular destination in the neighborhood. There are a bunch of other children in line waiting to get candy from the old couple sitting in lawn chairs in the driveway. Oliver joins the end of the line and swings his trick or treat bag.

"I called him again today," Rafe says in a quiet voice.

Immediately I understand he's talking about Kevin Walsh, the ex husband of Oliver's mother. The last time Rafe spoke to Dana, when she was heavily pregnant with Oliver, Rafe was told that Kevin and Dana would be raising the baby and that he would not be welcome in the child's life. Rafe had always assumed that Kevin Walsh was raising Oliver as his son. He assumed this until the day he was called to Kevin's office to be informed that Dana was dead. And so Rafe was given a choice; take custody of his child or turn him over to the foster care system. Kevin Walsh is a heartless man and Rafe would prefer to never think of him again. However, he's the only link to Dana. He's the only one who knows of the details surrounding her death. Oliver's therapist agrees that learning some of these details might help unlock the door to Oliver's anguish.

"He didn't answer, did he?" It's not really a question. Kevin Walsh has never taken any of Rafe's calls, nor responded to any of his email attempts. The one time Rafe received a call back it came from an assistant at the law form where Kevin works. She'd been instructed to tell Rafe that if money was what he was after then he would need to apply directly to the trust being held for Oliver's expenses. He hung up on her.

"Course he didn't answer," Rafe says, revulsion thick in his voice.

Oliver turns to make sure we're still waiting at the end of the driveway. We wave to him. An orange paw waves back at us and then he takes a step forward as the candy line moves up.

Rafe grunts. "I think it's time to go to Houston and look that cocksucker in the eye."

Every time he mentions taking a trip to Houston I cringe. It's a terrible idea. Kevin Walsh is a powerful attorney and can't be trusted. Rafe has a criminal record and no tolerance for anyone who gives him the runaround. If Rafe shows up in person all it would take is one phone call from Kevin to send Rafe's life into a tailspin.

"We'll figure something out," I promise Rafe, hugging him around the waist. I've already brought up the idea of asking for my father's help but Rafe was vehemently opposed and I can't go against his wishes so blatantly.

When the pumpkin bucket becomes so heavy that Rafe needs to carry it, Oliver announces he's tired. He wants to go home and take stock of his candy. Rafe reminds him that he's not allowed to eat anything without adult approval.

"I got at least five HUGE chocolate bars," he informs us with pride.

Lana and Shane are still handing out candy, though the traffic has slowed to a trickle. Oliver immediately dumps his bucket on the kitchen table and Rafe helps him sort through it as I run a bath for him. He's already pulling his costume off and muttering that he's had enough of being a cat.

Oliver is allowed to eat two pieces of candy and then he needs to get ready for bed. I keep thinking about this Halloween versus last Halloween, when I bar hopped with a big group of friends and someone puked on the bosom of my sexy pirate costume. As I stand in the doorway of Oliver's room and watch Rafe tuck his son into bed my heart is full. I could never have foreseen such a dramatic shift in my life when I decided to move to Hutton. This feels right. Everything about being with them feels right.

Rafe shuts the door to Oliver's room and smirks before closing in.

"Costume change time," he growls in my ear and backs me into a wall, sucking my neck like a vampire.

I wiggle free and walk backwards toward the bedroom. I slide my dress over one shoulder. And then the other shoulder. "This way to my dressing room."

Rafe's response is to seize my waist and throw me over his shoulder. Suppressing a shriek of laughter, I allow him to carry me to bed and pull my clothes off. He's in a hurry now and I am too. We kiss, we tease, he slides into me with a low groan and I wrap my legs around him to pull him in deeper. I didn't even get a chance to show off my alternative Halloween costume. It will keep for another night.

And there will be *many* other nights. So many.

19

RAFE

My phone begins ringing when I'm cleaning off the patio furniture and I don't recognize the out of state number. I'm about to reject it and then change my mind.

"Hello?"

"I almost lost her in a shopping mall food court once." The voice, deep and vivid, is one I recognize instantly.

"Deck." To say I'm surprised to hear from Izzy's dad out of the blue is an understatement.

"Rafe," he replies like there's nothing weird about this conversation. "It was a week before Christmas so the mall was packed. Izzy was three and I'd taken her shopping to pick out a gift for her mom. She wanted some frozen yogurt and we were standing in line when an old buddy tapped me on the shoulder. I hadn't seen him in ages and we weren't talking more than a minute or two before I realized that Izzy wasn't holding my hand anymore. In fact she was nowhere in sight. That moment of panic. Fucking hell. Nothing else like it. I found her only about thirty feet away, standing by the mall carousel and watching the plastic horses spin past. She didn't understand why I hugged her so hard. She asked me why I didn't have her frozen yogurt."

I get it now. Izzy must have told her parents about the pool.

With a ragged sigh I admit to the terror that still keeps me up at night. "I almost lost him. I wasn't asleep on the couch for more than a couple of minutes. That's all it took."

"It can happen to the best of us," Deck says. "It's hard and it hurts to know how close you came to disaster. Doesn't mean you're a shitty parent. All you can do is try to be even better from now on. Tell you one thing. I never came close to losing her in a shopping mall again. Don't beat yourself up so much."

I appreciate his words more than I can say. I get the feeling he knows this. "Thanks, Deck."

"You take care, Rafe. Take care of that kid. And tell my daughter she should call her old man this weekend."

"Will do."

When the call ends I stand in place for a moment and look at the pool. There's an eight foot tall fence surrounding it now and the gate stays locked at all times. And I have signed Oliver up for swimming lessons at an indoor community pool. The instructor assured me that the first priority is teaching the kids how to safely exit the water if they fall in.

A chime sounds as I open the door to go back inside. The sensor is set off whenever someone opens the door. At night we switch it to the louder alarm setting. Lana and Shane even put the sensors on their side for the occasions when Oliver is spending time over there. It's now impossible for Oliver to open any door of the house without making a sound.

In the kitchen Izzy is putting the final touches on dinner. For days she agonized over what to cook when Caris and Jay come over. She spent hours on the phone with her mother going over different recipes. In the end she decided to make spaghetti with meatballs.

"Were you talking to someone outside?" Izzy asks. She appears to be going for artistic meatball placement as she sets one atop the pile of spaghetti. She squints and then moves it to the left with a pair of large plastic tongs.

"I was talking to your dad."

Her mouth falls open. "My dad?"

"Yeah. He just called to say hi."

"Really?" She's extremely pleased.

I grin at her. "Really."

Oliver is in the living room and zooming his little racecars across the carpet in front of the television. We just bought it the other day. I haven't had a TV in years but it's kind of nice to hear his cartoons playing in the background.

The doorbell rings and Izzy's got her hands full of meatballs so I answer it. Caris walks in carrying a freshly baked apple pie and Jay follows. He hands me a plant.

"Uh. Thanks." I'm not sure what I'm supposed to do with it.

Jay snorts at my confusion. "Caris says you can use it as a centerpiece or something."

"Got it. Thanks again."

We kind of stare each other for a few seconds.

Oliver runs over and his uncle cracks a grin before swinging him in the air. "How's my favorite nephew?"

"Good. Come watch TV with me."

Oliver pushes his uncle into the living room while I go outside and stick the plant on the patio table. It looks all right there.

Dinner turns out to be fun, although I find myself wishing that Shane was around. He always manages to be a friendly link between Jay's awkwardness and mine. I shouldn't need a link of any kind in order to communicate with my own brother but whatever.

After we've all stuffed ourselves with spaghetti and made short work of Caris's pie, she asks Jay if he still needs to work tonight.

He wipes his mouth with a napkin. "Yeah, I've got a few small jobs coming up and I just need to pick up from the supplier and move everything to the warehouse. I won't be gone long. A couple of trips with the pickup bed filled should do it."

"I can help," I say.

He looks at me.

I shrug. "I've got a pickup too. It'll save you some time if we use both our trucks."

He thinks it over and then nods. "That'd be great."

The supplier is only open for another hour so Jay decides to drop Caris off at home and then meet me there. Next week he's installing a custom home office and a floor to ceiling library. Between our two trucks we manage to get everything loaded up in one shot and won't require a second trip. Jay gives me the address for the warehouse where he keeps his materials and does all the prep work. I trail him the short distance to a strip of old brick buildings that was once a shopping center and is now is seeing a renaissance as small business owners search for space.

We unload in silence and get everything sorted and stacked in record time.

Out in the parking lot Jay looks me over with new appreciation. "Hey, thanks for helping out. This would have taken me a couple of trips."

"No big deal." I hesitate to say goodbye. This is the first time it's really been just the two of us and while a dark parking lot isn't a great place for a brotherly showdown I don't know when I'll get another chance. I keep hearing Izzy's voice in my head.

"Talk to your brother. REALLY talk to him. You don't have to wait for him to take the first step."

Jay is bundling the straps we used to tie down the wood.

"You got a minute to talk?" I ask him.

He's surprised. "Sure." He sets the straps down. "What's up?"

"I was just thinking about Arcana." I scratch my head. I suck at this. I should have thought through what I want to say but I don't even know what I want to say.

"Arcana." He's puzzled. And wary. "What for?"

"It was just a hell of a shock hearing the truth about our grandfather. I kept waiting for you to bring it up and I don't think you ever will so here we are."

Jay is silent for a few long seconds and then exhales loudly. "Caris mentioned she told you."

"About the fact that Billy Hempstead was no killer? Imagine that coming out decades later, after we grew up with everyone in town looking at us like we were evil since we were born. And yeah, Caris did tell me. Months ago. But only because she thought you already had."

He kicks at a loose piece of asphalt. His posture has stiffened. He obviously doesn't like discussing this. "I guess I should have said something. No one will ever know for sure one way or the other. I don't know if Caris told you the rest of it, how all the physical evidence was destroyed a long time ago so there's no way to confirm a thing. And the guy who confessed on his death bed to the murders of Richard and Nancy Chapel isn't capable of talking to anyone anymore."

"Why didn't you think I'd be interested in knowing all of this? After the way people always sneered when they said our last name. After they stuck me with the nickname Killer on the high school football field."

He crosses his arms. "I've never known you to put up this kind of drama act, Rafe. You forget that I was there, back in Arcana. You liked the attention. You liked being called Killer."

"I didn't argue about it. Doesn't mean I liked it. But if people believe you're sadistically messed up then they won't fuck with you. Being called Killer was better than getting my ass kicked around Arcana."

He gets angry. "You mean like me?"

No, I didn't mean that at all. "That's not what I said."

"Because the truth is, I *did* get my ass kicked all over Arcana. By you, Rafe."

The stab of remorse in my gut is real. That's not enough to fix what's wrong between my brother and me. "Then hit me, dammit."

He snorts. "Oh, shut up."

"No, I mean it. Hit me. You should. I fucking deserve it. I am sincerely sorry and I want you to hit me until your fucking arm hurts."

He scowls and starts to walk away.

I follow and shove him in the back. Hard.

"Hit me, you little shit! Just like I used to hit you. I used to provoke you on purpose. Know why I did that? To get you to take the first swing. And it always worked. You'd get mad and come after me with your worthless little fists. Then I'd be justified in hitting you back a lot harder because I was a lot bigger. Don't you think I should get the piss knocked out of me for the way I treated you? So go ahead and take a piece of your pride back if you're not too chicken shit."

He's facing me again, his arms at his sides, but his right hand makes a fist. "You're being a real son of a bitch right now."

I mock him with laughter. "We're both sons of a bitch. Now you're big enough to give your big bad brother a taste of his own medicine so fucking do it."

He's practically smoldering yet he makes no move. I conjure up the old nickname I used to taunt him with.

"HIT ME, LIMP DICK!"

Then he does and I don't even see it coming. His right hook connects with my jaw and it's a solid punch. In a second I'll feel the copper taste of blood in my mouth. But he's not finished. He lowers his head and rams into me like a gritty offensive lineman. My back slams into something hard and there's an almighty crash because we've collided with a dumpster.

"Fucking asshole," Jay curses in my ear. "Fight back."

I don't, not really. I shove him off just so he'll think I'm doing something but this just makes him angrier and he tackles me to the ground. He punches my face again, this time beneath my right eye. My shirt rides up and I feel my back getting scratched to hell on the crumbly asphalt while Jay continues to rain down blows.

He gets me in the ribs. Once, twice, three times. One thing life on the streets taught me is that I can take a hell of a beating before anything gets cracked.

He's still snarling at me to hit back and after a stomach punch that knocks the wind out of me for a few seconds, I decide to give him his wish. I roll over, climb to my feet and deliver a blow to his face. I meant to get his jaw, the same way he got mine, but I miss and my knuckles crush his nose.

"FUCK!" He's bent over now, blood pouring from his face and seeping between his fingers.

The fight is over.

I take a few seconds to catch my breath. Then I pull off my shirt and hand it to him. He ignores me, blood still gushing everywhere. I ball up the shirt and press it to his face.

"Take it."

He lifts his head long enough to glare but he swipes the shirt and uses it to soak up the blood. My ribs are on fire, my eye is on its way to swelling shut and a wave of nausea makes me gag. Nothing comes out but I feel the blood in my mouth from the hit to my jaw and I spit a mouthful of it on the ground.

Jay watches me from a few feet away. "You all right?"

I cough out a laugh. It hurts. "Yeah. You got me pretty good though."

He takes my shirt away from his face. The thing looks like crime scene evidence now. "Pretty sure my nose is broken."

"I'm pretty sure it is too."

He laughs but there's no humor. "Shit."

Jay pulls down his truck's tailgate and takes a seat. He waits for me to join him and so I do.

"Throw it out," I say when he tries to hand me the bloody shirt.

This was stupid. Nothing got accomplished except we'll both look like we've been in a bar brawl for the next week.

"Some father I am," I mutter. I had not planned to say the words out loud and they hang in the air like an accusation.

Jay gives me a hard look. In the dim light I can tell he's still got blood smeared all over his face. "Caris and I have been talking."

I spit out a glob of my own blood. "Yeah, you should talk to a girl you plan to marry."

"We've been talking about Oliver."

"What about Oliver?"

"You've got options, Rafe. If you feel like you can't raise him, we can."

I'm so stunned that I can't even respond. He takes that as a cue to keep talking.

"It's just an option. I know that being a father has been a lot for you to take on. If it ever gets to be too much, we're here. You could see him whenever you want. Of course you should be part of his life."

Part of his life.

Like Caris's pet cats are part of his life. Reduced to a supporting background role and nothing more.

I hop off the back of the truck and walk away. If I don't do this there will be another fight. I can't promise how the second one will end.

"Rafe!"

I don't have anything to say to him. No, that's not true. I have one thing to say. I turn around and say it.

"Fuck you. *Jonathan.*"

He calls my name again. He shouts the words, "I'm sorry," but I don't want to hear it. I climb into my truck and drive off without giving him a second look.

There's not much I can do to hide the damage. When I walk in shirtless and with my face bruised to hell Izzy gasps. Oliver sets his glass of milk down, his eyes wide.

"Did you get run over?" he asks.

"No." The act of sinking into a chair is a painful one. If it hurts this much now it's going to be hell tomorrow. "Your Uncle Jay and I had a little bit of a wrestling match."

"Oh." Oliver loses interest and finishes his glass of milk.

Izzy is here at my side, touching my face. I try not to wince.

"You need to put some ice on that." She finds a couple of bags of peas in the freezer and gingerly presses one to my swollen jaw and one to my puffy eye. My ribs ache like a motherfucker and no little bag of peas will help with that. I know she wants more of an explanation but she won't push for one in front of Oliver.

"Can I hug you?" my son asks after he returns from brushing his teeth. He's hesitant, shy, unsure how to handle the fact that I'm obviously in pain.

"I'd love a hug." I open my arms and he's gentle, even giving me a comforting pat on the shoulder before letting go. This kid. He's my heart.

Izzy stands nearby and smiles, although the worry in her eyes remains. After she ushers Oliver off to bed she urges me out of the chair and into the shower. It's not a bad idea because I'm already getting stiff in the hard-backed chair and besides, my back is all cut up to hell after scraping against the ground during the scuffle with my brother.

The cuts aren't deep but Izzy wants to put some antiseptic on them and I let her. I'm face down on the bed with my eyes closed and enjoying the feel of her fingers on my skin as she dabs ointment on my cuts. I flinch when she brushes against a tender spot on my ribs and she sighs.

"Rafe, do you want to talk about what happened between you and Jay?"

"No." I roll over and reach for her hand. She's already dressed for bed. No bra and those little pink gym shorts that make her ass look fantastic. I'm hard already and I show her this by putting her hand on me. "Make me forget, honey."

The corner of her mouth tilts up. She's amused that I'm thinking about sex after I've just gotten the shit kicked out of me. But she's glad to cooperate. She slides my boxers down and removes her shirt before bending low to take me in her mouth. My girl sucks dick like it's her passion in life. Just one of the things I love about her.

"Fuck, I love you," I groan while my hands twist in her hair and she teases my balls. It's something that's been in my head and I don't mean to say it in this moment, when it seems like they're just words that come out when I'm on the verge of defiling her mouth.

Izzy stops and pulls her shorts off. She's open and ready when she straddles me and I need to take some deep breaths in order to hold off until she gets what she needs. It doesn't take long. She rides me slow and deep, her head thrown back, her bare tits front and center. I'll never see anything more beautiful. She comes in no time, as hard as she ever comes, and while she's still shaking I allow my own release to happen. I grip her hips and come inside of her, not exiting until I'm finished squeezing out every drop. We don't take this chance often, not even with her on the pill, but it's something we both need tonight.

"I love you too, Rafe," she whispers when the light is off and she's nestled against my chest.

I refuse to think about my brother and the words we said to each other because I'll just get angry.

I don't want to be angry.

I've wasted too much of my life being angry and I'm finished.

I just want to hold the girl I love and feel her fall asleep in my arms.

20

IZZY

Rafe is agreeable to the suggestion even though he doesn't think it's going to work. "As soon as you tell him why you're really calling he'll hang up so fast he'll probably break his screen."

"Maybe." I kiss him on the cheek. The swelling on his jaw has disappeared but the bruising beneath his eye remains very visible. "Maybe not."

Rafe hauls me into his lap while he finishes his coffee. Days have passed and he still won't say much about his fight with Jay. Caris is equally bewildered on her end. After Jay strolled through the door with a bloody face and a broken nose, he admitted that he and Rafe both lost their tempers and since then he's been quiet. Sad. When she prods him to talk he shuts down and changes the subject. Caris dropped by yesterday but Jay hasn't been around since the dinner party.

Caris and I definitely agree on one thing. This is between the brothers. We cannot solve their problem for them. Rafe and Jay need to figure out how to move forward themselves.

Oliver just woke up moments ago. He's still in his pajamas and he yawns into his cereal bowl. For weeks Rafe resisted my offer to drop

Oliver off at school on weekdays. He doesn't want me to feel obligated to participate equally in Oliver's care. He was being silly. It's no obligation. I *want* to take care of Oliver. Besides, the arrangement makes sense. I never have a class before nine and this way Oliver doesn't need to wake up before dawn and then spend time in daycare before the first school bell even rings.

Rafe's mind was finally changed when he realized this would be best for Oliver. So now Oliver and I enjoy a leisurely breakfast every morning after Rafe leaves for work and then I drop him off at school. I love it, this feeling of being part of a family. This train of thought reminds me of something.

"My Aunt Stephanie called me yesterday."

Rafe's brow furrows. He's definitely trying to remember who Aunt Stephanie is in the labyrinth of my family relations.

"She's Derek's mother. Married to Uncle Chase. Derek's getting married next month."

Rafe still appears rather nonplussed. "Okay."

"Aunt Stephanie wanted to make sure I was aware that both you and Oliver are invited to the wedding. It's the week before Christmas, remember?"

Rafe's expression is difficult to read as he gives this some thought. He doesn't like crowds. And the prospect of meeting my entire family is likely a little daunting. But he surprises me.

"We're coming to a slowdown at work so I'm sure I can get the time off. You think we could drive? I know it's a hassle but flying really sucks."

Oliver takes his spoon out of his mouth. "You said a bad word, Dad."

"You're right. I'm sorry." Rafe still breaks into a smile every time Oliver says the word 'Dad'. These days Oliver says it more and more.

I'm so excited I could clap my hands. "Driving is an excellent idea. There's so much beautiful scenery for Oliver to see between here and Arizona. We'll take my car."

Rafe slides his hand up my thigh. "What's wrong with my truck?"

"It's not an Escalade."

He grunts.

Then he notices the time. If he doesn't get out the door he'll be late for work. He kisses me before I exit his lap. Then he kisses the top of Oliver's head and instructs him not to forget to comb his hair before school.

I'm already dressed but Oliver is not. He wants to wear shorts but I talk him into a pair of jeans after explaining that the weather is cool and rainy. Rafe already made sure to pack up Oliver's backpack, including his lunch. I'm less organized. I nearly forget my laptop bag on my way out the door and then step in a muddy puddle when I cut across the front lawn.

The rain is coming down pretty hard but miraculously lets up when I reach the front of Oliver's school.

"Bye, Izzy," he says.

"Have a good day." I watch him jump down and then run straight for the door. He disappears into a sea of children and I wave from the window, just in case he turned around for one last look.

School remains a struggle for him. His teacher has assured Rafe that Oliver is one of her brightest students. But even though he hasn't been in any fights lately, he has difficulty making friends. He watches the other kids from a careful distance, wistfully observing them at play yet never joining in, even when they go out of their way to invite him.

Evidently I am lingering too long on the drop off line because the car behind me honks.

Before driving off school grounds I make a silent wish for Oliver to have a nice day. There's an hour to kill before my first class and the HSU campus is only minutes away. A trip to Ruby's Bakery sounds like a fine way to eat up some of that time.

The place is crowded with college kids in search of a sugar fix before sitting through class. Shane is taking orders and he doesn't notice me until I'm standing right in front of him.

Before I can say a word he tells me that I'm absolutely not allowed to leave until I agree to sample one of his brand new cinnamon apple muffins. His face is a bit sunburned following his trip to Hawaii with Lana. She returned with a souvenir. They are engaged now.

Shane acts like he's not going to take my money for the bag of muffins and cookies I've ordered but he never wins this argument and this time is no exception. I get one of his employees to process the transaction and then stick my tongue out at him. He laughs. He's made no comment about the fight between Rafe and Jay. He's Jay's best friend but odds are if Jay is unwilling to confide in his fiancé then he's unlikely to confide in anyone else. Not even Shane.

Bag of goodies in hand, I pop a cinnamon apple muffin into my mouth before storing the bag on the passenger seat. Oliver will be excited to have an after school treat when he gets home. The rain is coming down in sheets once more and I decide this is a good time to give Kevin Walsh a call. Rafe might be correct in his skepticism but I'm willing to give it a try. Oliver's therapy sessions have reached a roadblock. He still refuses to discuss any subject that involves his mother.

The law firm's receptionist answers and I ask to be connected directly to Kevin Walsh. She explains that he is not in the office at the moment but I am free to leave a voicemail. This is fine. I can leave a voicemail. In my message I try to sound a little ditzy. I'm a rich girl who just moved to the Houston area because I've inherited the family business. I don't like my current lawyer and I've heard so many fantastic things about Kevin Walsh that I'm hoping he'll please please *please* take me on as a client. My hope is that the flattery will work.

And it does.

Two hours later, after my class ends and I've retreated to my favorite isolated third floor enclave of the library, my phone rings. It's a Houston area code.

"This is Angie." I answer using the fake name I supplied in the voicemail. Which was Angie Menagerie. My creativity skills could use a boost. It sounds like the name of a cartoon character. Or maybe a porn star.

"Hello, Angie. This is Kevin Walsh." His voice is filled with bored arrogance. If I knew nothing about him I would guess him to be a pompous ass. But I do know a few things about him and so I know he's worse than that.

"Hello, Kevin. Thank you for returning my call." I take a deep breath and drop the act. "My name isn't Angie. It's Isabella Gentry. And I'm calling about Oliver. Please don't hang up."

The noise on the other end is a cross between a snarl and a sigh. But he doesn't hang up. Not yet. "How can I help you, Isabella?"

I should have planned this out better, what I wanted to say. "Oliver is doing well. But he has been having trouble dealing with his mother's death. I understand she died very suddenly of an aneurysm. But we don't know the specifics."

"We?" He's suspicious. "You mean you and *Rafe*." It's downright venomous the way he spits out Rafe's name.

I don't have a convincing lie handy. "Yes. I'm Rafe's girlfriend."

Kevin Walsh exhales loudly, obviously disgusted.

"It's not about money," I blurt. "That has nothing to do with this. We're worried about Oliver."

"I have nothing to do with the boy. Nothing at all. He isn't my problem."

Blood roars in my head. I'm glad Kevin Walsh cannot see the look on my face. I'm sure it isn't pleasant.

"You've made it quite clear that you want nothing to do with Oliver."

"Then what is it you expect?"

"What happened on the day Dana died? Was Oliver at home at the time? Please tell me. He's lost his mother. He has suffered enormously. Rafe is a good father to Oliver and he's just trying to understand his son."

Kevin is so silent that in the background I can hear the ticking of a clock. Thunder rumbles overhead here in the library. At least no one will scold me for disturbing the peace. The only other sign of life I've seen is a couple who were all over each other and disappeared into one of the small meeting rooms. They did not look like they were heading in there to study.

Finally Kevin sighs. "Dana's time of death was likely in the late morning or very early afternoon. The boy was at a play date with a friend and she never came to pick him up. She was found on the floor of the kitchen and since her phone was inches away it's assumed that her death was so quick she did not even have the opportunity to call for help. The boy stayed with a neighbor while I searched for Rafe Hempstead and made funeral arrangements."

I swallow hard. "I see."

Poor Oliver.

Kevin Walsh becomes agitated. "Now, this neighbor, she's elderly and not very intelligent and couldn't bring herself to tell the boy his mother was dead. So she told him that Dana had left on a trip and no one knew when she'd be returning. Maybe she meant well, but it was left to me to explain that Dana was dead and that no, she wouldn't be coming back. The funeral was quite small but the boy was so hysterical that I thought it best if he didn't attend. He would have made a scene."

"You didn't let him go to his own mother's funeral?" I'm outraged. And horrified. At a time when Oliver needed compassion and honesty more than anything there was no one around to give it to him.

His voice rises. "The boy was screaming at the top of his lungs like a wild animal. He's obviously disturbed. I even had to arrange for a doctor to come in and give him a sedative."

The boy.

The boy.

He won't even say Oliver's name. How could anyone be so evil as to despise an innocent child?

I don't know. I don't want to know.

Kevin Walsh is wretched enough to hate a little boy for the crime of resembling his father. He is a horrid man. Just talking to him makes my skin crawl.

"Thank you for your time." I press the button to end the call and sit there in the library chair. I'm shaking.

"Oliver," I whisper and a tear slides down my cheek.

The couple comes busting out of their conference room erupting in giggles while rearranging their clothes. The girl looks at me with curiosity but says nothing and they walk toward the elevator.

No wonder that sweet little boy has been in such pain.

He was lied to. He was rejected. He was ripped from the only parent he'd ever known.

And he was not even allowed to say goodbye.

21

RAFE

When I tell Izzy my idea she thinks it's a good one and suggests calling Oliver's therapist for her input. Nicole is enthusiastic and so I invite her to attend. Shane and Lana are also invited, as are Jay and Caris.

Oliver was deprived of the chance to attend his mother's funeral.

We're going to give her one now. Her son is going to have the opportunity to say goodbye.

Caris suggests using the park in her neighborhood. It's large and it's grassy and there's a picnic area that can be used for seating. Izzy and Lana arrange for the balloons. After a short ceremony that honors Dana's life we're going to release them.

The morning of the funeral, Oliver and I go through the contents of the box that's been sitting in his closet. We look at his baby book together, every milestone, all the ones I missed. The first time he crawled. The first time he walked. The first time he got a haircut and cut a tooth. There is much love in these pages and it's a treasure. An envelope falls out of the book. It has Oliver's name on it but it isn't sealed. Inside is a single piece of handwritten notebook paper.

My dearest baby boy,

Right now you sleep soundly in your little bed but one day you will be older. You will have questions. I'm writing this down in anticipation of that time.

Before you were born I thought I was doing the right thing when I turned your father away and chose Kevin Walsh instead.

As you are likely now aware, this was not the right thing.

Kevin is not a good man. And he is not your father.

The man who is your father is named Rafe Hempstead. I do not know where he is now. Perhaps someday you will want to find him. That is your choice. You may think to judge him harshly but please do not. He was very young and uncertain about his path in life. He walked away only because I asked him to. You look so much like him and sometimes when I notice this I am very sorry indeed that I did not give you both the chance to know one another. I'm grateful to him beyond words. He gave me you.

And you, sweet Oliver, are the darling and the joy of my life.

You always will be.

Love you forever.

Love you most of all.

Mommy

After I've finished reading the letter aloud, Oliver is silent. I fold the letter along its creases and return it to the envelope. Izzy stands in the doorway and our eyes meet. Hers are filled with tears. Mine are too.

"Oliver?" I reach for my son's hand. He lets me, although he remains still.

His lip quivers and he swallows. Then he finally looks up. "Mommy used to make me peanut butter and banana sandwiches."

"That sounds good. I can make those for you anytime you want."

"She would put a little bit of honey on the bananas."

"I can do that too."

A tear falls. Then another one. "I miss her very much, Dad."

"I know you do." I open my arms. "You can talk to me about her anytime you want."

He jumps into my hug and a sob wracks his little body. I kiss his cheek and hug him tight.

"I love you, Oliver."

He cries in my arms for a few minutes and then notices Izzy is here. He wants a hug from her too and she's only too happy to give him one. Then she gently reminds us that it's time to leave. The others will be waiting.

My son and I wear dress shirts with matching ties and Izzy has even dressed up Cliff by tying a purple ribbon around his plush neck. Oliver is very solemn as he holds his stuffed toy under one arm and a framed photo in the other, the photo of him and his mother that was sitting on top of his dresser.

Lana and Shane have already left to go help set up at the park. Izzy holds my hand on the short drive. She frequently looks into the backseat to give Oliver an encouraging smile.

The day is crisp and cool but the sky is clear. We are the last ones to arrive. Nicole is here with her husband. Caris and Jay stand side by side. Lana and Shane are arranging the trays of food Shane prepared. The photo of Oliver and Dana is set down in a place of honor. Cliff watches over it.

Nicole has already offered to read the eulogy, which was written with Oliver's assistance during his latest therapy session. Lana hands each of us a purple balloon before Nicole begins speaking.

"Dana McDaniel Walsh liked flowers and green apples. Her favorite place was the beach and her favorite color was purple. Her favorite animal was the cat and she would always leave out bowls of food and water to feed any strays that happened to be in the area. She loved her son Oliver very much and she was a very good mother. She was never too tired to read bedtime stories and she laughed a lot. Her death was sudden and painless but she will be forever missed by those she left behind. Goodbye, Dana."

Nicole releases her balloon.

"Goodbye, Dana," says her husband and does the same.

"Goodbye, Dana." Shane and Lana release their balloons at the same time.

"Goodbye, Dana." Caris gives her balloon a kiss before allowing it to leave her hand.

Jay looks at me. The swelling in his nose has gone down but

there's bruising under his eyes. We stare at one another and his throat bobs. "Goodbye, Dana," he says and then his balloon is freed.

Izzy cries openly. "Goodbye, Dana." She blows a kiss to the sky.

The string of my balloon remains twisted around my finger. I didn't want to risk letting it go too soon. Now I unravel it. "Goodbye, Dana. And thank you."

Oliver is the last one to release his balloon. He takes a deep breath and separates his fingers. We all watch his purple balloon climb high to join the other distant purple dots that are beginning to drift in separate directions.

"Bye, Mommy," he says softly and slips his hand into mine.

Izzy comes to my other side and I slide my arm around her. We all watch the balloons for a long time, until not a single one of them is left to see.

Oliver tugs on my hand. "Dad, is it okay if I go on the swings?"

He points to a little playground about fifty yards away.

"I can take him over there," Izzy offers.

"Yeah, it's okay." I bend down and give my son a quick hug. Then I watch him reach trustingly for Izzy and the two of them walk toward the playground.

The other adults are all talking and I know I should go over and join them but I don't. Not yet. Nearby is a small cluster of trees and I choose one to lean against as I watch my son select a swing and wait for Izzy to push him.

When I hear a noise I see Jay approaching, a little cautiously.

"Hey. You in the mood to talk?"

"Sure. Pull up a tree."

He leans against the tree directly opposite and I gesture to his face.

"Looks like you took a beating."

He throws me a wry grin and jerks his chin. "Funny, looks like the same thing happened to you."

We both get a chuckle out of that and then after the laughs die we stand around in silence for a minute.

"Rafe, you're a really great dad to Oliver," Jay says. "You've turned your life inside out for him and he's better off with you than with anyone else. I'm really sorry that what I said came out wrong. What I meant is that I'm here for you, both of you. Me and Caris are."

I let this sink in and for a second I try to put myself in his shoes. After a rough childhood and so many years apart it was never going to be an easy task to win over my brother's trust. He has his wounds and so do I.

"Thanks, Jay."

He looks up at the sky. "That was a nice ceremony."

"Yes."

Silence reigns once more. It's not uncomfortable this time.

He crosses his arms and blows out a long breath. "I was a real asshole to her at first."

"Who?"

"Caris. When we both wound up here in the same place after having nothing to do with each other since we were kids, I was awful to her. I acted like I didn't know her at all, that she wasn't worth remembering."

This is the first time I've heard this story. "Why would you do that?"

Jay shifts his weight and peers off into the distance. "I spent so long trying to escape my own damn self. I even changed my name. I didn't want to be weak little Johnny Hempstead, town trash, grandson of a murderer. I didn't even want to remember who he was."

"And so you became Jay Phoenix instead."

"Yeah." He hangs his head for a few seconds and then raises it to meet my eye. "I'm changing my last name back to Hempstead. It's kind of a hassle but I need to do it. In a few months Caris is going to take my name and I want it to be *my* name. Not one I just pulled out of thin air when I couldn't stand to look at myself in the mirror."

"That's good. So we'll be the Hempstead brothers again."

He flashes a sad grin. "We always have been." The grin fades. "She hated you, Rafe. Our mother. She didn't have much love for me either, obviously. But especially after Dad died she hated you because you reminded her so much of him."

"Lousy fucking Hempstead," I mutter, echoing her words. "She once told me I'd be dead in a gutter somewhere before I turned twenty."

"She was wrong." He's angry now, angry on my behalf. "She was so fucking wrong."

Yes, she was. But she's not the whole problem.

"Know what I hope?" I ask him. "I hope that someday, a long time in the future, I'll be able to look back and instead of being ashamed of the way I spent the first twenty-five years of my life, I'll feel proud of the way I've lived the years since then."

He's quiet for a long time. He uncrosses his arms and drums his fingers on his thigh. "I've been thinking about something."

"What's that?"

"The world is full of brothers who fight like cats and dogs the whole time while they're kids. But then they grow up and they get a chance to change. They get a chance to appreciate the things that bind them together rather than the things that would rip them apart. You and me, we never got that chance, Rafe."

"We could have it now, Jonathan."

He nods. "I'd like that."

Then he smiles. So do I.

"Are we supposed to hug now or something?"

"Or something." He puts his hand out for a handshake, then changes his mind and grabs me in a bear hug.

"Watch the ribs," I croak, hugging him back. "Some fucker pounded on them."

He releases me with a laugh. "Maybe the same fucker who broke my nose."

Oliver sees us talking and jumps off his swing. He barrels in our direction like he's trying out for the Olympics. He runs right into my legs and then grins up at me.

"I got you, Dad."

I tweak his nose. "Yeah, you did."

Izzy has kicked off her shoes and holds them in her hand as she daintily jogs over.

"That kid is quick," she laughs and steps right into my embrace.

"Uncle Jay." Oliver hangs on my brother's arm. "Can you turn me upside down?"

Jay obliges and Oliver howls out a laugh.

Caris is here now and says there's food available on the picnic table if anyone's hungry.

"I'm hungry," Oliver announces and begins pulling both her and Jay in the direction of the picnic tables. He notices that Izzy and I aren't moving. "Dad, are you guys coming?"

"In a minute," I tell him. "Save me a cookie."

Izzy reaches for a kiss and then together we watch Oliver as he joins the group.

For a large chunk of my life I was completely alone and I didn't think about wanting something different.

"Say hello to your father, Oliver."

That is and will always be my pivotal point. When a sad and angry little boy looked up at me. And I saw myself in his eyes.

Now I think about life in a new way. I think about love. I think about a family.

Turning, I cup Izzy's face in my hands and then brush my lips across hers. "I love you, Isabella."

Her smile is just about the most valuable thing I've ever earned. "I love you too, Rafe."

She's startled when I pick her up in my arms but even with my ribs aching it has to happen. Her shoes are still off and I'm going to carry her. I'm going be that duke (or was it an emperor?) who makes heroic moves like this out of the blue and only for her.

Always for her.

22

IZZY

"Who was that guy again?" Rafe points to my cousin Thomas and thinks he's being subtle when he asks this question but Gracie, Thomas's girlfriend, is sitting right on my other side at the table.

She hears him. She laughs.

"That's Thomas." I pat Rafe's arm. I know my family tree is confusing. There are many branches and endless names. "He's the youngest brother of the groom."

Rafe jerks his head to Uncle Cord. "And that's his dad."

He's so proud of himself that I almost hate to burst his bubble. "No. That's Uncle Cord. Thomas and Derek's father is Uncle Chase."

"That guy." This time Rafe points to Uncle Creed. Cord, Chase and Creed are triplets. To me they don't look alike. But I'm sure to someone who's never met them before it's a different story.

Rafe is trying really hard. I don't want to discourage him. "Um, yeah."

Gracie laughs again.

I pinch her. She's a sweetheart. I'm so glad Thomas found a nice girl. He's my favorite cousin.

I elbow Rafe. "There's Derek over there. I haven't had a chance to talk to him yet. Do you want to come?"

Rafe looks around and scratches his head. "I should probably locate Oliver."

"He's probably still hanging out with my parents. You'll have to pry him away. They've claimed him as theirs."

"I should go over there anyway. Your dad and I need to have a talk."

"What about?"

He gives me a cryptic grin. "Man shit."

"Well. Excuse me for not having testosterone."

I roll my eyes and leave Rafe to his chuckling and his masculine pursuits. Derek gives me a nod as he sees me approaching. He's been joined by his eternally sarcastic brother, Kellan, and I brace myself for some teasing.

"Izzy!" Kellan exclaims and tries to offer me a high five for reasons unknowns. "We were just talking about you."

"No, we weren't," Derek assures me.

"Yes, we were," Kellan insists. "We were taking bets on whether Uncle Deck will have your little boyfriend in a headlock before we cut the cake."

I smile at him. "My boyfriend is hardly little, Kel. And no one will be putting anyone else in a headlock. For your information, my dad loves Rafe."

"Rafe. What kind of a name is that? It's like 'rake'. But not."

I have no idea how to respond to such a stupid comment. "So I heard Taylor lost her mind and agreed to marry you."

He beams. "She did!"

"In that case, congratulations. May she never come to her senses."

"Thanks. By the way, Izzy, I like your dress. It looks like the one Derek ruined that one Christmas when he threw some sauce-covered meatballs at you."

I throw him a withering look. "That was *you*, Kel."

"Was it? I apologize." He looks up and sees Thomas beckoning from across the dance floor. "Hey, I've got to go. I have important things to do."

We watch Kellan flee as if his pants are on fire.

I shake my head. "He's still nuts."

Derek snorts. "Forever."

I grin at my cousin. We haven't always gotten along but that was just good natured childhood bantering. In truth I adore all of my cousins. Even Kellan.

"Congratulations, Derek. Paige is wonderful. You two will be very happy together."

"Thanks, Izzy." He gives me a hug. Then he looks around and leans in a little. "Want to know a secret?"

"I don't know. Is it about Kellan? Is it going to make me nauseous?"

"Neither." He shoots a look at his beautiful bride. Paige is being embraced by Aunt Stephanie, who looks beyond thrilled to welcome her new daughter-in-law.

Derek heaves a happy sigh. "I'm going to be a father."

My jaw drops. "No kidding?"

"Shh." He puts a finger to his lips. "It's not common knowledge yet."

"Oh my god. Derek!" I hug him again. "You'll be a great dad. I'm so happy for you."

"Thanks." He becomes a little wistful as he looks around at all the people we know and love. He zeroes in on the sight of his own father, who appears to be perplexed by something Kellan is whispering in his ear. "I've got a damn good example to live up to."

"We all do." I see my own parents now. They have joined the action on the dance floor. My dad's not a guy who likes to dance in public. But it's a semi-slow song and my mother loves to dance, especially at weddings, so he's got his arms around her as they sway gently in time to the music. He says something and she looks up and laughs at him. They kiss and it's not a quick kiss either. They're in love. It's the kind of love that I thought I might never find.

Until I did.

Derek excuses himself because Paige is motioning to him.

My father takes notice of me standing at the edge of the dance floor. He smiles but it's a melancholy expression and I don't know why. No one is sad here.

Kellan floats by. His grin reminds me of the mad Cheshire cat. "Wait till my brother sees his truck."

I know that Derek is a gearhead and he doesn't like having his vehicle messed with. "What did you do to it?"

He shrugs. "Nothing permanent. But I hope he's not in a big hurry to get to the honeymoon because this will take some time to undo."

Kellan then proceeds to make a spectacle of himself by coercing Taylor into waltzing around the dance floor with him when he clearly has no idea how to do it properly. It's a good thing there are so many heat lamps out here because even though a tent has been set up in the giant backyard it's still a December night and it's chilly.

Kellan bumps into my dad, who glares at him. He seeks protection behind Taylor. Thomas and Gracie are trying to persuade some of my teenage cousins, Rider and Ethan, to join the fun but they balk. Then Uncle Creed decides to step in and drag them to the dance floor whether they want to be there or not. Aunt Truly grabs his hand and announces that now that he's set foot on the dance floor he's not leaving until she gives him permission. Their daughter, my cousin Zoe, looks to me and winks before a couple of my youngest cousins start begging her to twirl them around.

I'm just standing by, laughing at all the madness, when I feel little arms around my waist and a child's voice says, "Izzy!" in a way that makes me feel like the most loved person in the world.

I bend down to hug the little boy. He looks extra adorable in the little suit we got him for the occasion. He's been having the time of his life ever since we got here. My folks have a stack of Christmas presents for us to carry back to Texas when we start the drive back the day after tomorrow. Most of them are for Oliver. They will be flying out on Christmas Eve to spend the holiday with us but it would be a pain to check all those gifts with their luggage.

I straighten up and crane my neck around. "Where'd your dad go?"

Hands around my waist, a rumbling voice in my ear. "Right here, baby."

I melt. Every time I melt.

"Dance with me," begs Oliver and pulls us to the dance floor.

Of all the Gentry family weddings I've been to, and there have been many, this one is my favorite.

At the end of the wedding reception, Derek is not especially pleased to discover that his brothers have covered every inch of his truck with plastic cling wrap. The doors can't even be opened. Rafe is among the volunteers who help clear it off while Kellan stands around and offers helpful guidance while holding a giant piece of wedding cake in a napkin.

We're staying at my parents' house, which is nice because we get to spend even more time with them and because I want Rafe and Oliver to see where I come from. Oliver sleeps in my old bedroom and I know my folks are thrilled to have a child in the house again. In a nod to both reality and my adulthood status, Rafe and I are given the large guest room with a king sized bed.

Before we left for Arizona I informed Rafe that there was absolutely zero chance I'd be willing to have sex in my parents' house.

I lied.

Oh, how I lied.

But I did warn him I would make him suffer if he moaned out loud.

He must have taken my threat seriously. He didn't make a sound, not even when I got on top and rode him like I was a jockey on derby day.

Afterwards, when I'm sweaty and satisfied and still slightly breathless, I get comfortable against his broad chest and stroke his skin.

"What did you need to talk to my dad about?" I yawn.

He had been running his fingers through my hair and now he stops. "I needed to ask him something."

"Advice?"

"No."

I'm curious now. I prop my chin on his chest and feel the thump of his heartbeat underneath. "Then what?"

"A blessing."

"You needed to ask Deck Gentry for a blessing?"

"Yeah, I think that's what they call it."

"I don't understand."

Rafe slides out of bed and searches around on the dark floor. I don't know what he's doing. He's naked. He must be searching for his clothes.

"I think I threw your boxers in that corner." I point out the location helpfully and then realize it's too dark for him to see where I'm pointing.

He switches on a bedside lamp. He's got something in his hand and he kneels beside the bed.

"Isabella. We haven't been together for very long and if you can't give me an answer right away I will understand. " He takes a deep breath and shows me the little box in his palm. "I love you, Izzy. I already know that I want to spend my life with you. And if you think that maybe there's a chance that someday you could say the same-"

He can't talk anymore because I've covered his mouth. I kiss him like crazy and fall off the bed into his embrace. We hit the floor with a thud and I laugh because now we are really not being quiet at all.

"YES!" I kiss him again and again. "Yes, Rafe. I love you. I'm ready to say yes today."

When I finally get a chance to look at the ring I see that it's beautiful. Rafe admits that he got some help from Lana when picking it out. He starts to apologize for it not being a big, expensive rock. Silly boy.

I shush him with a finger to his lips. "I love it. I love you."

We kiss slowly, tenderly. We make love again, this time with a gentle kind of passion.

And then, when I'm once again in his arms, I inform him of one very serious fact. "There is someone else besides my dad who needs to give his blessing."

He gets my meaning. "Oliver."

I smile. "Oliver."

EPILOGUE

RAFE

"Happy birthday, dear Oliver. Happy birthday to you."

The last note fades and Oliver considers the six burning candles for a full minute before sucking in a huge breath and blowing them all out. Applause erupts in the room.

"Happy birthday, Oliver," Caris calls as she stands nearby in Jay's arms. He touches her cheek and they share a quick kiss.

"What'd you wish for?" Shane wants to know.

"He can't tell us," Lana scolds him. "Or it won't come true."

"Oliver, say hello to Grandpa Deck and Grandma Jenny." Izzy is holding up a tablet so that her parents can participate in Oliver's birthday celebration via videoconferencing.

My son looks up and waves. "Thank you for my presents!"

"We love you, Oliver," says Izzy's mom.

Deck grins and waves on the screen. "Eat a piece of cake for me, okay kid?"

After digging the candles out of the cake, which was generously baked by Shane, I begin carving out pieces. The birthday boy gets the first slice of chocolate on chocolate with cherry filling. Izzy is still wrapping up the conference call with her parents so I pass out wedges of cake to the others first.

And then, before I take one for myself, I hand a piece of cake to my wife.

I married Izzy Gentry four months ago, the day after Christmas. Her parents were already here visiting for the holidays. We didn't want to wait. So we went down to the county courthouse and promised to love each other forever. Oliver was proud to stand by my side as the best man.

Her folks had one condition. Weddings are a hell of a big deal in Izzy's family. We needed to promise to come to Arizona this summer and have a second ceremony in front of Izzy's dozens of relatives. They'd all never forgive us if we didn't.

That didn't sound like a bad compromise to me.

Izzy and her mother have been busy planning out every detail for the June wedding in Arizona. The other day she modeled her dress for me. When I asked if that was bad luck or something she shushed me and said there was no such thing. Not for us. She looked like a dream in her dress. Sometimes I still can't believe she's mine.

My cake slice is untouched because I'm watching my son. He's shoveling forkfuls of chocolate as fast as he can. Izzy kisses his cheek and tickles him. He laughs with his mouth full.

If I try to think back to what I was doing exactly one year ago I can't remember. This would have been just an unremarkable day on the calendar in my solitary life. I had no idea that it was my son's birthday. I had no idea that in a few months I would be confronted by the challenges of parenthood. I had no idea that I would meet a girl who would change the way I looked at the world. And the way I thought of myself.

Izzy calls me over. "Rafe, you are needed for this picture."

Oliver stops devouring his cake long enough to wipe his face with a napkin and smile. My hand is on his shoulder and my arm is around my wife.

"Smile, Hempstead family," Caris commands before she snaps multiple shots with her cell phone.

Family.

It's only a word, yet it's everything.

Jay finds me in a little while and we lean against the wall together in identical poses.

I nudge him with my elbow. "Your wedding's up next."

He glances at Caris, who is in the middle of a lively chat with Izzy and Lana. "Four weeks. I'm ready." He nudges me back. "Hey, I know tomorrow's Sunday but do you want to grab some lunch and talk a little business?"

Last month my brother made me one heck of a generous offer. He wants to expand his carpentry business but doesn't feel like he can take on the burden alone. He's asked me to be his partner. I'm going to work hard as hell for it. I don't want something for nothing. And I won't let him down. Not ever. I've got another week left of my current job and after that I'll be working with my brother every day. We're going to build things together. A business. A brotherhood. A future.

"Name the time," I tell him.

He grins. "I'll call you."

After the presents have all been opened and Oliver has had his fill of chocolate cake, the rest of the party leaves and it's just the three of us.

"Kitchen duty or bed time?" Izzy asks me.

"What do you want?"

"I asked you first."

"Then I'll take bed time."

"Lucky." She pokes me in the stomach and then begins rinsing off cake plates.

Oliver wants bubbles in his bath before bedtime so I pour half the bottle in. There's now a mountain of suds that wind up spilling out on the floor but he's delighted. When he's had enough of smearing soap bubbles on the wall he gets into his pajamas and brushes his teeth.

"You ready for bed?" I ask him. He's got some toothpaste on his chin.

"I gotta say goodnight to Izzy." Oliver runs off to locate his stepmother while I wait in the hallway.

Izzy exclaims over his new pajamas, which are covered in sharks, his new obsession. She wishes him a happy birthday once again and reminds him that he's so very loved.

"I love you too, Izzy."

The two of them share a very special bond. Izzy encourages him to talk about Dana. She helped him write a letter this morning. It was addressed to his mother and so it will never be opened. But he wanted to tell her about being honored with Student Of The Week at school and let her know that he's six years old today. The letter has been placed in a special box that was carefully decorated by Oliver. Izzy tells him that anytime he wants to share something with his mother he should write it down and place it in the box.

Oliver scampers off to bed and waits for me to tuck him in.

"Happy birthday, buddy." I kiss his cheek and nestle the stalwart Cliff at his side.

Oliver wraps his arms around my neck. "I love you, Dad."

I bottle this moment up inside my head and vow to keep it forever. "I love you too, son."

His eyes are already shut when I turn out the light.

Izzy is not in the kitchen or anywhere else in the apartment. I find her out on the back patio.

"What are you drinking?" I gesture to the tumbler in her hand as I take a seat.

"Water." She sets it down on the table and pulls her legs up, allowing my arm to circle her. "What do you think he wished for when he blew out his candles?"

"I don't know. He asked me the other day if we could get a boat. I hope it was just a passing thought. There's not exactly a ton of beaches within driving distance."

"There aren't *any*."

"I know. So it looks like we won't be getting a boat."

"Know what I wished for when I was his age?"

"What?"

"A sibling. I wanted one more than anything else in the world. I was so jealous of my cousins because they all had siblings."

"You think Oliver wants a brother or a sister?"

"I don't know. But I imagine he'll get used to the idea when one shows up."

I never claimed to be the quickest guy in the world. I need a minute to catch up to what she's really saying.

"Izzy."

"Rafe."

"You're not…"

"I am." She swivels and becomes worried over my silence. "You know I went off the pill a few months ago because I kept getting migraines."

"Yeah."

"And you know how babies are made, right?"

I place my hand on her belly. A fierce wave of protective love surges through my blood.

She covers my hand with hers. "My cycles have been irregular for ages and I didn't think much of it until I had my annual doctor visit yesterday. A routine pregnancy test came back positive and they were able to do an ultrasound. I'm nine weeks along. I heard the heartbeat! Of course, I'll need to have my dress altered because I'll be showing by the time we have the wedding in June." She pauses. "Rafe. Say something."

"God, I love you, Isabella Hempstead."

"You better love me," she teases. "Because I'm not going anywhere."

"I don't know about that. Frankly, I think we should all go somewhere."

"Where?"

"A bigger place. Looks like we'll need it."

"Way ahead of you. Caris says there's a house for rent on her street. I didn't tell her why I was interested, of course. I just mentioned we might be looking for more space. It seems like a great idea, especially now that you and Jay are going to be working together." She bites the corner of her lip. "What do you think?"

What do I think?

I think there's not another man on this planet (or any other) who is luckier than me.

In fact I'm sure of it.

And this is what I tell my wife.

THANK YOU FOR READING STRAYS!

Writing this story was an incomparable emotional journey and I was sorry to see it end.

I hope you have enjoyed being in Rafe and Izzy's world.

Love,

Cora

P.S. Want to read more about Caris and Jay's love story?

"Our families have been enemies for generations.

But fate had other ideas for us…"

Now available on Amazon, free in Kindle Unlimited.

CLICK HERE == LONG LOST

STAY IN TOUCH!

MAKE SURE YOU SIGN UP FOR MY NEWSLETTER TO RECEIVE UPDATES ON NEW RELEASES, SALES AND GIVEAWAYS.

CORA BRENT'S NEWSLETTER SIGNUP

You can also find me here:

Check out what's happening on Facebook:
www.facebook.com/CoraBrentAuthor

Join my exclusive reader Facebook group:
https://www.facebook.com/CoraBrentsBookCorner

Add future releases to your TBR list:
https://www.goodreads.com/CoraBrent

Follow me on Instagram: CoraBrentAuthor

Worked Up

<u>FIRED</u>

<u>NAILED</u>

Stand Alones

<u>UNRULY</u>

<u>IN THIS LIFE</u>

<u>HICKEY</u>

<u>SYLER MCKNIGHT</u>

<u>LONG LOST</u>

<u>THE PRETENDER</u>